The Savage Place
Seesaw Sunday
The Twilight's Last Gleaming

ONE
FINE
DAY

W·W·NORTON & COMPANY
NEW YORK LONDON

ONE
FINE
DAY

LEON ARDEN

Book design by Antonina Krass

W. W. Norton & Company, Inc. 500 Fifth Avenue, New York, N.Y. 10110
W. W. Norton & Company Ltd. 25 New Street Square, London EC4A 3NT
ISBN   0   393   01423   1   cloth edition
1 2 3 4 5 6 7 8 9 0

FOR FRANKIE
without whom this novel
could never have been
rewritten

ONE
FINE
DAY

Oh, how I hated life's endless beginnings. A savage alarmclock, the awful struggle to climb out of bed, the tedium of shaving, the long march to work. And I have never cared for quaint tales that open with a newborn infant crying at the indignity of being alive. Childhood bores me; especially my own. All I can recall is myself miscast as a hypersensitive misfit housing an atomic pile of carnal need. For years I was trapped in nonsensical littleness, when almost everything was a beginning. I even found distasteful the initial maneuvers with a new woman, those superficial conversations, that first move toward the bedroom door.

One day I discovered at least how to avoid each morning's assault of shattering noise. It was a small victory. I simply wired my tape recorder to an automatic timer. Thus I was able to record at night a comic monologue with which to bring myself alive the following morning. "Wake up you lazy bastard." Those were my opening words and I shall never forget them. Soon you'll see why. Anyway, there I was shouting at myself as I lay asleep. From the very beginning it was unreal—and typical of my luck that on the worst day of my life I was finally able to get up on time.

Pressing the stop button made my harsh stranger's voice cease. "Thank God," I said and, pleased at being so fully awake so early in the morning, I took time out to notice with pride my new acquisition. On the wall was a Vermeer reproduction, with the tide of sunlight from my window touching the lower right corner of the frame. For a long moment I was as one with the painting's exquisite serenity.

Two minutes were lost looking for my left slipper. The radio promised traffic jams in the morning and in the evening, rain. The air, it said, was unacceptable. Yesterday's reheated coffee had lost its taste, and I spoiled the Familia with sour milk.

As I went out the door the phone rang. That would be Milly. It was depressing to know that I'd be seeing her so soon for I was chagrined at how deeply involved I had become with someone I no longer wanted, whom it was hard to believe I had ever wanted, and, to make it truly absurd, with whom I was forced to live, like it or not, every day from nine to five.

With two keys, I twice double-locked the door. Down the hall the attractive red-head, new in the building, stepped into the elevator on her way to work. I yelled and she dabbed at the button, but the door closed anyway and she vanished. I waited in bad temper, surprised that I could still hear my phone's faint ring. Was it important? Should I run back? When the elevator returned it brought the wasted magic of perfume.

The walk to the subway is vivid in my memory, but I'm not sure how much of it I noticed at the time. A minor accident in front of my building had both drivers out of their cars to engage in a churlish inspection of their bumpers. A bleached cathedral stood in the sky, floating east. A man's hat popped off in the wind. I bought a *Times* from the always moody newspaper vendor and galloped down the subway stairs. The headlines told of an American ambassador kidnapped in Brazil not to mention the Energy Crisis, the dying oceans, runaway inflation, a predicted depression, poisons in our food, mounting lung cancer, heart disease, and street crime, plus, of course, imminent war in the Middle East. Nothing new this morning. The train came. I squeezed in with the crowd and stood unable to move or read as we rocketed west. Each day, even to my daily pledge to escape this rut, was the same.

Back on the street I saw an old man in shapeless clothes lose his balance amid the hurrying crowd and fall. Several people, not relishing the task, helped the derelict to his feet. He thanked no one. He was wearing a pathetic pair of soiled tennis shoes.

INSTITUTE FOR THE APPLIED STUDY OF SOCIAL RESPONSE, read the sign on the door. Vince, our elevator man, short, and manic, provided my first social response of the day.

"Pick a number from one to ten," he demanded.

"Three."

"Wrong." He shook his head. "Boy, were you way off."

"Vince, how many years until you retire?"

"If Bela Lugosi married Bella Abzug, her name would be Bella Lugosi."

Motion ceased; the doors parted. "Vince, we all admire your efforts at humor."

"I don't retire for another nineteen years," he said and disappeared humming.

To arrive on time, I discovered, was to be way ahead of everyone else. The hallway was clean and dead, each empty office a calm shambles. Best to leave my door ajar so the boss would notice me when he arrived. Since I was so early I sat at my desk and did nothing, pleasantly discombobulated by it all. From the roof of the building opposite a sheet of brown wrapping paper was lifted in the wind and sent slowly undulating above the city.

I had set an unpleasant task for myself this day. After numerous postponements of courage the time had come and gone and come again to break with Milly. But to cease as lover and continue as employer involved such tactics of heart and mind that it boggled them both. For the last two months postponement had been the easiest ploy. Now I was spurred into action by a dinner party to be held next week by Milly's dreaded mother and populated as usual by her mad friends and bizarre relatives, among whom Milly stood like a lone mourner grieving at the loss of her family's sanity.

I met the mother through the daughter but I don't even remember meeting the daughter. She had worked in another part of the office as a secretary for so long that I'm not sure if she was hired before or after me or when, if ever, we were introduced. We greeted each other casually for some three years and spoke together occasionally in the elevator amid Vince's comic assaults. Eventually I came to think of Milly as a brother might a sister, someone with whom I had a boringly permanent and insignificant relationship and one with no remembered beginning. And so it continued until Miss Ausubel, a nose-blowing nineteen-year-old who spelled with surrealistic originality, learned the secretarial ropes in three weeks only to abscond with a delivery boy to Port au Prince.

My fantasy was to fill her post with a lovely young woman who would also be a prize-winning spelling contestant. This gift of spongecake would be sent over by the employment bureau for me to inspect, approve, seduce, and marry. But Scanlan vetoed bringing in someone from the outside, which immediately crash landed all such flights of fancy. The upshot was that Milly was switched from the computer department, where rumor had it that a middle-aged mathematician was making a fool of himself over her to the point where she complained to Scanlan, who then gave her, as it were, to me.

Upon closer examination there was nothing that would make one believe or even invent such a rumor. Luckily she had nothing of her mother's physiognomy. Her features, however, suggested nothing—not passion, or purpose, or an acquaintance with aesthetic heights. Here were no beaming smiles or astringent expressions of imminent wit. Just a plain face grazed with sadness. How a mathematician could make a fool of himself over such imprecision was beyond me. And her body was so thoroughly disguised with appalling garments, it was simply unaccounted for. No magic here, that was certain.

What also became certain was that working with Miss Madeleine Hawkmann would be easy. She viewed her job not as a way to meet men, at least not any more, and not as a way of filling time until more exciting work came along. Men seemed to figure marginally in her life. There were no efforts to glamorize herself for a big night out. Each time I asked her to stay late at the office she acquiesced at once. Whenever I phoned her apartment on some point of business never had I to wait for more than two rings.

Yet, when the mathematician persisted, so did she persist in her unrelenting apathy. He left notes on her desk, sent flowers to her room, delayed her in the halls. Finally he became such a laughing stock that he left to take a job in Boston. That day I broke from the routine of the office to hazard a personal question.

"Wasn't your heart melted just a little bit?" I asked her.

"Don't know about that but everything else froze."

"He seemed like an OK guy."

"We had nothing in common. But he wouldn't listen. Do you realize what he loves most? Camping. I mean like in the woods, outside, camping. Me, I swallow bugs. The minute I step into the woods, I swallow bugs. And he has no dignity. He never touched me but he was like all the time raping me with his love. Understand? And there's more. He offered me money. Swear to God and hope to die. Actual money, can you imagine? I asked him how much. You know, curious. Seventy-five bucks, he said. I didn't know whether to be flattered or insulted. He finally went up to a hundred and fifty. I called him a schmuck. That's a word for all seasons. And you know what? Are you ready? He didn't even know what it meant. That's what a schmuck he was. No sympathy left. I said, be gone. Faretheewell, Schmuck. What was the question? Did he melt my heart? You've got to be kidding."

She went back to her typewriter and didn't speak for the rest of the day. Such a flood of words was a jolt. I had been given a quick look into a younger, cruder person. But, contrary to earlier findings, alive.

For the next few weeks she was again a self-effacing slave bringing me offerings in neat triplicate. One Friday a problem developed in a project we were working on to see if female college students did better on tests when questioned by women than by men. Normally this wouldn't have called me out of the office, but our man who was to conduct the test in Vermont had been bumped off a flight on his way to Bennington. So an emergency developed and Scanlan, of course, decided I should go. When Milly heard of this she actually offered to drive me there. It seemed she had to go to Vermont anyway to visit her mother, who had a cottage near Arlington. It had begun to rain. Since I wasn't in a mood to struggle onto the train, I accepted. Milly was delighted. She took me home and waited, double parked, while I ran up to pack an overnight bag.

ONE FINE DAY

She drove skillfully and talked ceaselessly, her oral history jumping backward and forward in time until I was never sure whether any given event had happened years ago or last week. But little by little I realized that I was being turned into a sexless confidante.

"My mother keeps telling me to go out more with men. She never stops. In fact everyone tells me I should go out more with men. Even Mrs. Scanlan. She, bless her, has to fight them off with a stick. Do you know that even my cleaning lady dropped a hint. Said she cleans twice a week the pad of this nice young banker in Maspeth. Boy that sounded Jewish, didn't it? Twice a week the pad. Anyway, I guess my being like not the number one raging beauty of this world makes some people become desperate on my behalf. They think it helps giving my number to an army of creeps. Point being the men who like me are not to be believed and the ones I dig are booked solid for decades. I've had three proposals of marriage if you count The Mad Mathematician and would they ever make one great police line-up. Be gone. And you know? Are you ready? I don't *want* to get married. Pain. Boredom. Yuck. So this conspiracy to introduce me to a nice Jewish type is like comic in the extreme. I tell my mother that it's anti-women's lib. That's what I tell my mother."

"Why?" I asked.

"Shit, don't break in like that. You scared me."

"Why is it anti-women's lib to get married?"

"It's not, but I have to tell her something. If you ever meet my mother you'll understand. She's like sick, my mother. It's what keeps her such an entertaining person."

"When's the last time you met a man you really liked?"

"I met plenty. But they're always celebrating their tenth wedding anniversary or some such nonsense."

"Be specific."

"Ah, specific. Last year I got asked out by my chiropodist.

He was OK I guess. Then his brother came over one night and tried to rape me."

"What happened?"

"I found a new chiropodist. Hey, are we still on the right road?"

Whipped by night rain and burned by occasional on-coming brights, she drove on, declining my repeated offer to take the wheel, and asked, "What d'ya mean?" when I said that I wouldn't be surprised if, in this weather, we came across Heathcliff hitchhiking. Told that he was someone in a book, she asked, "Do you remember the title?"

"*Wuthering Heights.*"

"Did it just come out?"

"No, no. It's a classic. It's one of the five greatest novels written in English." She looked doubtful. "It's by a woman," I added, hopefully.

"Nope. Don't think I know it. Is it about wind and rain and like that?"

When I conceded that, in a sense, it was, she mentioned a favorite novel of hers that was also about the wind and the rain. *Lovers in the Storm* by John Royal. It was the first hint as to how much she and I lived in different worlds, literary and otherwise. She was an avid reader. So was I. Yet it turned out that neither of us had ever read a book the other recommended. Works by Proust, Joyce, Faulkner, Conrad were countered by such names as J. Roland Reynolds, Jessica Gilbert, Wolf Allison, T. S. Tubbs. As far as I was concerned, mythical authors, every one. My chauffeur, in turn, was disappointed in my rather parochial grasp of literature. She struggled to remember another author she liked. His writing she described as very gripping. Blacksomething was his name. Though it was useless, I tried anyway. "Blackwood? Algernon Blackwood writes stories about—"

"I hate the supernatural," she interrupted, quickly. Then she remembered. "Irving Blackstein. That's it. *Hitchhiking in the Holy Land.* It was real exciting."

But for a moment there our worlds had overlapped. "You read Algernon Blackwood?"

"No, never."

"How did you know he deals in the supernatural?"

"From my mother, who else? She'll believe anything if it makes no sense." She smiled. "Know what?"

"Tell me."

"Here we are."

We wound our way up into greater darkness and Bennington College. I leaped out and was stricken by rain-lashed blindness until at last I found a door that opened and someone who knew about the project I was supposed to supervise. A female professor of biology, as it turned out. Then the blow fell. My colleague, bounced from his flight, had found his way to Vermont after all and was now here, asleep, in the only bedroom available. I had come for nothing, had no place to stay, and no way to get home. I was wet, tired, and hungry. To commit murder would have been easy. Knowing precisely whom to kill was the problem.

"Well, I'll be fucked," I growled. The biology professor blinked.

To make it worse, Milly, sweet Milly, was on her way north to food, drink, and a dry bed. Then perhaps with cognac standing on her night table she would enjoy a drowsy hour's read of one of those internationally unheard-of novels before drifting off to sleep while the rain, her distant drummer, kept a drowsy rhythm for her dreams.

I was rescued by my own imcompetence. Stupidly, triumphantly, I had left my overnight bag in her car, and so back Milly came knocking on the thick floor-to-ceiling glass panel beside one of the locked doors, tapping loudly with her car keys, clutching my heavy valise, rained-on, grinning, waving her arm, only too happy to be of help.

Ten minutes later her mother's cottage, fully lit in the wuthering mess, appeared above us like paradise. Our headlights revealed a dirt road, a crushed mouse, shrubbery, a pebbled parking area. We dashed giggling up the steps and into the house, where Mrs. Hawkmann sat filing her nails and looking for all the world like Charles de Gaulle in hair-curlers.

"Milly," she said, good-naturedly. "In all this rain you've found a man."

"What?" I said, my reverie shattered as I sat in the office.

"Why so early?" Scanlan repeated. "You don't want to wear yourself out."

Taking my gaze from the sliding, flapping, floating brown wrapping paper, I focused on Scanlan's massive, double-breasted, well-pressed, pin-stripe business suit. His ludicrous baby-face, usually at the verge of a frown, gleamed with that special serenity it achieved just before a sarcastic remark.

"How come you're on time? Your home burn down?"

"Got up early to get in a full day of anxiety."

"You finish the Hilton job?" he asked. His face, as usual, resisted jokes and aging.

"It's been on your desk since nine P.M., Friday."

"Stayed that late, did you?" An eyebrow arched skeptically.

"If you didn't always dash home at closing time . . ." It was a joke of sorts, so I smiled, which didn't seem to make it one as far as he was concerned. He came a few steps closer and straightened a ragged line of books on my desk.

"My wife is dropping by today. She asked if you would write out your Quiche Lorraine recipe for her. We're having some guests over in a few days. She still remembers that time when you made it for us."

"Will do."

He waved and walked out. Immediately I jotted down the ingredients and instructions. I was slightly hurt by her asking this of me without also extending an invitation, yet somewhat relieved that I wouldn't have to undergo another evening's exposure to her charms. Why then was I getting such pleasure out of performing this menial task? I even took time to drop in a few light witticisms and wondered why. I went so far as recommending wines and what to put into the salad. Far too much time is being spent on this already, I thought. But it didn't look neat enough so I wrote it all out again. Then I folded it into an envelope, wrote "Mrs. Philippa Scanlan" on the outside, and slipped it into my jacket pocket.

It still seemed too early to start work. I opened the *Times* again and read about arson in the Bronx and a cop shot dead on the Williamsburg Bridge. Milly walked in. I expected a comment on my miraculous early arrival, but she viewed me sadly, went into her own office, reappeared without the purple, gift-wrapped package she had been carrying but with the same morose expression. She had all the pathos of someone who had just discovered how vividly unbeautiful she really was. For several weeks she had dwelt in gloom. Now, intensified, it punctured what little courage I had to articulate that which would have made her sadder still.

"Good morning," I said too loudly.

Her attempted smile gave away all the anguish she was hiding. Hurriedly I dictated several business letters, which she took down at equally great speed. My hope was to out-distance the gloom, and we seemed to do just that. Progress was made. Pitfalls, avoided. Saved, you might say, by the Protestant Ethic. Bless her love of work. Leave it to a Jew to really understand the Protestant Ethic.

"Are we through?" Milly asked, as if to prove me wrong immediately.

"Almost," I said. "Just two more."

I began to wrestle with the problem of an opening sentence.

"We are, aren't we?" she asked, looking like someone expecting to be slapped.

"How do you mean?"

"Please, Rob, just answer. Do you want us, you know, to break up?"

On the edge of her chair she sat, her beads becoming a pendulum. Numbness took hold. "Do I want to break up?"

"Do you want to, yes or no?"

I thought, better place the order for morning coffee or it'll be delivered late again. This nagged me for a moment. How did I ever get involved with this girl? That nagged me too. On the electric clock the digits 10:59 blinked and became 11:00.

"Do I want to break up?" I repeated.

My hesitation gave me away.

She nodded and climbed to her feet. I had no idea what she would do. Nor did she, it seemed. She stared out the window, walked toward the door to the hall, remembered the pad in her hand, came back, stared out the window.

"Milly, I'm very sorry that—"

"Sure. Listen, that's how it is. Talking's no good. Aspirins neither. Wow. Be all right in a minute. Not your fault. Sort of hung on, hopin'. Son of a gun. Really got shot down this time. Not too good as a tragic figure, am I? All mush, that's me. Shit, it's worse than with the chiropodist."

"Milly."

"Don't. Once I start cryin', wow. Intensive-care ward. Milly's gonna be all right. Milly's gonna pull herself together."

"Look, perhaps you'd like to take the day off."

She sat down and shook her head. "I am taking myself to the john. When I . . . when I return. New Milly. Fuckin' a-right. Then we work. We cut the shit. Really work."

"Sure thing," I said, close to tears myself.

She slapped her knees, stood up, and was out of there fast. I didn't think she'd return soon or be in good shape when she did. Yet back she came in five minutes, grim and white as when suffering her period. She worked hard, both of us did, toiling away cordially in the presence of that one person we each wanted to run from screaming. An hour and some minutes later while baking to death in this chilly atmosphere, I was saved by Scanlan wanting to see me. I left Milly and went across the hall.

It was as if I had stepped out of a decompression chamber. Scanlan's room, larger and more elegant than mine, enjoyed a daily flood of morning sun, a view of the park, and Philippa. Of all the wives who on occasion visited the office, only Philippa gave the impression she was trespassing and enjoying it. The lady turned and offered me the pleasure of her hazel eyes, concave cheeks, and warm, slightly mocking smile. What it was she mocked was never clear. Today it seemed to be the office I had just come from, with its need for new paint, a better lamp, and someone, anyone, other than my red-eyed stenographic albatross. Traveling from there into Murray's business temple of sunlight, with the riveting presence of his wife, made it seem as if I had come not from across the hall but all the way from the other side of the tracks. Or was she savoring the fact that as a subordinate to her husband's pleasure, I was to some degree subordinate to hers as well? Her smile seemed to imply all these things; it always did. It also implied that she knew how much I yearned to strip off all her Bloomingdale's packaging and skewer her on Scanlan's fur couch. The idea was to partake of her naked spongecake to amend for the vast unfairness of life—which makes no sense, of course, for life had been reasonably good to me. Still the worm of yearning came alive whenever Philippa entered the room. It was a constant much like, in Milly's phrase, the noodging of time.

Mrs. Scanlan's presence put a stop to work. We all chatted

as if waiting for a bus. Murray sat on the edge of his desk glancing through his newspaper—a sure sign that work had been suspended—while his wife asked after my health. I spoke of jogging and vitamin C, but all the while her eyes seemed to ask if I were finding her as lovely as ever. How cosy she was inside her beauty. Refusing to quench my need to look at her, I contemplated instead her huge husband, who often gave a faint smile at things said while continuing to read. Then he spoke; did she want him to get two tickets to this new Pirandello production? "Three," she said, sitting down on the furry expanse of couch, "one for Robbie." As usual, politeness was something he left to his glamorous wife. Wearily he stared at me for confirmation. They hadn't known of my affair with Milly and now, with its rupture, there would be no need to tell them.

"Would you like to?" Philippa asked, as she slumped against a pillow, her crossed legs predominant in dark stockings.

"Yes, I would."

"Three tickets, then."

"Three tickets," said Murray, returning to his paper.

"Robbie, did my efficient husband mention perchance a recipe?"

I removed it from my pocket and handed it over. She studied the instructions slowly (they were both reading now) while I imagined, with all her clothes still on, parting those long dark legs, tearing off her paper panties (which she once confessed to wearing) and thrusting home to produce (what?) a silent grimace as if holding to a thin line between pain and pleasure or loud, exhaustive gasps, as if appalled by her own approval.

"Thank you very much," she said, warmly. "It's not only a good job but so amusing. And how many recipes can you say that about? With me it's usually the results that are amusing."

"I hope your guests like it."

"I'd invite you, Robbie, but they're all such bores. Relatives of Murray's."

"Now, now," Scanlan said.

"The kind that talk baseball all evening."

"Like that weekend in Westport," I reminded her. She gave two slow nods of ironic understanding.

It had been a "working vacation," with clients and wives. The men were bankers to the last, displaying their mastery over the art of controlled boredom. Saturday evening, however, was meant to be fun. But at the restaurant, from cocktails to cognac, they talked nonstop about Watergate. Nixon was innocent, they argued. If you can't trust the president, who can you trust? If you didn't have faith in our system, what do you have faith in? Philippa was having trouble staying awake. Murray handed over his car keys and asked me to drive her back to our motel.

In the warm August night, she, to my suprise, rallied quickly. It was our first time alone together, yet how unselfconsciously she took my arm, how pleased she seemed to be with me. All at once the arthritic formalities of the evening were gone. In the car she made fun of everyone at the table, including her husband. Slowly and portentously she articulated a complex sentence of business-jargon which wound its way through an undergrowth of split-hairs and which finally and very precisely said nothing. I asked her to define her terms. She produced an invisible gun and shot me.

She decided to use the motel pool and insisted that I do the same. Standing in the doorway to her cabin, she tossed me a garish example of her husband's beach wear, and I went back to my room to find ways to keep the pair of trunks, once on, from falling off. I was swimming in them even before hitting the water. I didn't look like a man in a bathing suit; I looked like a man who had been jumped and robbed of his clothes. In the now somewhat cooler night, I sat waiting in a beach chair near quivering water and a flickering neon sign that read, VACANCY.

Philippa emerged in a bath towel, which she kept wrapped around her while we called each other cowards for not going in first. She held it around her as she approached the edge, descended several steps into the shallow end, the water reaching to her knees, and even then held it around her. At last she dumped the towel on dry concrete and sank quickly, clad in a pale blue bikini, until all I could see of her was her head. I stood up. She didn't comment on my voluminous swimming costume. When I dove in she kept to herself as though sharing the pool with a stranger. She practiced modest strokes, absorbed in keeping her head regal, her hair dry. I debated whether her cautious distance wasn't a bit insulting. I was mistaken in thinking her a flirt or maybe it took the safe company of her tall husband to bring it out. Actually I never seriously believed in myself as her lover. The danger of losing my job was too great. This kept the idea on the farcical level of erotic fantasy. She was elegant, a rare woman, but married. All of life's unnamed treasures, for years searched for, perhaps only imagined, were glimpsed at last and too late, in the hypnotic sculpture of her face. I climbed out of the pool, dripping and chilled. I hugged myself, searching for stars and finding none. Crickets throbbed. I felt thin and weak, like a boy again.

Philippa called from the water. "Hey, you look cold. Use my towel."

I thanked her and picked it up while she did another lap, craning her neck as though trying to see the cabins and then the return lap as though trying to see the road. She climbed the ladder, glazed with water, and strolled toward me in the flattering clutches of her bikini. Her compact, breath-catching figure suggested she be swallowed whole like an oyster. I offered up her towel. She became enveloped. We sat in the beach chairs as she rubbed and cuddled herself dry.

"Rob, you're still cold."

"No."

"Here let's try this." And she scraped her chair closer to spread the towel over us like a blanket. We lay there staring at the black sky, her smooth arm touching mine.

"Do you toss and turn?" I asked.

"No. Do you snore?"

"Nope. Talk in your sleep?"

"Never."

"Fine."

"Night, night."

"Pleasant dreams."

"Jesus," she said after a pause, "it really would be nice to sleep out this evening, wouldn't it?"

"We'll need another deck chair for Murray."

"For him anything less than a king-size bed is roughing it. Once when we were, as they say, courting, I tried to get him to spend the night with me in a hammock. Refused. Bad for the back, he said. You know how Murray can get. Well, I called his bluff. I climbed in and waited. If he didn't join me in an hour then I planned to give up and go to him. Stupidly I fell asleep. Spent the whole night in that Goddamned hammock."

"How was it?"

"Lonesome."

"I mean sleeping."

"Next morning I was one of the walking wounded. I never let on."

"Kept a stiff upper lip and lower back."

"Exactly."

A car pulled into the circular driveway. Murray climbed out

and the car moved off. He approached, circling the pool.

"Don't say anything," she whispered. "Let's see what he does."

"Cold?" Murray asked. "On a night like this?"

"We lost our bathing suits," his wife said.

"You lost your fucking brains some time ago."

"Why, thank you."

Murray's tie was loose, his collar undone, his jacket hanging over his shoulder. His other hand was undoing the buttons of his shirt. I asked how the dinner went.

"They're going to call us on Monday. I think they'll go for the full fifty thousand."

Philippa sang, "Mur-ray's slight-ly *plas*-tered."

He paid no attention. Frowning into the pool, he asked, "How far down is the bottom?"

"Just keep going," I said, "you can't miss it."

The motel lawn rang with her single volley of laughter.

"I'm wearing your bathing suit. You want it back?"

"Naw."

"Go for a swim, Murray."

"Go for a swim, Murray," he repeated, imitating his wife's condescending tone.

"The water is lovely," I suggested.

"You have the roast beef? Lousy, wasn't it?"

"I had the fish."

Philippa said nothing. The crickets seemed raucous. Murray pulled his shirt free of his trousers.

"Let's go," he said to her. "Come on."

"It's pleasant sitting here."

"Come *on*. Time for bed."

After a while she struggled to climb out of her chair, slipped back, offered a sigh and her arm, then grunted as he pulled. Standing with eyes averted, she said good night, left me the towel, and walked away. He seems stuffed and lumpy compared to her sleek nudity. His arm goes around her shoulders. She hooks her thumb in his belt. They become smudged in the distance and the moonlight. They turn into a naked boy and a grown bear. Then, man and wife again in the bright overhead lamp of their cabin porch, he bends and fiddles while she raises both arms to shake loose her bulk of black hair. The door opens; she slips past as his surreptitious hand does something quickly just below her pale blue bottom. A faint yelp. The door shuts. I watch the window light up. Much later I notice it has gone dark. Sounds of crickets and air-conditioners are vibrating and pulsating thoughts of smooth Philippa. How the others feasted on her during dinner. Her towel around me. Warmth and chill. Too much of something. Insistent. I come alive with a backache. The harsh, open sky is pouring down its sharp light. In the dregs of the dawn there I am still in the sagging beach chair, shattered and astonished. I feel like a trapped vampire decomposing at sunrise. The turquoise swimming pool was undulating in its solitude. An inverted, quivering turquoise oak tree joined trunks with a tall, brown motionless oak tree standing above ground on the other side of the water. I strained out of my chair and, despite a seizure of old age, walked.

"Yes," she said, "just like that weekend in Westport. They were so boring, Murray got drunk and you ended up spending the night in a beach chair."

"If you can't afford a room," Scanlan suggested grinning at the newspaper, "you should say something."

"Could have slept with us," she added, merrily.

One of the mathematicians leaned in and beckoned Murray out. Philippa stood up and came closer. "I never got a chance to tell you." She glanced at the door. "After we went swimming I dreamt I was lost in a forest. Lo and behold what do I see? A hammock. When I come closer, I find you inside fast asleep. True. I must not wake him, I thought. He looks so peaceful. But I was frightened so I climbed in just to be safe. Trying not to wake you."

"And?"

"I woke you. Didn't mean to."

"Then what happened?"

"The hammock broke. Kerplunk."

"A likely story."

"Really it did."

"How come?"

"Faulty construction, I guess." She gave a tiny smile. "Anyway, what I'm getting at is this. First there was the incident of me minus Murray in the hammock, right? Then you fell asleep outdoors just as I did, correct? Next came me finding you in the woods. By the way, did you have a dream that night, as well?"

"No, but that just might have been a coincidence."

"All right, Mr. Skepticism, what would you say if I told you that Murray also had a dream that night."

"Too much roast beef, for a start. OK OK, tell me what it was."

"He dreamt he came awake and found me gone from our bed. He went outside to look around. And there, Mr. Skepticism, there was I asleep in a chair, alone, by the pool. Voilà." She gave her head a toss of triumph.

"And what is it all supposed to mean?"

"Perhaps it's a sign."

"A sign of what? That we have a collective unconscious of three?"

"For a start, as you would say, yes. Perhaps it's a sign that we're all about to share a special destiny."

"In a hammock? I sincerely doubt it."

She didn't hear this. She stared at me for a moment as if trying to decide whether or not she should disclose one final, lethal bit of news.

"Go on. Tell me," I said.

She lifted herself onto Murray's desk and folded her hands in her lap.

"I should tell you, should I? All right, I will. He carried me back to our bed. In his dream, that is. Trying not to wake me." She paused to let that sink in.

"But you woke up anyway."

"Yes."

"I saw that one coming. OK. You woke up. And then?"

"I woke up. And then, well, Murray decided it was as good a time as any to get a little, oh, to get a little sex going."

"Ah, zo."

"But suddenly there's this terrible knocking on the door. And who is it? It's you with some unimportant business detail. Murray gets absolutely furious. You're just standing there, smiling. Murray grabs hold of your throat. You try to say something but can't. You're choking."

"And?"

She nods. "He kills you."

"Kills me?"

"It shook him up, afterward. When he woke up, that is."

"*Well!* Perhaps I should start wearing a neck brace. Or you should stop making love to your husband."

"Always skepticism. Well, one of these days, Robbie, one of these days—"

"*Damn it to hell,*" boomed Scanlan's voice as he entered the room. "Did you rewrite this?"

He held some printed matter near my face, tapping at an open page with his finger. Feeling myself tighten, I steadied the bouncing print.

"Not me," I said.

"Not *there! HERE!*" He stabs at the pamphlet again, knocks it to the floor, retrieves it, shows me the paragraph in question, one I recognize, didn't realize was his, and do remember changing. Philippa tries to calm him. He silences her with a loud bearlike growl. Turns to me again. His screams splash like hot grease. I reply in a cracked, unfamiliar, adolescent voice, suddenly terrified of all manner of loss, loss of my job, my pride, even—why do I think of this?—of my life. And, of course, my anger. I hang onto it and apologize. Philippa observes me without expression. Again I apologize. Hadn't intended. Didn't realize. Very sorry. A deadness is upon me like an armored suit. Yet my nakedness is outside of it floating on the air. I finally escape. People have gathered in the hall but I walk away from them, holding my breath, into my office, closing the door. Milly is in her room, out of sight. I wait until my pulse comes down from three floors above. For no good reason I check my watch and fail to register what it says. This day will be a long ride and I am as brittle as glass. At my desk I sharpen pencils. I've often seen Murray explode this way, always at others, while I stand by silently. Into Milly's room I go to hear a comforting voice. A note on her desk says, GONE TO LUNCH, BOSS-MAN. I left-hook another glance at my watch. Eight past eleven. That's odd. Lunch so early? I put the crystal to my ear. No sound. Dead. The phone tells me that when I hear the toe-un the ty-um will be tway-elve thirty-fouor. I hang up and move time forward with a thumb and a finger.

Food and wine. Just the thing. A whiskey first, perhaps. I make it unseen to the washroom. Splash water on my face. Adjust my collar, fingers quivering. In the hall again, I round the corner to the elevator and meet Philippa. Her hand touches my sleeve.

"Oh, Robbie. He's insane sometimes."

"OK," I said.

"He doesn't really mean it. That doesn't help you much, I know."

"Hate to be there when he does mean it."

"I've been there," she murmured, glancing at her shoe. Then with a shrug, "You're too passive, Rob. That's how he thinks of you. Defy him. Walk out. Take the rest of the day off. Be defiant. Really. Listen, why don't we go to a museum or someplace?" She smiled. I was appalled at how beautiful her eyes were. "You must take hold of things, Rob. Stand up for yourself. Hell, walk out. The two of us together, spending the whole damn day together, that should fix 'im."

I become worried again. Murray's recent behavior falls into perspective. If that's what happens if I tamper with his prose, what if with his wife? Or was she simply casting hints to sound the depths of her appeal?

The elevator arrived and Vince watched Philippa enter his domain. To my amazement he fell silent. But as we descended his squalid stare never left her. A married couple entered and stood in constrained idleness, the man spiriting glances at Philippa's beauty, the woman at Philippa's clothes.

Indeed, on her the most neutral garments spoke out and said woman. Lines were traced, secrets whispered, and always the gist was woman. Philippa seemed unable to prevent it. Each new posture or shift of weight made something else salient, brought forth yet another annunciation. It was as if she possessed fame, or carried a contagion, or, on the strength of a whim, had the power to change our lives.

In the lobby we were alone again. Vince, with evident regret, had gone up to fetch others. "Are you coming with me?" she asked. "Do we strike a blow for freedom?"

"I would love to, really. But there's this luncheon—"

"Tsh, tsh. You'll have to take hold of things better than that."

"I'm sorry. Truly."

"Remember, I know the secret."

"Of what?"

"Of how certain people should be handled."

"Murray, you mean. Yes, I'm sure."

"You're missing your chance."

"Well, perhaps some other time."

"Some other time. Yes, why not?"

All happiness went with her as she swept out of the lobby in a mild display of sporty theatrics. For her the day was vast with possibilities and I would take part in none of them. What bliss to walk off with her for a while. My own fault to stay so rooted in myself. I watched her fast dark legs, her lovely floating hair. Suddenly her arm stretched upward. I watched her as the taxi stopped; she bent down slightly to say something through the open window.

Her lilt stayed with me all that day and made life worse. If I backed off from her after what had happened in her husband's office, then surely I always would. Just as she would continue to insinuate what I must always pretend not to notice. We had become permanent accomplices in an endlessly incompleted act.

After lunch I felt ill at the very thought of work. Milly's presence, Philippa's absence, and mad Scanlan made it all seem too much. She was right. I must show that I am not a man who can be talked to in that way. Then I remembered how Murray never means for others to take his rages as anything more than momentary irritations instantly forgotten, at least by him. And does it make sense that the next in line, namely myself, should threaten all he worked for simply over a bruised ego, a bit of pique? There was Milly, too, alone now in my office, left to face her pain without the distraction of work. Lastly it just would not be right to appear afraid or deeply wounded. To return was the manly thing to do and in the end I did it. I spent the day at my desk with Milly's behavior cold and correct and without Scanlan coming to apologize, not that I really thought he would.

At 5:31, Milly left without a word. She stood in the doorway sending me a festering look which I took care not to notice. Then she was gone. Soon, so was I.

In front of my apartment building, when I got home, was some finely shattered glass where the cars had collided. My fifth-floor living-room window was opaque with a gleaming rectangle of orange sunset. No red-head was in the hall this time. I picked up the mail and rode the elevator. Amid several surprisingly large bills, there was a birthday card from my parents, who were living in retirement in California. A little verse inside invited me to have a happy and healthy birthday ("healthy" underlined) on this my thirty-fifth. And why didn't I write? Lots of love. Mom and Dad. It had arrived a day early.

I put on some Mahler and he boomed and dredged, writhed and whispered, as I made hamburgers and poured myself a beer. The first symphony seemed right for my mood, flooding this two-room pad with loud banalities and soft flights of lyrical magic. I needed mountains, chunks of majesty covered in catsup, huge indiscriminate things under which to bury sadness. Hell, I lost two women today. Carelessly tossed them both away. Christ, more rancid verse. Despite the music, bits of the trauma kept floating back. Philippa saturating the office as she lay on that couch. Milly-the-Martyr spilling invisible blood all afternoon. Scanlan's wild infant's face. Enough.

I replaced Mahler, who had struck out, with Chopin. The Nocturnes. Almost at once the undertow pulled me far beyond hearing. I was soon busy having a romantic reunion with Murray's wife, drinking chilled wine, and rocking gently with her in mid-pool upon a white air-mattress. Only to come

awake, so to speak, to find myself along with Artur Rubinstein
rummaging about in my soul.

Books then. Funny-writing was what I needed. I tried several and found their pages offering nothing more than print.
But Thurber helped. *The Night the Ghost Got in.* Except the
phone begins to ring. That'll be Milly. Right on time. Just
when I'm getting my head together. Damn her, we ended it.
Let it *be* ended. The phone is screaming in rhythmic waves of
pain. I'm not home. I'm not here. Let it be ended. A pause
lengthens. It's over. Peace at last. The sadistic device, a few
seconds later, rings again. Eight more times before the torture
stops.

The eleven-o'clock TV news, filled with disaster and killings, is nicely interspersed with sprightly, mindless fragments
from a mythical world, a place where lovely people are made
ecstatic over a new brand of coffee or by a magical pair of
panti-hose.

Amid inflation, pollution, corruption, and war, much time
was given to the loss at sea of a Pan Am 707 some hours after
takeoff from Kennedy Airport with 192 on board. A bomb, it
was thought, had exploded. Then my attention was caught by
a story of violence committed this morning in my neigh-
borhood. A woman had gone into the laundry room of her
apartment building, and there two youths caught and raped
her. Drawings were shown of the accused: a thin face with a
Fu Manchu mustache and another, fatter one with small eyes
and a scar. Both were referred to as "Hispanic." The woman's
name was withheld. Time of the rape, exactly nine forty-
seven. Her wristwatch had been smashed in the struggle.

Going to bed seemed by far the best idea. This time at the
tape recorder I was a little more gentle with myself. "Wake up,
Rob, old friend, old buddy. Awaiting you is a great day filled
with magical panti-hose and delicious freeze-dry coffee plus

the collapse of life as we know it. So get up, time's-a-wastin'. Oh, yes, we're out of milk and sugar. And no more chopped meat for a while, OK? And get your damn watch fixed. Rise and shine, Robbie. Hurry up. Oh, and happy birthday. Almost forgot. And many happy returns of the day."

The automatic timer was still set at seven-thirty. All was well. Lying in bed with a large delicate glass that cradled a puddle of cognac, I tried to plow further into my free set of Will Durant's *History of the World*. The Dark Ages were upon me but I couldn't care less, for Philippa kept insinuating her magic into the room. My hand resting casually on my own thigh was enough to summon up a terribly vivid Mrs. Scanlan tightly clasped in her blue bikini. We were in the water again, this time playful as dolphins. She came close and we touched. I carried her to our hammock in the woods and we put into motion a pendulous joy wherein I strove to make clear to my mystical Philippa all that was firmly evident and provable in this world.

2

As soon as I heard that unfamiliar, crude, slightly offensive voice that I could never believe was actually mine, I knew at once what the trouble was. I had stupidly set the tape in the wrong place last night, so entranced was I with recording clever things to be awakened with this morning. Instead I was again bombarded with yesterday's *Wake up you lazy bastard*. How's that for starting one's birthday off on the wrong foot? Well, at least it was 7:30 and I was awake again to see it. Two days in a row without oversleeping. Surely a citation was in order. And speaking of the wrong foot, I got my slippers together quickly this time. The left one was evidently making a habit of hiding itself under the dresser. My splendid Vermeer was all bathed in sunlight. *The Kitchen Maid*. Plump lass pouring out fresh milk.

Remembering that my milk was sour, I decided no Familia for me this morning. But true to my pledge to get out of this rut of mine, I passed up the news and fiddled about with the radio for some decent music, found Vivaldi, sat in luxury on my living-room couch and had purposely temperate coffee and two pieces of hot toast, all splendidly unrushed; a morning of efficiency and calm spoiled only by some butter-drippings on my trousers.

This time I was out in the hall and double-locking the door when I heard my phone come alive. Damn her. It was over. We agreed. Did she have to invade this lovely, hopeful, rut-free morning as well? I walked away and saw the red-head (must learn her name) reaching the elevator. Perfect timing, lad. And I trotted up as she stepped in. On closer inspection she had a face that exuded, along with a touch of perfume, the slightly vulgar suggestion of her own superior breeding. I lashed out with a jovial "Good morning" that sounded as if it had been recorded the day before and a bit too loudly at that. Her Majesty swiveled her head slowly in my direction indicating that there was something decidedly uncalled for in her having to do so. She nodded, barely, and swung her face away with all the ominous quiet of a pivoting turret on a Sherman tank.

"You just moved in," said I with fatuous panache.

She hummed in minimal agreement.

"Well, if you need any help. Borrowing salt. Lifting objects. Let me know."

"Thank you but the superintendent has been most kind."

My audience with Her Majesty was evidently at an end. I would have to look elsewhere for a romantic replacement for my two lost ladies. The doors parted and Her Majesty walked across our lobby, passed through the front door, and disappeared toward the subway.

I stepped onto the sidewalk and jumped as an automobile rammed another in front of the building. Wow, two days in a row, I thought, and moved on with the detachment of a true New Yorker. I looked back and saw one of the drivers, a tall bald man with a deeply disgusted look, climb out and adjust his tie. Ahead of me Her Majesty bought a paper and descended into the subway. I hurried, snatched my *Times*, paid, and cantered down the steps to catch her. I walked the platform but she had vanished in the crowd. The final snub.

A crowded train ground to a stop and I squeezed in. As usual I couldn't read. I could barely breathe. My hunt for Her Majesty left me at the wrong end of the station in Manhattan and I had to walk back to reach my usual exit. The final insult.

A stirring pair of bare legs led me up to the street. Since they were going in my direction, I followed, curious to see the lady's face. A good distance ahead of her a commotion was taking place. Some people stopped walking, others turned to look. When I came closer and realized what had happened, I went rigid. It was that sudden chill when your wallet is missing. He was a broken, disheveled, gray-haired figure and now that he had been lifted back onto his feet I even noticed his tennis shoes.

Someone walked into me from behind. I moved on and stopped by the curb to let the others pass. Quickly I glanced at my paper. Another American ambassador had been kidnapped in Brazil. The date at the top of the page said April 15. Today wasn't my birthday. Or had the bastard sold me yesterday's *Times?* I dashed across the street ignoring an angry car horn and came to a stop in front of another newstand. There was a stack of *New York Times* beside a taller pile of *The Daily News.* The date of each edition said Monday, April 15.

"Wuha' d'ya read?"

"Ah . . . nothing."

Turning the corner, I moved on. I stopped. There was no way to walk to where I had to go. Standing with my back to the wall of a building, I didn't move. Perhaps I couldn't move. The sky was beautiful. Just as it had been yesterday. Just as it often is this time of year. I watched the tedious blending and parting of the traffic. A slowly strolling black man glanced at me as if I were high on drugs. He and the trucks and the buses and the noise and the steep walls of commerce threatened me with their impenetrable indifference. I was too terrified to move or speak or even know that I felt any terror at all. A loose manhole cover made a comforting clop, like a horse's hoof, each time the wheel of a car passed over it. Gradually I was able to think again. I kept it safe and businesslike. There was, I decided a need for more data. An error of memory must not be ruled out. Overwork had brought about a short circuit in the brain. That was it, surely, I would go to the office. I'd be safe in the office. Things must be counted on to right themselves without my help just as they always had. Wasn't that so? The sign itself was comforting. INSTITUTE FOR THE APPLIED STUDY OF SOCIAL RESPONSES. And there was good old Vince.

"Pick a number from one to ten," he said.

"You pulled that joke yesterday."

"Yesterday was Sunday. Come on, pick a number from one to ten."

That terrible chill. "Seven," I whispered.

"Wrong! Boy were you way off."

I stared at him like an actor who had forgotten the next line.

"If Bela Lugosi married Bella Abzug, her name would be Bella Lugosi."

Was it conceivable that an elaborate practical joke was being played on me? Breathing became difficult.

"Your floor, Chief." The elevator had stopped. The doors were standing open.

This time I sat at my desk straining to recall yesterday, or was it last Friday? Frantically trying to find differences. Murray had been the first to enter. He had made a wisecrack about my being early and then requested that I write out a recipe. I waited.

A sheet of wrapping paper was dipping and tumbling in the wind. I leaped up to escape my view of the window. I bit a knuckle and felt terribly alone. Yesterday's letters! The carbons! Should still be here. I went and pulled open the file cabinet beside my desk and began fingering through the manila envelopes.

Jumping: "Wha?" I spun around.

"I said how come you're on time? Your home burn down?"

"No," I all but shouted.

"Looks like coming in on time doesn't agree with you."

"Ah." I discovered sweat on my brow.

"You finish the Hilton job?"

"It's on. Your desk."

"Fine, listen." He took a few steps closer. I almost screamed when he straightened the books. "My wife is dropping by today. She asked if you would write out . . ."

Didn't really hear the rest. Saw his jaws moving. Felt the sounds of his voice like cuts from a razor. He finished. I nodded. He waved and walked out. It was so early that even my doctor's nurse, when I phoned, wasn't in. Hand trembling, I hung up. I tore through the file cabinet but yesterday's carbons were gone. I sat down, got up, rushed to the john. The mirror framed a startled, ashen, opened-mouthed oaf. I walked in a circle and returned to my friend in the mirror. Neither of us had answers or knew what to do. Against my better judgment, I went back to my desk and, like a spy on the earth, I waited.

Milly appeared doing a flawless imitation of her previous morose entrance. And with that same mysterious purple package. When she reappeared from her room I waved her over. She stood by the desk in her usual bad posture, her clothes, a drab hulk of an outfit, were the same, a combination of leftovers from several equally unsuccessful ensembles.

"Milly, you want to say, to ask me, something. You came with a question, if I'm not mistaken. Or *am* I mistaken? Go ahead."

Her mouth hung open.

"Go *on*."

"What are you trying to say?"

"Will you ask me the question," I growled, impelled by a masochistic fatalism, "or not?"

"What question?"

"You mean you didn't come in today ready to ask me something?"

She looked as if some cruel trick was being played on her.

"No," she said, but not at all firmly.

"Good, then we can go to work. By the way, those letters you typed yesterday. Where are the carbons?"

She frowned. "You mean Friday. Yesterday was Sunday."

"I say we wrote letters yesterday."

"Say it. Terrific. Look, Friday we worked on ways to equate sexual morality and police ethics, remember? No letters. No lunch, even. Just dull committee meetings and a dry cheese sandwich."

We argued a bit more and then I gave up.

"OK, OK, take a letter."

She sat down. The only thing worse than doing boring work is having to do the same boring work all over again. I was able to get through only one, the effort shredding the last of my calm.

"Type that up," I ordered. "The rest, the rest we'll do later."

"Rob, is there something wrong?"

"I'm not sure."

"It's happened, hasn't it?"

I looked up, "What? What's happened?"

"You've decided you want us to break up. Have—haven't you?"

"Oh, Christ." I got to my feet and walked away.

"Haven't you?" came her pathetically irritating voice.

"Yes. You know damn well the answer is yes. Has everyone gone mad or what?" I swirled on her. "You mean to tell me you don't remember asking me that very same question just yesterday? Just yesterday, sitting like that, pad in hand, looking just as pathetic and bizarre?"

A phone in another office rang once only.

"Yesterday was *Sun*day." Then Milly whimpered. "All day Sunday . . ."

"Yes?"

"Spent trying to get up courage. Courage to ask." Her eyes glistened. "Been trying all week."

She was quietly weeping.

"Milly, I'm sorry. I'm very sorry."

She stood with dignity and, carrying her pad, left the room. I sat down in my unoiled swivel-chair, started to toy with a ruler, and broke it. The room seemed cold and I phoned to have coffee for two delivered. Later I heard Milly typing in her office. Later still, her face distorted in an effort to look natural, she brought in the letter and one of the containers of coffee. For two hours I waited until at last the phone rang. That would be Murray. I barely had the strength to go.

With all my heart I hoped that Philippa would not be there to turn and offer me the pleasure of her hazel eyes and that her husband would not be seated on the edge of his desk nor would a pigeon be taking flight from one of the sills; but they were. The spacious office with its huge panes of glass seemed that much more likely to expose everyone in it to any of life's un-catalogued horrors. Philippa's faintly mocking smile this morning seemed absolutely venomous with secrets.

I was determined to steer our talk into uncharted waters, away from this repetition of a day mysteriously cancelled. All my manic energy, however, couldn't distract Murray from his paper or derail his suggestion that he and his wife see that play by Pirandello or her invitation that I join them.

I altered the script with a no but thanked her all the same.

"Okey doke," said her son-of-a-bitch husband, making not the slightest effort to persuade me.

Philippa looked hurt. "It's a lovely play, wonderfully surreal."

"Ah, huh."

"You see there are these six characters—"

"I know the play. I know it. It's just that I'm not . . . free."

"Sounds like some girl's got him all wrapped up." Then to me, "Can't you spend at least one evening with us?"

"Will you lay off the poor boob," said Murray, over the top of the paper.

"Shush. How can I manipulate with you butting in?"

"And this one thinks *I* lack subtlety," he informed me, lifting his chin in her direction.

Philippa touched my knee with her shoe from the couch. "All right, who is this vision? This wild thing who keeps you from your friends. I want to meet this girl."

I told her there was no girl.

She threw up her hands. "I discreetly drop the subject. I now move to a new topic. Robbie, did my husband mention, perchance, a recipe?"

It was no use. I felt drained and helpless. Mrs. Scanlan looked at me from the couch exactly as she had the day before: her head tilted, a finger drawing aside some strands of hair from her face, the legs crossed in dark stockings with the tip of one shoe making small circles in the air.

My explanation for not producing the recipe as ordered was

that I just couldn't remember it. But I promised to phone it to her tonight. When Murray was called from the room right on cue, I sat down like a frightened child beside her on the couch, my hands tickled by the fur. Her eyebrows lifted ever so slightly in curious expectation. I asked if she had the feeling of living today through a second time.

"No, my dear. I can't say that I have. Why do you ask?"

"I've got this terrible feeling of déjà vu."

She was intrigued, of course, and made sad as well. "Nothing like that ever happens to me. Can you tell me what I'm going to say next?"

"Not at the moment. But Murray will come thundering in here in a minute, furious as hell. All about the wording in a pamphlet, believe it or not."

I felt like a fraudulent clairvoyant.

"Let's wait and see," she suggested, then smiled. "Unless you prefer to play it safe and run for your life."

"No fear."

And I had none, not even when Scanlan burst upon us raging in front of my clinical detachment. Philippa, delighted by her sudden state of fright, gave a little squeal. Murray just screamed and screamed. It was like watching a film I had already seen and now disliked even more. I remembered it as drama. This time it dwindled into farce. Philippa sat with a hand over her mouth.

As the scene continued, Scanlan's voice, his outrageous behavior, his vulgar loss of control even as he tried to control others, got on my nerves. I snatched the pamphlet from his hand, tore it to pieces, screaming "SHUT UP!" and he did. The whole building did.

Murray frowned. "Oh, I should, should I?" Deflated into a normal tone.

"Yes, you should." I threw the shredded mess into the air.

"Merry Christmas." Philippa's hand was still on her mouth. "Put me down for a ticket, after all," I told her. Exit. It was, I thought, a much better performance than last time.

One look into my office (Milly was gone, of course) decided me that to stay here on this rerun of a day would be agony. I was close to screaming as it was and once I started I might not stop. At the elevator I pressed the button and puzzled over how lucid one could feel while going bananas.

A woman's heels clamored up behind me. With her arm through mine, her face beaming, Philippa exclaimed, "It was wonderful, Rob, the way you stood up to him."

"Guess so."

She straightened my tie and gave me a suspicious look. "How did you know he was coming in angry?"

"Today is a repeat."

"Of what?"

"Of today."

"Again, please."

The trouble was in knowing how much to tell her. She was enamored with the occult for she was one of those who found it rather exciting to believe in all the unprovable things. Not that she believed there was "someone up there" but rather that there was "something somewhere." To her, the supernatural was the workings of a secret and busy department of the mind that the mind knew nothing about. My little magic show in Murray's office she weathered rather well, I thought. After all, to predict anger in a cranky man might not seem so miraculous to the man's wife. But what I had to tell her was so far outside her fashionable range of mystic beliefs that in the end I edited my answer.

"Today is being repeated," I said, "at least for me it is. No one seems to know this. Don't ask me to explain because I can't."

"You're teasing me."

"I am not."

She was delighted. "What happens next? Tell me."

"Let me see. Vince will stare at you as we ride down."

"I hate to be immodest, but he did that when I rode up."

"Then you flirt with me outrageously."

"I always do that."

"You try to get me to take the rest of the day off in defiance of Murray. That's what happens."

"Seems to me you were pretty damn defiant as it was."

The elevator arrived and took us away. Vince stared at her as if trying to bring off the world's first telepathic rape. The married couple (I had forgotten them) stepped on board several floors below, and while the man indulged in a little extrasensory molesting, his wife seemed to be trying to read, if not Philippa's mind, then at least the hidden labels on her clothes.

"Do you think I was too defiant?" I questioned her afterward. Thoughts of losing my job chilled the lobby as we peered into each other's eyes.

"You should always take hold of things as forcefully as that. It's the only trait you lack."

"And today I had it."

"Today you had it."

"And tomorrow I may lack a job."

"Why are you always afraid? Murray respects strength. We both do. Strength in a man means a lot to a woman."

"Murray's strong, no?"

"Murray's a bully." With a mocking smile, "Well, you haven't told me what's going to happen next."

"You are about to suggest that we both go some place together."

"Oh, and where exactly is this place you think I want us to go?"

"A museum?"

"I'm going to suggest a museum, am I?"

"I'm beginning to wonder."

"Sounds to me like you've found a clever way of putting forward your own suggestions."

"It was just an idea."

"Well, it's a charming idea but your ESP left something out. Something that I know and you don't. A secret."

"And what is that?"

"A man. A man I'm going to see in about five minutes."

"Oh?"

"My dentist." She laughed. "Sorry. Perhaps some other time. Now I've got to run."

Her movements were less sporty and theatrical than last time. The taxi was farther down the street and didn't notice Philippa's upraised arm but did the raised umbrella of a bent dowager and stopped for her instead. Philippa snapped her fingers in disappointment and I watched as her dark legs and lovely floating hair disappeared into the lunchtime crowd.

I still felt very much like screaming. Hoping to stave off a psychotic episode or a cold faint or whatever else was in store, I paid my way into a movie house and there remembered my doctor. I nearly broke my neck doing a fast two-step down the stairs to the lounge. There it stood, dark, upright, unoccupied. I dial his office only to be told by his nurse that his appointment book was filled for the next three days. I protested. Was it an emergency? It was. What was the nature of the emergency? I actually got as far as taking a deep breath to explain it all when I realized it was hopeless. I hung up. A thought had occurred. Perhaps you need a psychiatrist, you mad bastard. Good point. A cousin of mine once went to a shrink name Lumki. West Ninetieth Street. Yes, he was in the book but out to lunch. I sat like a catatonic in one of the leather chairs staring at the Coke machine and waited for eight million people to swallow their food. I had nothing to read. No one to talk to. I just sat and waited for madness to come and stake its claim, or someone to arrive and explain the joke amid grins and apologies. Then another thought occurred. Dummy, you're in a movie house! At that I dashed upstairs to watch a skulking, fixated, and apparently lustful vampire induce several excessively beautiful ladies into letting him come close enough to sink, of all things, his white teeth into their long necks after which they became even worse actresses than before. But soon the entertaining clichés of a spike through the heart, a yawning grave, the strolling dead, and several melodramatically farcical thunderstorms lost for me that distance of fantasy and became, as with everything else, real. I escaped into daylight, felt sick, and sought darkness again. Forty-second Street saved me. There I submerged myself in one movie after another. All I can recall now is a hodge-podge of killings, stabbings, shootings, and shoutings. It was an afternoon of blessed peace.

The night life of Manhattan, when I finally emerged, seemed plotless and pointless. Thinking of Philippa, I ate a cold slice of Quiche Lorraine (to go), which I acquired in a swank deli. Dismissing the day as just so much bad news to be gotten over with as quickly as possible, I took the subway home. The bills and a birthday card from my parents upended my efforts at calm. This time the verse took on new meaning.

> Ever have one of those
> Wonderful days
> That's almost too good
> to be true?
> Well, that's the kind
> of wonderful day
> I'm wishing right now
> for you!

Convinced that there were now two such cards, I searched my small rooms stubbornly. No luck. OK, I imagined the whole thing. I'll settle for that. Tomorrow is another day. I'll think about it tomorrow. Better yet I'll not think about it at all, ever.

When the phone rang, stopped, and rang again in eight more rhythmic waves of pain, this time I did scream. One good loud healthy cry to loosen up the soul. Then I got out the Chivas Regal to loosen it up even more. I was too tense even to choose a record for the hi-fi. All I could manage was to press a button to hear what the radio had to offer. As luck would have it, an announcer was rambling on and on.

"A short and curiously moving *grave* yields immediately to the section that best exemplifies the sonata's title, and this is replete with long trills over staccato eighth notes. Violinist Leopold Auer once said of this masterpiece: 'If it really was inspired by the devil, it proves that whatever his other faults, His Satanic Majesty is a musician of the first order.'

"Now, with David Oistrakh, violin, and Frieda Bauer, piano, here is Tartini's Sonata in G Minor, *The Devil's Trill.*"

Filling my glass and getting comfortable on the couch drew my attention away from the music; I wandered, unlistening, amid my problems. Then long, mounting, diabolic trills suddenly infused the room with an almost unbearably moving sorrow. Without warning the piano fell silent and only the devil played (or rather Oistrakh as his advocate), and I felt undermined as a most gleeful and terrible evil rushed upon me. I could almost see His Satanic Majesty amid flames and smoke, his great black cape flowing in the sulphurous breeze, as he spun out, with excruciating beauty, on that insidious instrument, the dark powers that now would surely engulf us.

The piece ended at the very moment I rushed to turn it off. Another scotch was called for at once. I left it to Vivaldi's smooth river to float me, without incident, through the rest of the long evening. When it came time to watch the news on TV, I told myself I shouldn't, while knowing all along I would. Of course, it was the same, word for word, each commercial and disaster right in place. The Pan Am 707 blew up, and the woman in the laundryroom was raped right on time, at nine forty-seven A.M.

I took the bottle of Chivas to bed. But first I made sure that there was nothing wrong with the tape recorder. I put in a new cassette and started from scratch.

"Wake up, Rob. It was just a bad dream. All gone now. God's in his heaven and all's right with the world. Happy days are here again. It's April fifteenth, old buddy. Happy Birthday, old buddy. When you hear these words, sing out 'cause a new day is upon us. You're a lucky guy with your whole life ahead of you. Stay in bed for all I care. Sleep till noon, if sleep you must. O happy, happy day, for whatever was wrong, old buddy, has now been made OK again."

3

I was doing a study on eunuchs in Middle Eastern harems to determine if they had encountered difficulty in acquiring employment as disabled members of the national work force or whether their unique qualifications overcame the usual reticence of management toward hiring the deformed. But then, to my amazement, I discovered that I had somehow become the victim of a typographical error through which I had lost my own manhood or, more specifically, the exclamation point that gave it emphasis. This was brought to my attention by Mrs. Scanlan, dressed as a bellydancer and lounging in a hammock. She kindly offered me Quiche Lorraine and carfare home when suddenly I was attacked by a number of muscular eunuchs who were enraged that I had lost interest in them as a minority group and who chased me through the Casbah hoping to tear me limb from limb when I burst from the dream like Moby Dick plunging out of the sea only to find no ocean to fall back into or dream or sleep either. I sat upright like a man allergic to consciousness but nonetheless relieved to have escaped back into a rational world. Then the memory of something I thought I had heard froze my blood into solid piping. Quickly I stopped the machine (it had played past my message and was running silently), reversed the tape, and listened again to "Wake up you lazy bastard. Hop to it. No more getting in late for you, buddy. Come on, come on, wake up—"

I pressed *stop* and stood up in an agony of silence. Running into the living room for no reason, I stood there, my back cool with drying sweat. I phoned the *New York Times* and said I knew it was a silly question but would they tell me please what day it was. The receptionist said, "Thank you" and switched me to the city desk to whose occupant I had to repeat the question before being told that today was April fifteenth. Are you sure it's not the sixteenth? "No, Monday, April fifteenth," said the amused voice uncertain if this was a practical joke or a call from a madhouse. I hung up.

My chest became a massive heartburn. I was dead. At last I understood. How simple. I was dead. How diabolical. In twenty centuries of theological discussion it was astonishing that no one had guessed. Hell is the eternal repetition of a single day. How obvious. How economical. And no one knew or would believe it if I told them. They were just phantoms anyway. It was I who was real because it was I who was dead. Only the victim knew. Victim of life after death.

At this point the phone nearly gave me a coronary. I reached out as if for a life preserver.

"Hello," I insisted.

"Hello yourself. What are you shouting for?"

"Milly."

"Son of a gun, he remembers my name. OK, question: Did you just call me a minute ago or not?"

"No, I didn't."

"'Cause by the time I finished breaking my leg getting to the phone it went dead. Since you never call at night anymore, I figured maybe he's calling me by day."

"Milly, what's the date?"

"April fifteenth, exactly ten days since the last time you took me out, took me home, didn't take me, and took off."

"What did we work on yesterday in the office, Milly?"

"Boy did you ever just get up. Have some coffee. Yesterday was Sunday. Friday we worked on sexual morality and police ethics. Don't tell me you forgot *that?*"

"No, no."

"Well, good morning, Boss-man. See you in a little while, eh?"

"Look, I've run into a few problems. I won't be in the office today."

The silence grew virulent.

"Are you there?" I asked.

Her voice went flat as if under a great fatigue. "Tryin' to avoid me in the daytime, also?"

"Don't be absurd."

"But I am."

"Milly—"

"—me that way."

"What?"

"I said, 'you made me that way.' Absurd."

"Milly, I don't have time for this. I can't talk now."

"Someone there?"

"No, of course not."

"Is she makin' you breakfast?"

"For God's sake."

"Is it on the . . . on the . . ." Her voice became a wreckage.

"Milly . . ."

". . . table."

She was gone. I phoned back but no answer. Had I the wrong number? I dialed again and, waiting for the first ring, hung up. A noise sent me hurtling to the window. A bald-headed man climbs out of a maroon Dodge to survey the damage done to it and to a green hardtop convertible he has just rammed and out of which is climbing an indignant dark-haired guy in plaid trousers. Down the block I see Her Majesty hurrying to the subway. A man is chasing his hat across the street. And in the sky floating east . . .

As if nothing was askew I ate breakfast, tasting none of it, and trying not to hear my heart's leadened beat. I was endeavoring to think. It was as if I had never tried before. I kept at it and in good time constructed a theory. Several, in fact. The first began with the assumption that I was dead. If not exactly gone. This presented a problem, to say the least, because for years now I had considered myself a lapsed Protestant. Originally I had attended church because my tired mother had taken me. After she stopped, I kept going, but mostly to meet girls. Reverend Davis had a sense of humor. The music was nice. I liked singing hymns. And at the church socials were always one or two heavenly young ladies. Salvation in those days was a concrete concept I could really get my mind around. But of heaven and hell I was never so sure. Weren't those places like elaborate toys one puts away with childhood? Surely grown-up people desired and feared much simpler things. Even God and Satan resembled borderline myths that were based, perhaps, on some distorted local truth of the kind that created the Trojan War out of a fist fight in a wheat field. Were not The Deity and The Prince of Darkness as quaint and faintly comic as grown men hiding in a wooden horse? But when archaeologists discovered the ruins of Troy and found them just where Homer said they were, one had to think again. Just as I, now, had to think again.

But hell, I decided, was not my dwelling place. There was too much fun to be had. A vast penal system such as that would surely disallow this earthly wealth of short-term pleasures: nights in Paris if I wanted them, freedom to murder for the harmless sport of it, or to rape like a marauding king. Hellish as it seemed, this afterlife was just not hellish enough. Something else was afoot. Could it be, could it just be, that each morning, each fresh start of this same dull day, would set me loose, again and again, in the workhouse of purgatory?

Now the hammering in my chest was quick like hope. Purgatory was a place from which you could earn your release. Not by serving your time like a sullen inmate but by becoming, somehow, corrected. How, though? What *do* people learn or purge? Perhaps the trick was to perform good works. Maybe then, at last, I'd be released into heaven. This stopped me cold. Then I *was* dead. Just like that. It was as if I had failed before to grasp its meaning. I had died. The loss of this vast life was all I could think about. My death, the cessation of time, of its lovely, slow, total slaughter. I grieved. I tried to imagine it. *Mr. Robinson Blake died today at thirty-four.* An immense sadness exhausted me. Such a small spill of years. All that was yet to come and now would never come loomed large like the earth. Marriage, children, a long career, new pleasures, autumnal satisfactions, having books and friends at hand, the love and anger I would never feel, events marching on without me—it was as if I had died a child.

But suppose I was released from purgatory and allowed to proceed with everyone else into tomorrow. It was almost too much to hope for. It would mean I was alive, for a start, and it would be hard to imagine a better start than that. Could it be that man had to earn his passage through time? Had others like myself been assigned to labor in behalf of the many? Or is this what madness does? No, I rejected that. It was all too lucid to be the figment of a deranged mind. And whether I was alive or not was beside the point. The order of the day was to do good works. Not accustomed to thinking in these terms, I fretted for a moment. What were they, these great good deeds that would free us all or perhaps just me? And could they be done and done in time? I let these questions pass unanswered. Best thing to do was get to work. "In theory," I said aloud, to give me courage, "this should be easy, lad. The world is filled with people who need help. Just pick one out and help the poor bastard." The idea began to appeal to me. My spirits soared. I decided to make a list of all the poor bastards I had known. I ran into trouble at once. Almost everyone I was acquainted with needed help or needed money, which was much the same thing. But I wanted my good deed to shine forth like a candle in a power failure. In fact, the deed should be something I didn't want to do at all, highly resistable, nearly unthinkable, and, of course, fantastically good.

My plan was simple. I would send a check for two thousand dollars (half of my life savings) to the United Cancer fund. I reconsidered and wrote in three thousand dollars. Kissing dirty feet would have been far easier. Almost anything would have been far easier. Surely here was a deed of enormous candle power and, of course, good beyond any singing of it. I carried the gift in an envelope downstairs to a mail box and quickly, before I could change my mind, pushed it through the slot.

Then I remembered that lady raped in the laundry room. Two good deeds were better than one, surely. So I went upstairs once more to empty my attaché case and place inside it a hammer, a kitchen knife, and a monkey wrench. Am I late? A quick glance tells me my watch has stopped again and this time, oddly enough, at 8:05 A.M. I reset it by the electric monster on the kitchen wall, which groans with unwavering constancy. Nine twenty-three.

In the street I hurry along looking to all the world like someone late for a board meeting. I find the building in a nearby back street and go directly to the basement. The laundry room has the faint smell of lime and soapsuds. Of the ten washing machines, one is furiously at work. I check my watch again; it and my heart are both still running at about the same speed. A green army locker at the far end of the room is perfect to hide behind. The room is hot, or is my sweating due to clairvoyance? Waiting proves to be more complex and agonizing than I ever remembered. After a final burst of spin-dry madness the lone machine stops. There is a long damp silence. I had fixated on 9:47 for it all to begin, which is why at 9:42 I nearly shriek as the door scrapes open and someone walks in.

It takes a while for me to get up nerve enough to peek out from behind the locker. A slim woman in patched dungarees and yellow hair-curlers keeps lifting her arms above her head to dump load upon load of moist laundry into a large basket while humming Bach's *Sleepers Awake*. She yanks the basket up with a grunt and bending backwards, shoulders high, hurriedly waddles out of the room. I am pleasantly appalled. Joy at not having to perform heroics balances out my need to pile up points for doing good works. Is there to be no rape? I had entered the wrong building, perhaps. Or is there more to this torture than I had imagined?

The door scrapes open. She is back. Ah, of course: her box of soap powder, her container of water-softener, her *Time Magazine*, all these had been left behind. In agonizing silence, I find myself urging her to get the hell out. Then it begins. The door scrapes open before she reaches it and in comes a tall man in a Fu Manchu moustache. His accomplice, who is shorter and stockier, has his back to me. They both wear crinkling leather jackets. Lifting a knee, I open the attaché case and take out a hammer.

"Excuse me, may I pass, please?" This from the lady. There is a cracking slap. The things in her arms are now on the floor. She leans against one of the machines holding her cheek. The tall man takes out a knife. He mumbles to her in Spanish. Then the shorter man speaks, " 'E says to be silent or 'e cut you." I can hear the woman backing away in my direction with the sound of their jackets following. When she is near me, still holding her cheek, continuing her retreat, my moment comes.

"S'okay."

With a yelp she jumps against a table knocking over two chairs and scattering a stack of metal coat hangers.

"I won't hurt you."

She seems paralyzed by the sight of my face. To clarify my allegiance, I scream at the leather jackets.

"Get the fuck out you stupid fucks."

The short fat-faced man quickly translates this for the tall one who studies me now with a delighted smile. I dump the attaché case on the table and offer the monkey wrench to the woman, who does nothing, just stares as if in this whole world I am her only cause for concern. I leave the weapon nearby for her possible later use, then taking hold of the kitchen knife I make a few ostentatious, loosening-up combat movements, hopefully to demonstrate my hidden talents at ferocity. This brings the tall man close to bliss. Meanwhile, sweat like an embarrassing secret, is oozing forth against my will.

"Did you hear me?" I screamed at them. "Get the fuck out."

The translater repeats this in their own language. Fu Manchu listens soberly and replies in kind.

" 'E says 'e think now 'e kill you."

"Tell him he's a lousy Goddamned Puerto Rican bastard."

"Naw, he from Coo-bah."

"Hot shit," is the lady's reply. "Who cares."

The two men ignore her and approach me, each holding a long blade at arms length next to his leg. I feel absurd holding my two weapons like a mad blacksmith thinking he can pound a kitchen knife into a plowshare. I also feel close to death, which now seems unquestionably the ultimate humiliation. And if I am dead already I have the definite impression this won't help me now, that dying, even a second time, is rough going and very painful.

"How loud can you scream?" I whisper, and she shows me.

A long hot primal screech scorches the room. It is so loud that I'm sure it will trigger a series of screams from other ladies, who in turn will set off still more screams like Tom-Tom messages until all the necessary alarmbells will alert all the nearby squad cars, in which are riding all the available patrolmen needed to come stomping down the only stairway toward this small laundry room to perform their hurried justice in the barest nick of time. It is a horrific scream and deeply comforting.

Both men flinch. Words are exchanged in perfectly clear but meaningless sounds and then they turn and run.

"Let's get 'em," I find myself shouting. In the hall a pair of feet are disappearing through a door marked EXIT. I leap over her laundry basket and follow at a bit less than maximum speed. Each door I come to is slowly swinging closed again. In the street two leather jackets with long legs are running madly. Following I yell, "Stop those men" to no one in particular and feeling like an ass. At the next corner they have, thank God, vanished. I lean on a tree quickly trying to consume all the available air in Queens.

"Hey, bud, which way to Jackson Heights?"

I pointed and the TV repair truck drove off.

Back in the laundry room a bit of spilled soap powder was all that was left of her. I collected my things and stopped in the lobby, but the names by the buzzers meant nothing. No matter, all things considered, I felt heroic. Not the phony Hollywood sort but a slightly fearful, glad-it's-over heroics of the kind that lends itself so well to TV talk shows, magazine profiles, and a successful lecture tour. I walked slowly in sunshine to enjoy my small allotment of hard-earned glory. But, soon depressed again, I went home to put away my attaché case of hero toys and make more coffee. I had remembered to buy milk.

An hour later I took a cab to Kennedy Airport. I couldn't recall the time of takeoff or the flight number. There was first a delay due to technical difficulties, that I recalled. When the 707 did take to the air, an explosion hours later sent it spinning into the sea. Of course I could have phoned-in an anonymous threat, forcing them to check all flights, both London-bound and those continuing on to California. But I feared a slip-up. Too many tons of luggage to examine. Too much of a gamble. Instead I spent hours endlessly checking the wall board and waiting for that all-important announcement: a flight delay.

Tourists sat and mostly did nothing. Loved ones ran at each other. Children went slack with boredom. Large suitcases were carried by people stiff with effort. Others calmly flipped pages at the newstand or debated the location of the washroom. My attention had been settled on one of those enchanting Dickensian children standing politely with his mother as if waiting to fly back to the quaint century from which he came. Then God or fate in the form of a pleasant, slightly uptight female voice announced that Pan Am Flight 428 for London would be delayed fifteen minutes.

I ran to a phone, fed it my dime, and dialed. Sorry but all the lines were busy, would I hold? I would and did, slapping the wall with impatience. At last I was let through to a sweet-sounding lady who introduced herself as Miss Vine and who wished to know if she could be of assistance.

"Listen, sweetheart," I said in a voice that was as strange to me as it was to her. "There's a bomb on flight 428 to London. I didn't put it there. Someone else did. But find it or 192 people will die. That's flight 428. Hurry."

I hung up. For all I knew she fainted. Another dime got me on the waiting list after I again promised to hold. In minutes I was put through to a cheerful chap by the name of O'Brien. I gave him the same message and left the booth, sweating.

I felt I might split apart at any moment. Joining others at the bar, I drank Chivas Regal and waited. When a roaring silence and a vast roguishness took hold of me, I paid the bill and walked carefully in splendid strides through a throbbing world to the restaurant and had some food and many cups of coffee.

Flight 428 was announced at last. This time two hours late. My table was beside a wall of glass with the airfield beyond. I had no idea which was the aircraft in question but I watched several distant speeding toys lift off, climb, and disappear.

I went back to my phone booth and called Departure Information, and, impersonating a reporter for the *New York Times*, I asked if it was true a bomb had been removed from Flight 428. They conceded this point but assured me that the "device" had been hours away from detonation. There was no mention of a phone call. I went and had a couple of *Chivas* to celebrate.

After a while I would find a bus that would take me home and there I would wait to see if I had earned tomorrow. I would go home and sit and wait—but not just yet. I had more coffee. I walked for miles through this peaceful non-place. To sit in a barber's chair was calming. Flipping through magazines at the newstand was another painless way of hurdling time. More Chivas at the bar helped. Then back to the restaurant I went to sip coffee again and watch more toys lifting off. After a while I went and found a bus to take me home.

Outside there was spilt blood on the sky. The day was dying in beauty and style. Back in the real world I found myself pouring sweat. It was the thought of returning to my apartment, climbing into the bed, waiting for sleep, knowing just how important this next morning would be. Then I panicked. It was at my door, key in hand, that I did an about face as if on parade, returned to the airport, marched to the nearest airlines ticket counter and using my American Express card bought passage on the first plane to Los Angeles. The idea was to put a continent between today and that bed. I could even pay a visit to my parents in Tarzania. I could swim in the Pacific. If you're going to panic, I thought, do it in style. I did: first class. I only hoped the day would come when I would have to pay the bill.

I fastened my safety belt, left the earth, chased the sun, was offered dinner, and drank scotch instead. As we approached L.A., my watch said it was ten minutes to midnight. Immediately I set it back to California time wondering who exactly I was fooling. If I was still cursed, was it according to Eastern Daylight Savings Time and if so then at what point on the clock would today begin anew or yesterday start again? Sweat glued my shirt to my back. Have a pleasant chat with someone and try to keep calm. I turned to the man next to me, who hadn't eaten, spoken, or, as far as I could remember, moved a muscle.

"Pleasant flight," I said.

"What's that?"

"I said, pleasant flight."

"What is that? That noise. Something's wrong. Miss! *Miss!* That noise. Hear it?"

"Oh, heavens," said the hostess bending over him, "that's

the landing gear being lowered. That's all it is. Now buckle up and don't worry, you hear?"

She left him as stricken as before.

"Don't worry. We'll land safely," I assured him.

"How do *you* know?" he asked bitterly and then forgot me, staring straight ahead as if into a firing squad.

"Try to relax. OK?"

"Shit," he snapped, not in reply but in protest as the plane banked and the city appeared far down at the bottom of a long, fatal drop. In the darkness were strings of electric pearls moving on the throughway or fixed at street corners. There was a power failure. The lights dimmed. Then we passed through a cloud and all the pearls were bright again. The magic of all this was lost on him.

"We're gonna crash!"

"Don't be silly."

"Why doesn't he straighten out?"

"He will, he will."

The eyes widened. Panic that deep was much like dignity. Both his hands clutched the same armrest. His wristwatch said three minutes to midnight.

"There," I said, "he's started his approach."

"*Ahhh*," escaped inadvertently from his throat.

The ground came up to meet us with a jolt like a running flop with your sled on snow which speeds along underneath just as the runway does during the harsh scream of the jet fighting to stop. As we touched-down my neighbor made several lurching, protective moves after which he mopped his face.

Eyes shut, I put my head back as we taxied-in, my fear remained, unlike his, but was much abated thanks to the comedy of his panic, to my own fatigue, to the suspicion that I had at last escaped, to Philippa remembered and reclaimed, to the calm of the aircraft safely down, all tensions gone, California outside, its warmth inside, the noise of passengers gathering their things, and the pilot's voice offering the cheerful greetings: "Wake up you lazy bastard!"

With a gasp, I found no cabin or people, just a stained ceiling, an old dresser, and a table on which a raving tape recorder was prattling away in an unconcerned and heartless voice.

I scurried to the bathroom and was aggressively sick. I flushed this away and then put more of myself into the bowl. Back in my silent room I sat on my bed and stared for no reason at the fixed slant of shadow across the lower edge of my exquisitely still, utterly calm Vermeer.

4

Later I found myself in the living room, sipping brandy to settle my stomach, and wishing to God I had someone to hold me as my mother had when I was a child. Panic came, but there was no where to run and all it did was set me shivering as if in a deep freeze. So this was what doing good deeds would get me. I felt cheated and bitter. What a self-deluding fantasy to think I had mapped out an escape route. Escape from what? I didn't even know where I was. I just wanted to be held. To be taken care of. There was a time when I could have gone to my mother and told her anything. She wouldn't have understood, of course. After all, what would I have thought had someone come to me with this? Anyway, my mother's cures are all the same: lemon in hot water, then straight to bed. But at least she would have been comforting. She would have been very comforting.

This need to be held and kept safe had me hugging my

knees and rocking to and fro. Then some words came to me. "Remember, I know the secret." Who said these words? "I know the secret." Then all at once I had it and with it the plan for the day.

I joined Her Majesty in the elevator as usual. Strangers once again, we stood like mannequins until we reached the ground. Perhaps it was the terrible shock of still finding myself trapped in this cosmic collapse of time. Or just the urging of the brandy. Anyway, I did something I have no explanation for. As the doors opened onto the lobby, I reached over ever so briefly and squeezed ever so politely one half of a high and royal rump.

Believe it when I say that I was as appalled as she. And amazed as well for she neither jumped nor yelped. Thank God, I thought, preferring tight-ass rancor to the big scene. Again like a gun barrel her half dead, half deadly face turned slowly toward mine. She placed her hand inches from my nose and with furious dignity snapped her fingers with a crack of profound disdain as if to send me spinning into the yawning cauldron of hell.

"Just for that, just for that, I'll file a complaint, I will, with the police, Oh, yes, I'll tell them your name, your address, what you did, with the police, oh yes, I'll bring charges, you'll see, you filth, we'll teach you to reach out, and molest, like that, just anybody, you'll see."

"I'm terribly sorry," I muttered.

"You'll see."

She was marching toward the exit. I hurried to keep up.

"I don't know what came over—"

"You'll see—"

"—under stress—"

"—to the police."

"Humbly sorry."

"Ha."

"Listen to me." I followed her into the street. "Will you listen to me?"

"Filth."

She was about to walk off. I took hold of her. She stiffened in fear.

"Listen to me."

"Let me go or I'll scream."

"If you don't listen to me I'll smash two cars together now, right behind me, in the street. That's what I'll do."

As her lips were forming another volley her body lurched at the crash. She looked into the street. Then at me again. My eyes had not left her face. Hers were frozen wide.

"A bald-headed man is climbing out of a Dodge, right?"

She checked, then gazed at me in even greater alarm.

"OK. Now that you're listening I just want to say, to tell you, that I'm sick. I think. I don't know. I'm not myself, is all. But I'm sorry for doing what I did. Very sorry."

I let her go.

She jabbed her thumb toward the street. "How did you do that?"

Unable to play the magician any longer, I simply walked away. What was I trying to prove anyway? Behind me I heard, "Stop. He did it. He had something to do with it. Stop that man."

There was nothing for it but to keep walking. I bent to catch a man's rolling hat, received his thanks, and, passing up the *New York Times*, descended into the subway feeling ever so slightly ill again.

I didn't go to the office, not right away. I couldn't. Milly's agony would be just too much for me today. Perhaps out of guilt toward her, I phoned the police and tipped them off to what was scheduled in the laundry room. I told the officer to hurry for there wasn't much time. Then I hung up. Should be getting used to this. All the same, both my hands were trembling. While I was at it, I phoned the airport and warned them about the bomb.

Scrambled eggs and onions with toasted bagels and hot coffee at a nearby café kept my mind focused and relatively sane. Except *All powerful and powerless* kept repeating itself in my mind. I was just able to keep my hand from shaking when I paid the check. No small task, this. Today there would be no small tasks. At least my watch kept going. Hadn't it stopped yesterday at an earlier time than this? My watch and I, the only things with free will. Never mind, I told myself and, delaying my entrance as long as I could, marched to the office, chose the number five this time, got from Vince the same tired joke, and, instead of going to my office, went directly into Murray's where Philippa turned and offered me the pleasure of her hazel eyes.

What followed was much the same as before except somewhat revised as though still in rehearsal. Murray made a sarcastic remark about my coming late, and I calmed him with a heart-rending admission of early morning nausea. His wife was duly concerned. Murray suggested a pregnancy test, and roared. Philippa examined a fingernail. I examined Philippa. When the right moment came I placed in her hand the recipe I knew she wanted. How amazed she was at this startling display of telepathy, which I unscrupulously took credit for. Murray looked bored and then, as if on cue, was called from the room. Now terribly excited, Philippa rambled on from telepathy, to parapsychology, to dream analysis, until lo and behold she was glancing at the door and telling me, as she moved closer, about hammocks.

Murray's re-entrance and rampage this time seemed even more unjust. Such sadistic, short-tempered self-indulgence; I had all I could do to keep from taking a swing at him. But I imitated as best I could the poignant exit of a crushed employee. I went straight to my post at the elevator. The wait was longer than I thought. Was she coming? I had imtimations of panic. The elements of a scream were falling into place. Then I heard her heels clamoring behind me and felt her touch.

"Oh, Rob. He's insane sometimes."

"Yeah," I said, trying to remember my lines.

"He doesn't really mean it. That doesn't help you much, I know."

"Hate to be there when he does mean it."

"I've been there." Then that charming, defenseless glance downward. The ill-at-ease little-girl shrug. She incited rebellion with her words and warm skin. The elevator arrived, and we rode down amid an ethos of lust until we were left alone again on the ground floor. My fear that something would go wrong vanished, and I almost kissed her there and then, when she lifted her chin and asked:

"Are you coming with me? Do we strike a blow for freedom?"

"Yes, OK let's go." With my arm around her waist, we even caught the taxi that had gotten away from her the day before.

Just sitting with her in the restaurant made me happy. Soon we talked as two people do who hope they are the converging halves of a great event. Never had I seen her more winning or seductive. She had decreed that our little adventure be a success and she had all the warmth and confidence to make it so. She seemed at the very top of her game. Her intelligence rendered everything easy and her spontaneity made it all seem new. Those hazel eyes rarely left my face and those silent lips conveyed all manner of pleasant things as she listened to me speak. To make a point she would touch my arm, while the resonance of her voice made points that had nothing to do with what was said. Occasionally I found her waiting impishly for me at the end of my sentences, often with that special toss of her head in laughter.

She was pleased that I ordered another half-bottle of Chateauneuf-Du-Pape and later she accepted the suggestion that we end our meal with Irish Coffee. She seemed to be saying yes, always yes, as if I could not possibly do or suggest anything that would not please her. I might lift and carry her out into the street with all heads turning and that, too, would only please her. All her expressions and her multiple proofs of beauty, especially her generous breasts, whispered yes, undeniably yes, so that surely the man farthest across the room must feel the radiating warmth of her determined acquiescence.

I was just a wee bit drunk.

Taking her hand, "I feel you have a special message for me."

She tilted her head. "Perhaps I have."

Our waiter presented the check and left.

"He has a message for you, too." She laughed.

I paid without concern and with a generous tip as well, for each morning it would be back in my wallet again anyway. Or if it wasn't I'd be too relieved to care. We rose to leave. Heads turned. She edged sideways, stomach compressed, between the narrow passageway of the tables and her clothes spoke again of woman.

"Anyway," I continued, "I'm much more interested in the one you have."

With mock caution, "The one I have—of what?"

"I get the feeling this message will, in some way, save me."

"Save you?"

"Will it?"

"Could be."

"It's got to be."

"You mean some sort of occult message, passing through me to you?"

I nodded.

"Suppose I don't *want* it passing through me?" she teased. "Suppose the message is, you know, obscene?"

"Look, it's important you tell me."

We were walking in the street in no particular direction. She took my arm.

"Robbie, I'll tell you anything you want to know.

"For example," she continued, before I could reply, "this car sitting here next to an expired parking meter. It's mine.

"Would you like to drive?" she asked, again as I was about to speak. "Here." And dangled the keys.

Inside she leaned against the door, arms folded, watching me as I watched the road, her legs crossed in those eternal dark stockings, her checked skirt with its grinning zipper, her frilly blouse spanking white, her lips amused and sly.

The safety button on her door was up. As I leaned forward to lock it, she moved ever so slightly toward me as if expecting to be kissed, or perhaps only to give me room.

We went beneath the river, emerged from the tunnel, paid at the toll, then followed the expressway past glimpses of grave-yards. She didn't ask where I was taking her. She requested music. With a press of my finger the radio offered gentle baroque.

"Vivaldi," we both said, and laughed.

She asked me if I often had psychic experiences like knowing what someone wants before they ask for it. I nodded. Then why on earth did I always argue against ESP and flying saucers and all the rest of it? Learning things changes one's mind, I explained. Like what things? She sat up. Go on, what things?

"Did you by any chance have an appointment today you decided not to keep?"

She stared at me while Vivaldi kept busy and I kept driving.

"An appointment with—let me see—with a dentist."

"Amazing. You are amazing. Murray didn't tell you, did he? No, how could he? Amazing. Yes, I just decided to go to the restaurant instead. With you." Staring hard at me, "How did you know?"

"I just knew."

"You just knew. Beautiful."

But the chill was on me again and she was much too far away.

"Philippa, sit closer."

She did at once. "Any special reason?"

"Frightened."

"Of the supernatural? Why? Think of the power it gives you. I only wish something like that would happen to me."

I took her hand and drove with my left. Almost at once I had to let go because of a turn. Now she started talking about herself. It seemed her husband ridiculed all her special interests: astrology, mind-reading, reincarnation. He made fun of everything but wealth. That and the common currency of sex. How she hated him at times. She had married a good provider; what she hadn't realized at nineteen was how little of what she really needed would be provided. They both got swindled, was her assessment. She ended up with a hard-working computer, and he ended up with, as she put it, "emptiness." She once reveled in her above-average intelligence only to learn that all she really had was above-average grades. "I got the marks. Others got the education. I never did figure out how that happened."

"You're not emptiness now. You're an intelligent and cultured woman."

"He doesn't think so. And I have the bad habit of becoming just what others expect of me."

"Then why did he marry you?"

"My looks, he says. Except in those days I was a stick. They used to chant, Philippa with bread, Philippa with meat, Philippa with anything, we got to make her eat. A friend of ours says Murray must have been clairvoyant to know what I'd look like six years after the wedding. Obviously, in knowing what he'd be like, I didn't have any such powers."

"What made you fill out, finally?"

"Unhappiness."

"Eat, did you?"

"He was, as I said, a good provider."

"Why do you stay with him?"

"Why do I stay with him? Convenience, you might say. I'm waiting for something to happen. I just don't want to go from him to another Murray. Don't want a whole series of Murrays added to my credit. Or should I say debit. As a single girl I thought I was a woman of experience. The truth is before I married Murray I used to date nothing but Murrays. Perhaps that's why when I met him he seemed so right, so familiar. As if we had known each other all our lives."

"Ever make it with a non-Murray?"

"Once. Once I made it with a non-Murray. A long time ago. My first, last, and only passion. The sort that afterward dulls things. Really wonderful, it was. A long time ago." She turned her head away and studied an MG that was keeping pace with us. The driver looked at her, his face nearly all mustache, glanced ahead and then at Philippa again. She turned to me. "I was eighteen and empty. He was—get this—fat and married. But, nevertheless, voilà: doom." She shook her head. "Really something, it was."

"What happened?"

"Died."

"It did?"

"He did."

She folded her arms and stared straight ahead. Her eyes, in the rear-view mirror, glistened. I took her hand again. She squeezed mine in reply. Two desperate exiles, we were, she unable to go back, me prevented from moving ahead. This and the wine and the Irish Coffee flooded the car with profound sadness. We drove like that, holding hands, both of us tearful and cautious, while Vivaldi, housed in yet another part of time, was busily telling us how beautiful and elegant life really was.

She carried her melancholy with her into the lobby and then when I fully expected her to ask where I had brought her, she didn't. Would this undertow of sadness wash away that special place I felt I had in her esteem? I eyed my mailbox but went no where near it. Hoping to get her thoughts off other men, I tried in the elevator to cheer her up with the first joke that came to mind.

"Pick a number from one to ten."

"This a game?"

"Yes, pick a number from one to ten."

To humor me, "All right."

"OK. What's your number?"

"My number is wrong and not even close." She couldn't keep from smiling.

"He pulled that one on you, did he?"

"Pulled it on my husband. All Vince ever says to *me* is . . ." And she bent forward to gawk at empty space with ecstatic derangement. "Murray claims these jokes are poisoning his mornings. I believe it, for then Murray comes home to poison my evenings. And here I am poisoning your afternoons."

"I only wish you were always here to poison them."

She looked refreshed.

Taking her into my living room for the first time, I saw it anew, found it disheveled, and was gratified when she made a complete circle of inspection, nodded, and decided, "I like it. Too neat. But it has warmth. All those books make the difference, don't they? How many, a thousand?"

"Close to two, I think."

"Wish we had walls of them like that. I see you take your dust jackets off."

"I want the place to look like a library, not a bookstore."

She laughed, and I suggested a pair of whiskey sours.

"Haven't we had enough to drink today?"

"No."

"Good."

She was a follower. She followed me into the kitchen and watched. She trailed into the hallway where I took the rye from the liquor cabinet and then trailed back again into the kitchen, with me all the while explaining how fortunate it was that her intuition had told her to visit the office this morning because otherwise she would have ended up in a dentist's chair instead of getting pleasantly drunk here with me.

"Is there a scheduled tour of the other rooms?"

"Room," I corrected. "Other room."

The bed looked as it usually did, slept in. A collapsed pajama top lay on the floor. For some reason a slipper was perched on the arm of a chair. As if visiting a playroom, she gave a condescending smile. My recently acquired Vermeer reproduction caught and pleased her appraising eye. Next she noticed—how could she help it—the tape recorder.

"For dictating your memoirs, or evaluating lady visitors?"

"Evaluating of lady visitors would amount to dictating my memoirs, would it not?"

"Hummmm. Good point. How about playing a few juicy bits?"

"Well, perhaps not."

"Oh, come on. Comeoncomeoncomeon."

Not sure if it was a good idea, or more to the point whether I could calmly walk over and do it, I calmly walked over and tried. Reversing the engine, briefly, I stopped it, gritted my teeth and played the now apocalyptic: "Wake up you lazy bastard. Hop to it. No more late start for you, buddy. Come on, come on, wake up. Today you're going to get places. This is it. On your fuckin' feet . . ."

She made that single guffaw of hers, doubled over, stood straight, and gave a totally different follow-up laughter, deep and resonant as if the universe itself had suddenly proved richly comic. All this without spilling her drink.

I put mine on the table and walked over to her. It was as if we had rehearsed it to perfection. A long casual harvest, it was, not a first kiss at all. One warm, emphatic unclothed arm went smoothly around my neck, the other reached out, placed her drink somewhere, and joined in the embrace making me feel incredibly safe until I heard her wristwatch ticking in my ear.

"Well, well." Her palms slid down my shirt front, as she moved away. "Now it's a whole new ball game," she smiled. "As they say."

"You shatter me, young lady."

"Oh?" She picked up her glass, watching from over the rim.

"I want to swallow you whole like an oyster."

She lifted her chin with pleasure, savoring the idea.

"You make me so very happy. I must see you every day. Suddenly all of life for me is you."

"Remember when you said you thought I had a message?"

"Yes!"

"Well, I have. I've had it ready for some time."

"Oh?" I could hardly stand it. "And the message is . . ."

"That I'm, well, terribly fond of you."

She smiled. She had finished.

"And? . . . Nothing more?"

"Nothing more? Well, I like that."

"No, no. I mean, thank you. That's wonderful. I'm not sure I know what I'm saying. Just a nervous wreck."

"You do act funny sometimes. Why are you nervous?"

"You," I said. "And life."

"Ah, life. I remember."

"Philippa."

"Yes."

"I love you."

"Ah, love. I remember that too."

"Will you sleep with me?"

"Will I sleep with you?" Slowly she took another sip from her whiskey sour. "Oh . . . probably. I wouldn't put it past me."

Stepping forward I undid the top button on her blouse.

"But I didn't mean now, sort of thing."

"Oh," I said.

She wanted to "consider it," was her phrase, "to consider it for perhaps tomorrow or some time soon." I felt my skull tighten. I wheedled and pleaded while she behaved as if there really was all the time in the world.

"If you had come to me it would have been different and it would have happened a long time ago. But I had to come to you. All those opportunities during three whole years. But in the end I had to come to you. Well, now, Robbie, I would like to take *my* time. And you, you can't even wait one day."

"Look, Philippa, believe me, this afternoon is all I have."

"Ah, yes. Your big important afternoon. I forgot how you struck this great blow for freedom. Funny because you're usually so cautious. Aren't you? Taking care of your safe little job and your very precious health. Looking both ways at crossings. Staying single. Playing it safe. Tell me, why today? Was it because Murray made naughty on you? Why did you pick this afternoon to kiss me when for years I waited. But why today? That I'd like to know."

"I always wanted you . . ."

"Oh, sure, you had a little lust going. A little twitching to stave off boredom. But why today?"

Between wanting to beat on her face and gather her into bed, a spasm of infant's fear vomited the truth all over her stable understanding of things. I told her of this day like a needle stuck in a groove, of being stabbed each morning by my own demented voice, of how everything was always the same and terribly wrong, how everyone always said identical things, flawlessly repeating all the trivia and tragedies until I thought I'd go through the roof. And I spoke of my need for her, for her to love me, to save me, yes, to save me from this terrible snare.

Her anger was gone. It wasn't until I finished that I saw in her rapt attention the comatose glaze of panic. Sex had run from the room like a rabbit. "Poor Robbie," she said. I didn't reply. She reached out and almost touched me. Her teeth clamped her lower lip. All over the landscape lay the wreckage of our solo flight. "How horrible for you," she suggested. Three fingers fastened a button on her blouse as if to secure herself against my presence. "How awful," she said. "Really." I was fighting tears. She offered a helpless smile. "Perhaps you're overworked, Rob." Her rasping voice was like a gentle touch. Her beauty was a comfort. She nodded with sympathy. Yet all the while she was watching not me but my dangerous unchained derangment.

Stupidly I went on about my plight as if a greater effort would make her understand. Seated in a chair, masked with a blank face, she watched, becalmed and alert, depositing her cigarette ashes in an empty walnut shell beside the tape recorder while I strode about like an attorney flailing the truth to make it credible. When I stopped she stood up and, signaling an end, stamped the table with her glass. She suggested that everything would work out, that tomorrow I should see a doctor, and that, unfortunately, she had to go.

I was desperate and it showed. I begged her to stay. "Tomorrow," she replied and moved toward the door. Strident with the truth, I explained that I'd love her always and needed her now. She picked up her handbag and said, "Tomorrow." It was the last day on earth and I didn't want to be left alone, to be run away from in panic, or be given coquettish delays. I followed her into the hall. She said there was no need. We rode down in the elevator together. She wished I wouldn't. What was she thinking? "Nothing," she said. That she should believe me mad was an intolerable insult that must be set right. Foolishly I tried to kiss her again. The doors opened and she elbowed her way into the lobby where, at the same moment, entering from the street, was none other than Her Majesty returning from wherever the hell it was she marched off to each morning (or each time this same morning) carrying her lofty, frosty virgin's vault to put it perhaps to some better, higher purpose than what she thought I might dare suggest, entering from the street, transfixed and aghast at what she saw, and started yelling.

"Oh, my Christ. At it again. Leave that woman alone. You filth. You hear? I have his name. I know his name. Robinson Blake. That's his name. Lives on my floor. File a complaint. Do it, Miss. Go to the police. I did. I really did. You filth. Twice in one day. *Oh!*"

I'm not sure which of us alarmed Philippa more. She hurried away looking once at Her Majesty and once at me as if hoping one of us might offer to explain the other. I went out into the street knowing it was pointless. From a distance she made bye-bye twice opening and closing a hand, then scurried off as if late for eternal salvation. Her Majesty, seeing me glance into the lobby, ran for the elevator. Boy, was I knockin' 'em dead today.

5

If I were shipwrecked and alone on an unnamed planet among all those receding points of light, hopelessly beyond reach of the earth eons away, I'm sure the feeling of isolation would be close to what I learned to live with on that recurring afternoon. How could I sit in a bar and chat with others while secretly serving a life sentence they could not even conceive of, or blurt out my grief to a friend, who would only think me mad and then, come midnight, forget I even spoke to him. If I was sane then this was as close as I could come to knowing what it was to be otherwise, to burn with a truth that no one would ever acknowledge.

And how very fatuous my high thoughts of good deeds now seemed. If I were to rescue that same plane-load of tourists a thousand times over, would the virtue of such an action be cumulative—especially when the very most I could accomplish, in the end, would be to save each person only once?

Why hadn't I spotted this fallacy earlier? Suddenly the whole idea of purgatory collapsed and all efforts at doing good deeds became totally pointless. But if I wasn't in purgatory, where was I? If the truth be told, I hadn't a clue. I was simply here, no where, lost, or, to be precise, wandering on Queens Boulevard. Perhaps, later on, when I was less confused, I would think of another theory to explain my inhuman condition. Perhaps, later on, when I was less afraid, I would be able to concern myself with something other than getting through the day.

Well, what now? Constant indulgence seemed the only way to maintain stability. No pleasure dare be postponed. Invitations for tomorrow would be like cruel jokes and the ingredients of a chance meeting could not be left to bake slowly into love. All that was possible had to be consummated in a single day, for tomorrow was off somewhere among those receding points of light.

As things stood now, one fact seemed proven: time could be erased. In the morning, Her Majesty would reappear as usual with no memory of anyone's hand having sampled her sponge-cake, her mind dormant once more. Time could be erased. But was this an opportunity or only a dead end? We would soon find out. Tomorrow I planned to see Mrs. Scanlan once again. Hell, if I was being given a second chance the only sensible thing to do would be to take it.

I strolled along Queens Boulevard on a bright and lovely late afternoon while all around me were innocent people re-enacting their seemingly pointless lives. Occasionally I passed a citizen whose face was grim with shallow sorrows. I wanted to tell someone my secret that, despite all evidence and popular opinion on the subject, the passing of time was the great gift. It was all the days dwindling and everyone's age mounting, that made dry and rare this wine of life. Death and nothing coming afterward is what gives us the worst and best of the shit and bliss. But what's the point of revelation if it frightens people even more? This business of God holding His tongue made more sense now, I had to admit.

Anyway, I was walking along Queens Boulevard trying to take things easy for a while when I discovered yet another problem, as if the one I had wasn't enough. Spasms of desperation such as I felt just before fondling Her Majesty began racing through me again, this time stronger than ever. I had an urge to enter a supermarket and knock everything to the floor. I hungered to slap every passing lass smartly on the rump. I longed to kick cops, ring doorbells and run, whisper dirty words to upright senior citizens. Was this the start of that downward slide into insanity? I kept walking. But the truth was out. I tingled with vandal lust and playful villainy.

I stopped walking and stood frozen by a thought. If it was pointless to demonstrate the same virtue a thousand times over, then just what were the restrictions against evil when every devilry would right itself by morning? Now, the most extraordinary things suggested themselves. Her Majesty, who I amazed myself by hating deeply, the stiff bitch, well, why not knock her around a bit? Why not rip off a rape, while I'm at it? Surely there was a good reason why not; but at the moment, oddly enough, I couldn't think of what it was.

I started walking again and before long I remembered that I was rich. After all, no bills need be paid and all cash transactions lost me not a cent. I could be a spendthrift without conscience. Vast sums spent on food and drink, on call girls, on the very best front-row seats, even on traveling thousands of miles to spend evenings in foreign cities; none of this was illegal or even unethical. It was simply no longer prohibitive. Then what wrongs were left for me to commit? I gave this some thought. Well, I could shoot Murray, for a start. The next day he would only reappear again anyway. Yet, think of the satisfaction. Was this psychotic reasoning or normal aggression? Did pain and grief caused by me really exist if afterward they were totally erased? In fact, these people to whom I did harm, were they real or only phantoms?

I kept walking and whistled a bit as though in the dark. People were everywhere. Simple folk belonging to happier, linear days. They were no less trapped than I, it seemed, although not knowing this, they were free to repeat themselves innocently forever as part of their imprisonment. They could be set loose on a different tangent only if I interfered. Unless, of course, there were others like myself, each unknown to the other but also going through this cosmic replica of life, this stuttering of God, this imaginative hell, this bad dream, this joke, this jewel set in a silver sea—*Vigilance!* "Hold onto the mind, me lad. Do not let it slide. Think of something sobering, something unexciting."

Like Milly. I even thought of calling her, since I had so very few ports in this storm. I thought of it. Then I remembered the vast bog of her depression, our affair gutted, both of us desperate. No, I preferred to stay away. This brought me back to that other conundrum, namely those four bizarre months together that began with Milly saying, "If you have, like, tears, prepare to shed 'em now." We had just parked in the rain in front of her mother's cottage. "Hamlet," she added.

"Julius Caesar," I corrected.

"Same thing. Point being my mother is not as a mother should be."

We ran across the threshold, out of the wet, and smack into a playful greeting, "Milly, in all this rain you've found a man." My hostess winked at me.

"Mommy, I'd like you to meet *Mr.* Robinson Blake, my *boss.* Mr. Blake, I'm forced to introduce my—I don't know what—my *trainer.*"

"How do you do, Mrs. Hawkmann?" I ventured, although

part of me wanted, despite her hair-curlers, to say *Mon Général*.

She responded with a slight bow from a sitting position before replying, "Trainer?"

"My cross to bear," Milly corrected.

"Cross to bear? What is this to call a Jewish mother?"

"OK. My Mt. Sinai."

"There, that's what I call respect."

"Huge, barren, and surrounded by desert," Milly continued, as if reciting an answer in geography class.

Above her close-set eyes, Mrs. Hawkmann's eyebrows met and made an arch. "The fruit of my loins tells me I'm barren. Logic, she hasn't. Mr. Blake—lovely name—my house is yours, my food is yours, my daughter is yours. We're gracious to a fault."

Milly turned to me, "Perhaps you'd prefer to take your chances with the elements?"

"I am more than delighted to be your mother's guest."

This was greeted by loud, motherly applause after which she tightened her pink terrycloth bathrobe. "And handsome. Milly, you never told me your boss was handsome."

"Why the big butter-up?" asked the daughter while taking my coat.

"No 'butter-up.' Mr. Blake knows he's handsome. Confidence he's got, which is more than I can say for the fruit of my loins. Mr. Blake, is she not the picture of loveliness?"

"Everybody knows that," Milly yelled with sarcasm from inside the closet, where she had pushed her way against a wall of clothes.

"But just look at her," said Mrs. Hawkmann. "Look how she dresses. Neo-Bowery at best. Some people wish to attract men. Others, women. My daughter is bait for social workers."

"Mother, he's still standing up."

"When a guest of mine is offered a chair, I want him to appreciate it." Another wink in my direction. "Mr. Blake, to save my Madeleine from nervous collapse, would you kindly be seated?"

"Call me Rob," I managed to get in as I took possession of a lumpy wicker chair.

"Milly, bring whiskey. Mr. Blake is gorna need it. And food. Rich we're not but food we got. Mr. Blake, I'm indeed glad you dropped in."

"Call me Rob."

But her roughshod heartiness trampled such fine points underfoot. Milly was impressive in her handling of this mother-run-amuck. Hers was a kind of compassionate fatigue born of having weathered the fire storm a thousand times too often.

My problem was somewhat different. When I addressed the old lady as Mrs. Hawkmann, I did so a bit fearfully, as if I were calling attention to a bad joke played on her by fate. Her nose, you see, was like a ship's rudder, the eyes small and close together.

But we did eat and we certainly drank. I had two grilled cheese sandwiches and four bourbons. And I enjoyed myself, if a man who is swept over Niagara Falls without a barrel or an injury can be said to have enjoyed himself. It was not, heaven knows, a slow evening. Mrs. Hawkmann, in her fervor, knocked my glass (empty as it so happened) across the room, where it landed unbroken at her daughter's feet. Milly brought it back filled. She announced she was bushed and going to bed. She made the living-room couch into a bed for me, then slipped away, as the rain, like dozens of skilled typists, recorded our conversation. Mrs. Hawkmann, now an old friend, was tireless.

"Daughters," she announced. The conversation, it seemed, was about to turn serious. "Daughters. Screw they do, talk they don't. Not to me, anyhow. I'm not prying. I just want to learn. In the modern world, sexually speaking, as far as the old standards are concerned, all bets are off, am I right? So tell me, says I to my daughter, what's it like? The ethos, I mean. What's all about it? Just want to learn. So what do I get? Mums the word. Wild horses couldn't drag it out of her. I don't know if she's a virgin or a hooker. That's how tight-lipped she is. If you'll pardon the expression. I love the girl. It's the best part of me, that love. I'd die for her. So is it strange that I'm concerned for her well-being? What I'm really afraid of, to put it on the line, is that my daughter, God forbid, is not, how shall I say, getting laid. A typical Jewish mother, I'm not. Children today, I'm told, are physically free. Milly? Who knows? I mean sexual problems can fuck up one's life. It's a thing to consider. Well, confess to me she don't. And I respect her for it. But I worry. It's what we Jews do best. Listen, two thousand years of worry wasn't caused by chopped liver. So do you see what I'm getting at? Daughters! That's what I'm getting at."

My contribution had been a cough, a few nods, and several Jewish shrugs: they were infectious. Now came my big chance, for she seemed to weaken, had fallen silent.

"Your daughter, Mrs. Hawkmann, is not only charming but she can take care of herself, I assure you."

"So you tried already. Don't protest, I'm glad for it. So tumble her. I wish you would. I really do."

"Mrs. Hawkmann, I am only her employer."

"Employer? You're not her boss anymore? I know from bosses. I may have voted for Goldwater but when it comes to bosses Lenin wasn't all wrong, you know. Nobody was really all wrong, am I right? I've worked for bosses. They usually want a finger in your pie, if you get my meaning. Oh, I'm not implying you. You're clean. You got à face that keeps no secrets. That's why I like you. Crap I throw, duck you don't. If you can take me, you can take anything. You make my house proud. My friend, go to bed. Look how bushed you look."

"A real pisser, my mother," said Milly at breakfast, with Mrs. Hawkmann in a back room, still snoring.
"She does command a certain authority."
"Like a Sherman Tank. More toast?"
"Thanks."
"Eat, eat, so we can scram before she wakes."
"I'm doing my best."
"And chew soft. She wakes easy."

Grazed as I was by that evening, I grew cautious about the daughter who had survived so many such evenings. If "survived" was the right word. In general, Milly Hawkmann's office personality was as enlightening as a bricked-in window. But even after our spending time together in Vermont, she returned to being the same secretarial stranger, selfless as a bank clerk, remote as tomorrow. When I asked after her mother, to remind her that the evening in Vermont was not forgotten, at least by me (I had taken the train home that afternoon, and she had gone straight back to her mother's cottage), Milly extended, or perhaps invented, her mother's regards.

Indeed, nothing was changed. Nothing was new. Except for the thought that here was a girl who so rarely found herself desired that should some of it come her way, it would surely let loose a grateful burst of erotic passion. This thought, arrogant and sexist as it was, stuck with me. Soon I became inordinately curious how she, who had no discernible self-image as a woman, would behave in a hardcore carnal situation. It became annoying how totally uninterested she was in flattering her boss or appreciating anything he did or said. That's what finally angered me. Half a year passed leaving her just as she was on the very first day she entered my office. This unleashed, to my amazement, at first a slight and then a determined desire to take her manless, unmalleable self to bed.

Late one night as the two of us were alone in the building trying to make sense out of a mass of answers to a badly worded questionnaire asking whether label A, B, or C was more likely, less likely, or just as likely to induce the customer to choose *Dante's Bolognese Sauce* over products 1, 2, and 3 and whether this choice took no, some, or much contemplation, I kissed her.

Milly 1. took it in her stride 2. acted as if it were long overdue 3. seemed very surprised 4. died of a heart attack? Closest to the truth, I fear, was Milly "3", seemed very surprised.

Did she A. take part in the kiss? B. resist? C. convey anger? The answer was "D" none of these.

Then was she a. too frightened to respond? b. asleep? c. trying to determine what I was doing? d. waiting until the kiss was done so as to receive an explanation? The answer was evidently "d," because when I released her, she said,

"I don't get it."

"I felt like kissing you."

"Oh, felt like." She flung away her beads and they swung back against her stomach. "I still don't get it."

"Did the kiss displease you?"

She gave an abrupt shrug. "Should we go back to *Dante's Bolognese Sauce?*"

"No, I'm taking you home."

"Out for the kill, huh?"

"I would like to kiss you again." She seemed dubious. "What say you?"

"You better go ahead 'cause by the time I make up my mind . . ."

I did and her response could be termed passive-curious. Her arms remained at her side but she lifted herself on her toes. My reaction the first time was confirmed on the second. She was like one of those foods whose appearance belied their tastiness: the slimy blob of an oyster, for example, or ink-dipped caviar. She didn't smoke, so it was not like mouthing an exhaust pipe, nor was there the clumsy jolt of teeth against teeth. It wasn't sexy either or filled with the busy skills of the virtuoso. It was simply unexpectedly delicious like a newly invented candy laced with habit-forming drugs. When we finished she looked at me searching for a clue as to how to behave.

"There's a couch in Murray's office," I suggested.

"There's a hatrack in the hall," she answered.

"The door locks on the inside."

"The elevator comes when you push the button."

"No one will think we're up here."

"That's cause we'll both be down in the street."

"All right, you win. I'll take you home."

"I, you know, can, like, go by myself."

"No, I'll take you home."

She acquiesced with a world-weary nod. Nor did she like the idea of us taking a taxi, as though their only legitimate use was in rushing people to the hospital. The taste of her was still with me, leavening into an incredible erotic memory while she sat innocently beside me looking to all the world like a sex-frightened proofreader for *The Christian Science Monitor*. "You hungry?" I asked, simply because I could not think of a single thing to say. Her rather candid reply was, "Fuckin' a-right." We got out in front of a brownstone in the West Seventies. She went upstairs and I walked off to buy pizza.

Milly, who lives in one room on the third floor of a musty building with eroding carpets, proved that office efficiency was often accompanied by a private life abounding in chaos. I burst into her apartment; nothing was ready. No plates or wine glasses on the table or even so much as a corkscrew anywhere. I said I'd like to know how the devil anyone can survive without a corkscrew? For an answer she shrugged and swung her beads away from her; back they came in a soft reprimand. So while the pizza went into the oven, I trudged up one more flight to disturb "Cranky Mrs. Manners," who took five minutes to undo all the locks on her door only to explain somewhat proudly that she has never owned a corkscrew in her life. I finally had to go and buy one. Plus sugar, coffee, lettuce, and Tampax.

To an untrained eye it would be hard to tell if Milly was moving into her apartment, moving out, or simply using the room for storage. Cardboard boxes everywhere, pictures standing on the floor, books stacked in tilting columns, an unlaid rug like a fallen tree, a floor lamp that was unplugged as I soon found out, a day bed buried beneath a groundswell of clothes and a hair dryer like a component part of an electric chair.

We ate and drank in intermittent silence and from the bemused look on her face you'd think she was eating leftovers from the last supper. Finally, we abandoned her wobbling kitchen table and repaired to comfortable sitting positions on the floor. During the meal I had pried out of her the reason why her room was in such a state. She just couldn't decide, after she had moved in, whether or not she really wanted to stay. She was determined not to unpack until she had made up her mind. That was four years ago. I laughed. She shrugged. We both sipped some wine. I took her glass away and kissed her. Milly gave herself to it on a "work to rule" basis: no more, or longer, than was necessary. Yet never in my memory did such an unexciting girl have such an erotic sting and never was I so provoked without any clear idea as to how it was done.

Getting her into bed assumed precedence equal, say, to reaching shore when drowning. I tried to undress her. She didn't so much resist as she busied herself working at cross purposes, zipping closed and buttoning up all that I had achieved in the way of unraveling the mystery. She just couldn't make up her mind, she said. Why? She didn't know. But she assured me that her ambivalence wasn't because I was her boss or in any way repellent.

"Look," she explained with irritation. "I just can never make up my Goddamned mind. It's a pain in the ass, I know. It's a pain for yours-truly, as well. Like with me it's always, should I? shouldn't I? and afterward, should I have? or shouldn't I have? and since I did, should I again? or never again or what? Fuck."

"Madeleine," said I, "Make. Up. Your. Mind."

Her reply was demented-playful. "Can. Not. Do. It."

"Flip a coin?" I insisted.

"That's stupid, isn't it?"

"No, it's not. It's not. Heads I go home and die. Tails I stay. Come on. OK? Come on."

She gave one of her lightning shrugs. Quickly I flipped a quarter, caught it and slapped the back of my left hand. I uncovered a small, tarnished American Eagle looking, I must admit, more glorious at the moment than at any time in our nation's history.

"Son of a gun."

"That's it," I said. "Tails I win."

"Best two out of three?"

"No, no. Be a man."

"Be a man?"

"I mean stick to your word."

She stood up. "I'm gorna take a shower."

"No, no. No need to do that."

"Point being I'm all grubby."

"Don't care. Never mind."

"But I do care. See ya in a while."

Yet it took a "while" for her just to get herself into the bathroom, what with hunting for her shower cap and nightie and stopping to finish off a few remaining pizza crusts and to reclaim her unfinished wine. Once the door to the john was closed behind her, it took another long while before I even heard the sound of water. With a "Wow" "Zap" "Hot" I learned that she was under the shower at last, a fact that struck me as deliciously erotic. I was so obsessed, it was like being fourteen again. How unnerving to discover one's rampant darker side—or at least lower half—and learn to what extent it can take on a life of its own. I felt almost broken in two by a lust not unlike arthritis. I had gone clear into heat like a four-legged beast. Surely howling would be next.

Well, to cut a long seduction short, I stumble to my feet, strip off my clothes and hobble past a pizza box, a carton of books, a fallen Mohawk rug-tree and on into a muggy and thunderous steamroom, where her voice is humming, then screaming, as I climb past the shower curtain, parting plastic ensembles of dancing bears and waddling ducks into enveloping clouds of a devil-devised sauna bath and seduction booth, where hot fluids, like the sacred lava juice of lust, pour down over her smooth, water-proof spongecake. She argues, scratches, growls, falls, pulls me with her, laughs, purrs, and holds on tight in the torrential downpour and hell fog as we grapple like two brain-damaged sea creatures, delirious in a warm, slippery, white-walled basting pit, gasping and writhing in a cataclysm of mock rape, she underneath thinking of God-knows-what and I on top, vividly envisioning Mrs. Scanlan.

6

A frantic police siren screamed on the avenue. With
sadly dripping hair Milly looked, if possible, even
more unglamorous than usual as we toweled each other down.
"Little tits," she conceded and shrugged. By the time I had her
dry I was inflamed once more. On her bed, with soft light
coming from her bathroom, we tangled again. Feet hammered ominously down the stairs past the door. A four-
engined monster grumbled in the sky. Life went on and so did
we. Afterward, as we lay gathering our strength, I had a
chance to look upon Milly plain. She had beautiful arms, a
rump to remember, and excellent skin. Her modest charms ig-
nited enough passion for yet a third assault. "More yet?" was
her comment, like a neutral observer. Hours fell away, forgotten like dreams. We flipped a coin. I got up and made the
cocoa. Another four-engined heavyweight growled overhead.
In the middle of the night I reached out and found Milly be-

side me, smooth like a salacious thought. The decathlon continued. "Son of a gun," she said, still half asleep. Mad, rhythmic, perpetual copulation during which my foot knocks over an empty cocoa mug that hobbles away on the dusty floor. The radiator ceases its bird imitations and hisses in outright disapproval. Milly asks, "You tryin' to kill me, yourself, or what?" Dawn's tubercular light reveals Milly face down, a pillow over her head. The alarm goes off. Morning is an old debt remembered.

There she stood dressed, a work-a-day rag-a-muffin.

"Hey, Boss-man. It's eight-thirty. I am going—guess where—to work. Faretheewell."

I sat up to tell her, wait. No one was in the room. My watch: nine-thirty. In the office she is again the efficient, hardworking secretary and stranger. Her IBM electric typewriter, humming at rest, displayed more inner life than she. When the phone wasn't ringing and people weren't dropping by and she wasn't fingering at top speed business letters in triplicate, I pulled her aside and asked if she had enjoyed herself last night. She made a circle with thumb and index finger and with her mouth open, closed one eye.

"This morning I could hardly walk," she whispered.

"I've never been like that before. On and on like that."

"Nice."

"Must have been the hand of God."

"Felt like two hands and a foot."

"We'll do it again soon, huh?"

"First I got to get in training. Road work, deep knee bends, all that. Last night, though, I only wished my mother could have seen me." Striking her head with the heel of her hand. "Boy, do I have a weird mind."

I tried to steer the mood away from flippancy by saying how wonderful she had been.

"Yeah?" A little grin. "Really?"

"I'm glad you were finally able to make up your mind."

A mistake. Her quick, spasmatic shrug told of lingering doubts. Immediately I tried to nail down another evening. Well, tonight was her pottery class and tomorrow she was baby-sitting for a friend and this weekend she was attending a wedding in Philadelphia. As she talked I felt these vacant nights like storage tanks filling up with lust. I had to do something. I asked her to lunch, didn't wait for an answer, dragged her downstairs, hailed a cab and gave the driver her address.

Milly looked at me. "There's a restaurant there? Who said?"

"Shush up."

"I think you're a nymphomaniac or whatever they're called."

"Satyr."

"Yeah, a satyr, that's you in spades."

"You bring out the best in me, I'm sorry to say." In my inflamed state, I wondered if I'd be able to hobble up those damn three flights.

"Do I get a last meal," she asked, "and a chance to leave a farewell note?"

"Afterward," I said.

It was the same each time we climbed to her little room where everything was boxed, or rolled away, breakables removed, as if nothing must be allowed to distract us while I ran amuck or, as Milly quipped, reclined amuck. Quite frankly, these fire storms baffled me, especially since the sight of Milly should hardly have summoned forth what she called my Olympic Games. She seemed infused each time with awe and apprehension almost to the point of dismay. I could hardly blame her. And sure enough, in all of this, there turned out to be a great and actual danger, something I would no more have predicted than my very sudden galloping lust. I fell, you see, in love.

Now I had to be with her all of the time, not just on top of her some of the time. To be there to suffer her platitudes and share her pizza. Then of course there was her eternal flippancy in the face of passion, her mental untidiness and, of course, her mother. Needless to say, Milly didn't love me in return. So here was misery. Oddly enough, the only one who I could talk to about it, who extended deep understanding and sympathy was once again, that great Frenchman himself, her mother.

One day, when I was deep in a Sunday-afternoon depression, she phoned.

"Mr. Blake? This is Mrs. Hawkmann. So tell me, about my Madeleine, what's gorna be with her? Suffer she does, talk she doesn't. You know where that leaves me, don't you? In the dark. So what else is new? Mr. Blake, I am forced to humble myself and ask you something straight out. My daughter's lover, no less. But first let me say that I know you're ga-ga over her. Don't ask me how I know; I know, that's all. A mother can tell these things. Especially if she's got a lumox like Madeleine for a daughter. You see, Madeleine is never so miserable as when a nice young man is in love with her. 'Cause then she really *has* to make up her mind. Unless I'm wrong. Unless she's doing right by you and the suffering is caused by something else—like fallen arches."

"Mrs. Hawkmann, your daughter is most certainly not in love with me nor anywhere near it and also—"

"Say no more. She's edgy, right? Prickly, you might say. In the office a regular Miss Goodie-Two-Shoes. But after hours she treats you as if your what's-its was made of frozen turd. Am I right?"

"Your description, Mrs. Hawkmann, is reasonably accurate, I'm sorry to say."

"You poor guy. I feel for you. Well, I give up. She's a real pisser, my daughter. She don't like me to use language like that. Think lofty, mother, she says, think lofty. Get her. Well, you can't say I didn't try. Motherhood, who needs it? But you keep punchin', you hear. Because I love her. What a burden is love. None greater on this earth. Look, I'll do all I can. I shouldn't, I know. She doesn't like it. Stay out of this, mother, she says. Stay away. As if I could. As if you could. I see trouble coming, Mr. Blake. Dead ahead. I'm an old woman, I am a tired woman. And love is a burden. It doesn't let up. I was married once, long ago. May he rot in New Brunswick. That's where he's living, my husband. I loved him. And what does he do? He walks out, the crummy bastard. Well, I'm not going to walk out on my baby. Not like he did. Just walk out. Not even so much as a note. It's . . . cruel. . . . Sorry . . . Mr. Blake. To cry like . . . this. Look at me. A mother crying. . . . . Think lofty, she says. Mind your own beeswax, that's what she says. Tsh. I got to go now. Don't tell her I phoned. OK? OK. Got to go. You wouldn't believe the people waitin' outside this phone-booth. And making faces yet, the stupid bastards. OK OK. Go, I will. Mr. Blake, good-by. God bless."

Not knowing from day to day whether Milly would break off, break down, balk, or just bitch was trouble enough without these monologues from her mother every Monday, Wednesday, and Friday, which I correctly anticipated would take place. But I had missed the point. It was for me a time of miracles. That I was blind to this was not, after all, very hard to explain. I had no idea, you see, that a true miracle, like so many other things, could also be just another pain in the ass.

Then it happened. I had spent, as usual, a dismal evening with Miss Ambivalence, who these days was always moody. Her previous complaint was that she was "over-fucked." Her present gripe was that I pestered her to death with all this "icky tenderness and devotion," which she now claimed "ruined all the screwing." And she was leaving me; but only for a few weeks. She insisted that we take our vacations separately. To make sure she took hers in mid-winter. The dismal evening consisted of my escorting her to dinner and then to the airport where she patted me on the shoulder and said, "So long Boss-man."

Wearing dungarees that made her butt look 30 percent again as large, and a short ridiculous jacket which appeared to be fashioned out of dangling confetti, she was easily identifiable from the observation deck as she ambled in line toward the aircraft, dropped her paperback biography of Marilyn Monroe, bent to pick it up, hurried to rejoin the fashionable women and distinguished men who were climbing on board, caught her beads on something, freed herself from the stairway railing, looked around for me, waved in the wrong direction, and bounded upward to disappear in the hole in the side of the plane.

At that moment, for the first time in my life, I suffered the deformity of being alone. I made for a movie, parked my sorrow outside, and saw a long, slow horror film whose most frightening aspect was the blood money I paid at the door. I came out, reclaimed my loneliness like a crutch, and hobbled in spirit home. A surprise letter was waiting in the mail box. I opened it in the elevator.

Dear Boss-man:
Re: our love affair.
Now please don't get pissed off or depressed or like that but I'm writing this to say that I think we should break up. I mean all we have in common is the horizontal. Vertically, already, we're in trouble. I talk and you get nauseous. You talk and right away I'm asleep. What does that leave us? Pain, boredom, *yuck*. So since I don't want anyone to get hurt & because I respect you tremendously, I figure let's call it kaput. At least think about it. I'll make a final definitive decision when I get back.

OK? We can always be friends. Can't we? Anyway, that's it. Give it some thought. Faretheewell.

With affectionate regards,

Madeleine

P.S. If you're really against it I guess we can continue a little while longer just to see. But consider this letter a second warning. (The first, I think, was when I threw up pizza all over my rolled up rug.)

P.P.S. I just read this over. Talk about sick. This isn't a Dear John letter. It's a Dear I-Don't-Know-What letter. Shit, next time I'll get you to dictate it.

The elevator stopped and I stepped out holding this typed reprieve in my hands only to notice down the hall seated on the floor, leaning against my door, wrapped in confetti, Milly.

"What happened?"

"I'm in love," she moaned.

My heart jammed. "Who with?"

"With you, you stupid fuck. I'm sitting but the plane's not going. Slight delay. So I start to plotz. I feel terrible. Sick, lonely, chilly, the works. Everything but my period. It's you I want. It suddenly dawns on me. I can't believe it. It's *him* you want? Schmuck, are you for real? *Him?* After writing that letter and everything? Yeah, him! But there I am stuck in a plane that's stuck on the ground and me seated next to a Priest. They're taking me to California. Away from Robbela. Then the P.A. announces a two-hour delay and everybody should go back to the waiting room and wait. I yell *Hot damn* and slap the Priest on the knee. Swear to God and hope to die. Well, here I am, my luggage is in L.A., and I'm in love and pissed off 'cause Love isn't what I bought a ticket for. Terrific, huh? End of story. Are there any questions? Oh, and would you please do me a favor? Would you hold me?"

Life, like Milly, was a gift. Badly wrapped and in poor taste, but a gift nonetheless. The miracle was that this girl, whom I didn't want and dearly loved, whom I resisted and cherished, whose unremarkable and sagging self turned me instantly into a diligent stud, this very girl now doted on me and with such cloying determination, that I suffered as never before the deepest of any disprized love: my own.

The miracle was that I didn't go bananas. Of this mutual amour I can only remember the general pattern, scattered fragments, and a sense of static anguish. I had all I could do to keep her from pinching my rump in the office during the day and at night, when the others had gone and we were working late, from dragging me at long last onto Murray's furry couch. Endearments like Robbela set me twitching. She clung like lint, wrote pornographic love notes, wept gently about she-knew-not-what, and, just as I did, had God-awful dreams every single night.

Mrs. Hawkmann joined this tug-of-love like a one-woman Greek chorus phoning-in her comments. What she wanted was not a progress report, oddly enough, but assessment as to my state of mind. When I described my mixed stew of devotion and misery, she recommended a combination of Bhuddist acceptance and Hebraic endurance—that, and trips with Milly to Vermont for clean air, hot cider, and long walks in the woods. We went, suffered, and drove back to our city misery. The trouble was that Mrs. Hawkmann had too much energy and hunger of her own. She loved her daughter with a tenacity few mothers could equal and she seemed to need us near her as if the musk of our passion would give her eternal life.

My belief that Milly got along well with her mother was shaken one afternoon when having had enough of Mrs. Hawkmann's ceaseless talk, I left the cottage and strolled uphill in the empty woods amid patches of clean snow. Milly had a cold and chose, or was ordered, to stay behind. A discovered pond was glazed with ice. Beauty, vivid and everlasting, was everywhere and the leafless trees seemed like so many good friends safely asleep. As I stood amid their solid cluster and tall sway, I almost felt that love was not so bad a thing at that.

Milly's basic decency, her straight trunk, her lovely arms, her hearty, barren, rooted permanence seemed well worth any man's celebration. Quickly, I strode back to the cottage to tell her so. They were having a terrible row. I heard it through the closed windows, yards away. Milly was screaming with such blistering rage that I grew frightened. At what, I don't know. Some five minutes later I returned again. They were still at it. I strolled back once more much later and it had finally stopped. Inside, each room seemed frozen with pain. Milly lay in bed asleep. Behind a locked door, bathwater was running. That night at a dejected dinner I did all the talking as they sat in anguished dignity.

Hours later Milly made love with such a clamor of gasps and exhortations that it seemed to me her mother could not help but overhear and I tried to contain with hushes what I was busily stoking into a roar. I also had the crazy thought that she was calling out to her mother in a strange language that I mistook for passion.

Then it happened.

Three days later I woke up, as usual, long after the alarm went off, this time however without the bad dreams and accompanying cold sweat. It reminded me of the time I had been taken as a child on a nonstop train ride that consisted of days of sitting, reading, washing, eating, and sleeping in a constant tremor and quiver of eternally maddening, jostling motion until I awoke one morning to find that during the night it had all blissfully ceased.

I entered the office and found Milly lifting her face from a container of coffee to smile at me with a mustache of cream and I knew I never wanted to touch her again. It was the suddenness more than anything else that appalled and puzzled me. Love like a great vibration had ceased. I felt exhausted as well as grateful. And just as trapped. She came over, kissed me, left part of her mustache on my nose, made me bow slightly as she gave a soft grab for the groin, and sedately moved away saying, "Yes, Mr. Scanlan, he's here among the living," into the telephone that had rung once and which she now handed over to me with a bit of mustache on the mouthpiece, as well.

7

Quite true. Her mother was not as a mother should be. But then neither was I the classic lover. Perhaps I was only a carrier of love, someone in whom the symptoms flare up and are quickly gone and who then proceeds, unknowingly, to infect others. Poor Milly. Thoughts of her were weights that sank me deep in recollection. I must do something to help, perhaps even find her another man—that is, if I ever wind my way out of here and into tomorrow.

In fact, nothing was as it should be. I ate alone in the most expensive restaurant I could think of, had a bottle of chilled Montrachet to accompany a splendidly cooked pheasant and a dessert such as a monk might damn his soul for. This was followed by a radiant snifter with its aromatic pool of sunburned gold. At that moment, while alone at my table in this vast cul-de-sac of uncommunicable misery, I was, despite everything, a secret, one-man enclave of happiness. There were, even now, secondary benefits. Then I copied down the serial numbers of three twenty-dollar bills and handed them away on a plate with the check.

Keeping an eye on the time, I walked, greatly stuffed, to a nearby tavern to watch the 11 o'clock news. Today there has been no air disaster. Instead there was a report admitting that there was nothing further to report on the kidnapped Brazilian ambassador. I felt splendid. The next item was also new to me. A cop was killed and two people were on the critical list because of a shoot-out this morning, said the reporter. I stared at the screen. I didn't breathe. The gunfire had taken place in the basement of an apartment building in Forest Hills when the police, alerted by an anonymous phone call, came to the aid of a woman being threatened with rape by two men. The dead officer had a wife and two children. The wounded man was from Venezuela. Arrested with him was an unemployed Cuban, age twenty-five. The woman, whose name was withheld, had been accidentally shot in the spine. There are fears that she will be paralyzed for life.

I saw and heard nothing for a while as I tried to tally up a scorecard of good works and bad luck in which a woman saved from rape is now bed-ridden for life and a dead policeman must be subtracted from a plane-load of safely delivered tourists. But I was never much good at arithmetic, moral or otherwise.

In the meanwhile, time kept closing in. I downed the rest of my Chivas and turned to a woman seated on a bar stool beside me. Clasping her hand I said, "Madam, I am about to leave you. Faretheewell."

In her embarrassment, she played her part too grandly, shook my whole arm and boomed, "Ta, ta to you too." I gave her a slight, seated bow, directed a mock-frown at her boyfriend, who was glowering at me from over her shoulder, saw the wall clock close its hands as if in prayer, and decided to play a little game with fate.

I patted the nice lady on the knee and winked at her protector. He was off his stool in a moment. *"Hey!"* He came toward me. *"Hey!"* I stood down from my seat and got pushed in the chest. I winked at the lady's ashen face. *"Hey!"* And with this her protector raised his fist, I hoped for the best. But, of course, the bar, the smoke, the woman, and the raised arm of her furious friend, not to mention my desperate panache, were all blown asunder with a vast, obliterating sweep of time, deep and slow, which took me at once to where I lay shouting at myself for being a lazy bastard. I simply sat up, pressed STOP, and felt myself shudder at the terrible thought that perhaps I was even getting used to it.

The magical lass pouring milk from a jug offered me a share in her tranquillity. The same lovely day was sending its triangle of light through my window to where it drew a line on the wall several inches below the cheap wooden frame.

I sprang out of bed and ran to the closet to get the slip of paper from my pocket, and, of course it wasn't there because I hadn't gone to the restaurant yet, and so the foolish idea about the serial numbers only gave me cause to worry as to what all this was doing to my intelligence. I snapped up my wallet. The three twenty-dollar bills were there all right; whether they were the self-same three twenties I could not now be sure.

Then I bolted into action again. Twenty minutes later, well before the phone rang, I was out the door and on my way. This time it was I who held the elevator open. There was a loud slam, quickening strides, and a weak, "Thank you" as Her Majesty stepped in and turned to face the closing doors. I almost said, "Hello again," switching in mid-thought to:

"Lovely fur-piece you're wearing."

"Thank you," she replied, addressing the space on the floor half way between us.

A row of numbers took turns lighting up and going dead. The silence chaffed.

"Beautiful day," I said, recalling how much I deplored people who force upon others such mind-draining small talk.

She nodded, almost pleasantly, considering the vacuous passenger she was trapped with. Unless this sort of thing was just her speed. But why in hell was I so eager to break through? That was the real question.

"Good for tennis, this weather."

"Is it?" Again not quite looking at me.

"And long walks in the woods."

With a brief hum of agreement, her gaze finally touched mine. At that my stomach sank. The door opened and off she went without so much as a word of farewell. The auto accident, the tumbling hat, the floating cathedral were now hardly worth noticing. That's what I told myself. Even better would have been to leave the building later, except I was lonely and too much in a rush, for there was one departure I didn't want to miss.

In fact, I almost blew it by nearly running into Murray. He came slowly down the steps of their Brownstone in the West Eighties, impressive in his new pin-striped, double-breasted suit, filing a fingernail while squeezing his briefcase under his arm. I paused, flat-footed and trapped—except that he walked the other way, up the street toward the café, where, as Philippa had told me, he always stopped for breakfast before heading downtown. I leap up the stairs and stab the bell. There is a considerable wait. Her voice sounds not a bit pleased at this door-to-door salesman or forgetful husband returning to intrude on her sleep, or her breakfast, or her bath. Not a bit pleased.

"Yes, who *IS* it?"

"Robinson Blake. Must speak to you."

The door opening the length of a short chain revealed her narrowly framed astonishment, girlish without make-up, the harmless glamorous guile replaced with an unmocking, more trustworthy face yet with her hardcore beauty retained, bone strong, comforting. The rest of her was kept out of sight.

"Who?" She squinted. The light was in her eyes.

"Me. Rob." I felt myself presiding over a massive blunder.

"You rob, me call police." A little smile; pleased with herself.

"Did I wake you?"

"What time is it?"

"After nine."

"Then you didn't wake me," she replied in quick self-mockery. "But you missed my husband."

"I came to see you. It's very important."

"Is it, you know, bad news sort of thing?"

"No, no. Just very important."

"I'm not dressed. I suppose you'll want to come in."

"If you're not dressed, I'll want to come in."

"Wait a sec."

For a good while the door stayed shut. I imagined her scampering naked up the carpeted stairs, where once we sat chatting during a party, to rummage through her several closets in their huge bedroom agonizing desperately over which seductive chiffon thing to wear for me, bending to brush her hair in the vanity mirror, then hurrying into the bathroom to hold that open-mouthed, skeptical, self-examination in the full-length mirror, a dab of Tabu, a rapid horizontal toothbrush spree followed by a tranquil descent in fluffy pink slippers down the carpeted stairs, as if the eyes of the world were already upon her, to slash the chain free of its hold and swing open the door with that curious, alert tilt of her head.

She was, of course, wearing nothing of what my clairvoyant

voyeurism had foreseen. Here was a simple white sweater that did not quite reach her beltless white slacks and which left a narrow suggestion of her bare swarthy self and the intimate blind eye of her bellybutton. She wore no make-up or bra or perfume or even shoes. Her fingers had gone through her hair a few times and did so again as she led me into the living room and up to that low, round, glass coffee table the size of a trampoline that was flanked by a right-angled couch of gold velvet into which she dropped, her legs tucked under her, tapping a cigarette on her knee, offering none, knowing I didn't smoke.

"Coffee is almost ready on the stove," she said, then lit a match.

We were seated some distance apart. I explained again that I had to speak to her, that it was most important.

"Have the phones all gone dead in New York?" she asked, pleasantly.

"For what I have to say, yes. I want to look at you as I tell you this."

"Christ, what can it be? The last time a friend came knocking on my door this way she was two months gone."

I took a deep breath. "I came to apologize."

"To apologize? You scare me. What have you done?"

"For three years I've wanted you, I've been completely obsessed with you. Stupidly I did nothing. I said nothing. I was afraid. But my need for you kept growing. Today I just could not stand it any longer. I thought, Who knows? Maybe Philippa feels the same way about me. Who knows? That's why I want to apologize. For saying and doing nothing. If I was wrong not to act, three years have been wasted. Coming here will waste only ten minutes. Look, I want you. OK? End of declaration of love. Wow, I could use that coffee now."

It was as if I had been lecturing on medieval place names in

Finnegan's Wake. As she altered her position on the couch she set into movement, briefly, all that was inside her white sweater. I waited.

"Well, this is the first time someone has apologized to me for *not* making a pass."

"Guess so."

"Black with sugar?" she asked, as if unable to find anything else to say.

"Yes, thanks."

"Don't go away." She stood up and walked off and even the light whispering of her feet said woman.

She returned with two flowered mugs of a slightly steaming brew, sat down once again, and, for want of knowing what to say, asked me why today, exactly.

"My need for you was getting out of hand, that's why."

"Your need for me."

"Yes."

She sipped her coffee. "This is quite a change of pace." She sipped again. "I'm not at my best in the morning." She put her mug on the glass table top. "I'll have to think about it. And you'll want to get back to the office now, I suppose."

"I had a dream," I said, as desperation took hold. "That's another reason why I came this morning."

"A dream?"

"That's right."

She leaned forward. "Tell me."

"Well, I was in this dark forest. I was lying, all alone, flat on my back in some kind of, how shall I say, hammock."

Her lips parted slightly. A hit, a palpable hit.

"Go on."

"I heard the sound of someone crying. It's you, sitting on the ground, dejected and miserable. I ask what the trouble is. It seems that Murray has been treating you very badly. You

just can't stand it any more. You're sobbing. I take you back to
the hammock. You climb in and ask me to join you. As soon
as I settle in, the damn thing turns into a flying carpet. We
each grab hold of the other but instead of feeling frightened as
we soar high above the woods, we experience together this
tremendous sense of joy."

She waited for more.

"That's all I remember, really."

"Fan-tastic."

"It was very vivid."

"Fan-tastic."

One speaks of the naked truth. The truth is, when I tell a lie
it's then I feel most naked. Philippa looked at me, however, as
if I had become clothed in shining armor.

"I must tell you something," she breathed.

It was all about similar dreams that she and Murray once
had. She didn't even leave out, though she left it for last, that
he strangled me. She paused to let this cast a cloud over our
joyful flight above the evil woods. The melodrama appealed to
her and left her free to savor her concern. She explained, with
her usual occult fogginess of thought, that if my dream meant
anything then so did Murray's. I must, she said, look to my
well-being, my actual physical safety. I almost laughed. My
safety now was of no concern. My well-being was something
else again, especially when, reaching for her coffee, she set her
sweater gently rocking, so afloat with youth, so filled with
promise, so persuasive in suspending my disbelief. I quickly
explained that my dream had not meant that we would liter-
ally fly away on a rug any more than his meant the physical
end of me. Murray's revealed his general hostility, mine
pointed the way to salvation. She agreed absolutely and so very
quickly that I didn't know if she had secretly thought this all
along or whether the great strength of her fogginess of thought
was that it could accommodate to anything.

"So what do you suggest we do?" she asked with a touch of malignant innocence.

"Become lovers."

"That was fast."

"But it took a very long time to get said."

"So I understand."

"Well, then?"

"You might get fired."

"Fuck it."

"They're waiting for you now in the office."

"I'm staying right here."

"Well, well."

"I'm home sick."

"You're *home*sick?"

"I'm home *ill*."

"Ah, then you should phone in. Let them know."

"I will. It'll be a pleasure. But first we make love."

"Love before pleasure."

We both smiled. I got up and sat down beside her. The refrigerator came alive in the kitchen. I took her mug of coffee and set it on the glass table beside a copy of *Time*. She remarked that I had changed somehow. That I was almost a different man. We kissed. It evolved, with some shifting of position, into a different one than I had planned, a more passionate one than I had hoped.

"Well, well," she said with wonder.

I suggested we go upstairs. She suggested that she go upstairs. I, on the other hand, should fetch a half-empty bottle of white wine in the fridge, run some hot water over it, then hunt up two stemmed glasses, and bring them to her with the bottle and myself. A little celebration sort of thing. She smiled, touched my nose with a finger, and left the room. When I did all this and finally got to her bedroom, it was empty. The pillows had been worked on, the blankets somewhat straightened, odds and ends most likely snatched up, carried, and dumped down again on the closet floor. Everywhere was innocence. All else stayed hidden. An exercise bicycle faced a TV set. Two night tables: one with the poems of Sylvia Plath, the other with a tome on real estate. On the walls were childlike little sketches that turned out to be original Miros. In a corner were back copies of the Sunday *Times*. I felt oddly at home in this place, where nothing was mine except perhaps the lady I now heard coming down the hall.

"To a whole new ball game," I said, as we drank wine, standing up as if at a cocktail party.

"To surprises in the morning," she said.

We touched glasses more than once. Soon I took hers away and put it with mine beside *Property, the Best Investment*. When I turned around she had her sweater off. I was, I think, sufficiently blasé.

"Sir, I believe you're a bit overdressed for this party."

As my shirt hit the floor so did her slacks. She had nothing on beneath them either. This lavish gift of her—it was as if I had come recklessly close to suffering a terrible loss.

"My God but you're beautiful," she said, teasing my portentous expression.

In the beginning we played but soon all playfulness ceased. With her face in something like despair, she gasped endearments as if she had run to bring them to me. Rasping fragments of love in fervent whispers, she was a heroine fashioned not from the real world but out of some playwright's deep disappointment with life. And she was the only woman I ever knew who used her hands as a man does, as if she was blind and wanted to learn all she could about this pleasing creature she was bedded down with, the multi-dimensions of him, the flat and fat of him, the up there and down here of him (mostly the down here of him) breathlessly engrossed in her amusing discoveries. While I could only think again and again, my God how long I've waited, how much I've missed.

And for a little while I even forgot about this day that I was anchored to. Nothing beyond our grasp was of the slightest concern. Afterward, becalmed, I studied her unmagical repose (it was now as natural to view her, nude, as Murray, dressed) and realized that I would never want to be with anyone but her, ever.

"Guess what?" She placed the phone on my groin.

I watched her rear dimples seesaw out of the room, then dialed the office to find myself up to my neck in the humid swamp of Milly's lowest mood.

"Don't ask," she answered when I asked how she was.

I explained that I was in bed and not about to come in and infect the world with flu. I said I felt more or less like death and that she, sweet child, should pray for me. I recited all this in a light-hearted hope that it would cheer her up.

"You don't sound like you got the flu."

I explained that I was trying to be somewhat stoic.

"You're also tryin' to somewhat avoid me in the daytime, isn't that right?"

Now I did feel sick. "A hell of a lot of sympathy I'm getting from you," I snapped, furious that my little lie was not endorsed at once.

"You don't give much either." Her voice crumpled. Then I was as wretched as she.

"Look, Milly—"

"She make breakfast for you?"

"Milly, for crying out loud."

"What are you two . . . going to do now?"

"Milly," I began with an authority born of desperation. But the lady of the house was approaching with quick light steps. "Milly, good-*by*."

"Everything OK?" She slipped back into bed.

"Fine," I said, as if with a mouth full of broken glass.

"Good."

"Guess so."

"What did you tell them?"

"That I had the flu."

"The twenty-four-hour sort?"

"Why not?"

"You'll be back at your desk tomorrow, I'll bet."

"Could be."

"Important thing is to stay in bed."

"Right-o."

"Who'd you speak to?"

"Milly."

"She believe you?"

"Why shouldn't she?"

"Well, she's on your side, I guess."

"Sure."

"She'll get a day off, too, more or less."

"That's right."

"Wish she'd find a man, that one. Poor Milly."

"Yeah."

She rested her head on my shoulder, her hand on my chest.

"It's lovely just lying here, isn't it?"

"Hummmmm."

"Heavenly. Like time has stopped."

"Hummmmm."

"By the way, have you eaten? Can I make you some break-fast?"

"In a while."

"OK."

The silence was total and chilling.

"I want us to spend the day together. The *whole* day."

She raised her head. "Murray comes home about five-fifteen."

"Can't you get the night off?"

"We've been invited to dinner."

"Can't *you* get sick?"

"Then *he* won't go. They're *my* friends."

"OK, OK. Until five then."

Her head went back on my shoulder.

"Until five," I repeated and, feeling the chill deepen, pulled the sheet over both of us.

We decided to skip breakfast and go out to lunch instead, for, on second thought, she didn't want to take the chance of her husband coming home. In a fetching flared dress with a low back she was Murray's wife again, but her smile and the lean of her on my arm in the street made Philippa mine once more. We studied a menu in a restaurant window.

"That reminds me."

"You want my recipe for Quiche."

"How on earth did you know that?"

"See, we're made for each other." Kissing her cheek, "I can even read your mind."

"You know, I think you actually can. That was amazing."

" 'Tis nothing." And I took her inside for snails and lemon sole.

Later we sat on the grass in Central Park, and I was aglow with that same happiness I felt when I took her from the office and we ravished each other with flirtatious attention, not to mention red wine and Irish Coffee, and then drove to my place in her car.

"Can you tell me what I'm thinking now?" she asked after we walked for a time and watched an old man holding a long string that led up to a swatch of color that seemed stitched into the sky.

"You're thinking that we should go back to your place and make love."

"Yes, well, perhaps I should have thought something less obvious."

In the bed that had now become ours, she dizzied me again, talking and touching, and it was so lovely that I almost ruined things by thinking for a moment that I didn't want this day to end.

I left at ten to five after she promised to find some way to see me tomorrow night. If nothing else it was at least comforting to know she wanted to meet me again. Meanwhile, the rest of the evening, hollow and ominous, was waiting in the street to get at me. I didn't want to leave but Philippa was eager to be alone and rush about erasing all signs of my existence. I didn't want to leave because I had nowhere to go until morning, at which time events would almost surely send me rushing to wake her up again. I didn't want to leave and yet I walked calmly down the front steps and stood for a moment watching the blood spreading over the sky. I didn't want to go home either, except it would have been harder still to wander again through more pointless night life, stuffing myself with food and drink. I descended into the subway, changed at Fifty-ninth Street, changed again at Seventh Avenue, and found myself squeezed into the same train, noticing the same faces, taking the same ride that we had all taken at this same hour, before, on this same day. I closed my eyes. A Goddamned rush-hour reunion, it was. Get out at the next stop, you idiot. Take the next train or at least another car. Hold on, lad. Don't be a coward. Panic, once begun, might never end. Stand firm. So I did. With my eyes closed. And I damn near missed my stop.

Climbing up to the street I recognized a pretty teenager, who would always be cantering down these subway steps at that precise moment tapping the hand rail, her hair bouncing, her brown eyes not seeing me, now or ever. On nearby grass a small tot and his dad were playing a dementedly simple game with a large yellow ball. Had I seen them before? Couldn't remember. I approached my dreaded building and eyed the debris from the morning collision. Not knowing what I hoped to see, I looked up as I always did at my fifth-floor living-room window. A nip of dazzling sunlight inflamed a corner pane. Behind the other squares of glass I could see magnified skin tissue. It was a cloudy membrane of books. This, too, oddly enough, seemed somehow different. I rushed to the mailbox. What hopes I had were quickly dashed.

> Ever have one of those
> Wonderful days
> That's almost too good
> To be true?

I tore the card to pieces, threw them back into the slot, and locked it. Upstairs I almost put on the radio again before I remembered Tartini's tricks and Oistrakh's magic and went, instead, to my record collection. I tried a new combination: Chivas Regal and "The Eroica." The blessed bottle was always full and so, for that matter, was Beethoven's Third. What I needed was spiritual strength shouted at me in unsubtle cannonades of sublimity and triumph. I drank until I heard the cosmos breathing. And I ate a stack of chocolate-covered graham crackers. Soon I felt better. No TV for me. And fuck books. No more fragile intellectual endeavors that tear apart in your hands when you need them most. I slumped in a chair, shoes off, surrounded by volumes I would never read again, while Beethoven kept giving me stunning encouragement and Chivas added a most regal surface humm. There were chocolate-covered smudges on my glass. My thoughts were smudged as well. Some mess, I, or someone, was making of things.

And, oh, how I needed her. So lovely she was. Those breasts! Here, too, were unsubtle cannonades of sublimity and triumph. To you, sweet lady, and to yet another parting of those long, willowy legs.

The phone rang right on schedule. I had finished all of the graham crackers and had worked my way through several other of the odd numbers all the way to the "Choral Symphony" when, as always, Milly broke into my life. I had consumed much of the whiskey, too, though not enough, evidently, for I still remembered that tomorrow I would have no hangover. "Let the damn thing ring," I proclaimed.

Then compassion broke through and flowed everywhere. I was aghast at the pain I knew she was feeling, as if I had just learned of it. Why hadn't I gone to her this evening, since I had nowhere else to go? And if she was down in her swamp then lift her up, joke with her, lie to her, say anything at all to her—what does it matter, since I was alone and she was in pain?

The ringing continued. Guided by that smaller, sober patch of me, the larger, roaring rest of me, helped by the majestic "Hymn to Joy," made it to the ringing phone and spoke a happy hello to one and all.

"This Mister . . ." A sagging pause. "Mister Robinson Blake?" It was a gruff male voice.

"Spleaking."

"Are you acquainted with a Miss Madeleine Hawkmann?"

"Umer ployer. Her ump-loyer."

"I am trying to ascertain the whereabouts of her mother, a Mrs. E. Hawkmann."

"Oh, whafor?"

"To inform the lady that her daughter has committed suicide. . . . Can you help me? . . . Hello? . . . Can you help me?"

8

The night air sent things spinning and it was difficult to walk, but a fixed stare kept me from being pulled into the vortex. I took a cab thinking that in this case Milly would approve. It was a long way just to sit still and feel sick, wanting to hurry and afraid to arrive. Closing my eyes seemed to activate the solar system. When I opened them again I saw on the street battalions of people her death would never touch. I loathed them for their immunity and closed my eyes again to swing out beyond Saturn to where the stars became windows of truth but were still too far away to see through.

At her downstairs door I am buzzed-in just as if nothing has happened and she is busy, as always, making that last-minute effort to finish dressing as I climb the stairs. In the doorway is the man who phoned me. Police Officer Dunne. He looks like a boy in a stolen uniform and seems to be assessing the exact extent of my sorrow. On the bed is the body covered with an unwrinkled sheet in which the symmetric folds from the Chinese laundry are still visible. A doctor, I am told, had come and gone. The young woman, he said, had killed herself with pills. An empty bottle of Nembutal was found. She was discovered in her bathtub, the over-flowing water had leaked into the apartment below, which was how they had known something was wrong. I couldn't help feeling that Milly had gotten confused. People use a tub when cutting their wrists, a bed when taking pills. She probably got it all mixed up. Very like her to do that.

"Left a note for you," the policeman said. He handed me a pale-blue envelope with "To R. Blake" on it neatly in pencil. It had already been opened. The note inside on matching pale-blue paper, and also in pencil, is in her usual scribble. He studies me as I read it, watching for I-don't-know-what.

Rob:

You don't love me. I've known that for weeks. I gambled and lost. That's me in spades. I've never won a bet in my whole life. Not ever. I just don't see why I'm alive. Life is shit. Mine sure is. Your love for me was a dirty trick played on both of us. Yet it happened and for a little while it was a wonderful thing. Now, suddenly, you don't care anymore. But I still care. I can't stop. I tried. No go. I don't blame you because it's not really your fault. It's my mother's fault. Yet even she wanted only the best for me. The bitch. Well I just can't stand this being miserable every single fucking day. All my life I wanted just to love someone and when I finally did what a misery it made of things. Now I want out. OK? For a while though it was pretty good, wasn't it? For a little while anyway. Well, that's that. Take care of yourself. I loved you. Sorry.

Faretheewell,
Milly

P.S. If you have any questions you just see my darling mother, OK?

And she lay so still beneath that sheet. Hard to see. Just a blur of white. I didn't go near her. Didn't know where to go. The depths of her love staggered me. But she'll be alive again in the morning, God damn it. Let us hope. Yes she must. It has to be. And then will I bawl her out. Oh, will I ever. What a cheap shot. Wait till I get hold of her. Just wait.

The cop was staring at my tears. Heartless bastards, even the young ones. Well, who cares? In the morning she'll be alive. She must. I glance at my watch. Nine-twenty. Can't be. The second hand has stopped. All ticking ceased. "What time is it?" I ask. He tells me. Is it that late? Four minutes to twelve. I go to the phone and dial. An almost human voice gives me the exact time. Two minutes and twelve seconds to midnight. I set my watch. The second hand reads a few seconds more. No matter. The very nearness of her salvation frightens me. What if, at midnight, nothing happens? What if life goes on again just as it should? And I have found out too late? Good works, indeed. This was what I should have prevented, and I didn't even know of it till now. I have trouble breathing. My watch says one minute and forty-five seconds to midnight. The officer takes Milly's note gently from my hand. Does he need it for evidence? I don't even bother to ask. I can think of only one thing. If we don't jump back to morning again it will be all over and dear Milly will stay dead. It really will be too late. Fear is dissecting me. "You OK?" the officer asks. "OK," I tell him but with pains in my chest. One minute and nineteen seconds to go. Oh, God, let this day be repeated like those others. Let it not be too late. The body under the sheet lies so very still. The young man glances around the room. "She just move in?" he asks. I shake my head. "Looks like she just moved in." I shake my head again and go to the window. Novels are stacked on the sill. I recognize not a one. Fifty-three seconds to midnight. "You sure you're OK?" he asks. I shake my head. "Perhaps you should sit down." Good guy after all. New young cops. Better breed than the rest. I sit down. A stuffed carton supports me. Forty-one seconds on my watch. "You expecting someone?" I shake my head. Sweat is on my face. I feel unwell. Rub my chest with my hand. The cop looks at the bedsheet. Shakes his head. "Young girl like that." I nod. Twenty-two seconds. Please let it be morning again. Seventeen seconds to go. "What was she like?" he asks. "Mixed." I take a deep breath. "Up." I realize I'm sober. Then why do I feel so odd? Ten seconds. There's laughter in the street. Men and women. A car horn. Eight seconds. It occurs to me what this feeling is. I'm going to throw up. It comes as a vulgar revelation. Bile seeps into my mouth. Must go to the john. I stand up. Two seconds left. Now. Please let it be morning. Now. Right now. It's midnight on my watch. *Now!* Then it's two seconds after. Then four. Then seven. No good. Lost. It's all continuing. Going to throw up. "Going to throw up." I run for the bathroom door. The cop mumbles something. I bang the door open. Nearly fall into the tub. The voice in the other room continues to mumble. Something about my being a lazy bastard and then there I am, on my back, twisting my way out of a turbulence of sleep.

My pajama top was soaked right through. My head throbbed and my hands trembled. I stood before my Vermeer to absorb quickly some of that cathedral calm. This time something was wrong, however. It was difficult to give myself over to the great Dutchman's therapy. Then I saw why. Of course. The sunlight from my window bathed the painting, the entire wall, in fact, so that I squinted in the glare as I had into the oncoming headlights on that drive through the rain to Vermont. At that moment, the belated and cataclysmic thought of Milly broke through the general night fog and discombobulation of the morning. I scrambled to the phone, dialed and reached a rudely awakened, fully displeased Bronx grouch to whom I stuttered apologies and hung up to dial again, carefully, only to have my finger slip which forced me, after a high-pitched expletive, to go at it yet again with moronic deliberation. The terrible thought that she just might happen not to be alive almost choked me. The ringing went on and on. Was she there hearing nothing beneath that white clean sheet? Oh, dear. Oh, no. And the ringing, on and on. Abruptly, hurriedly, that sweet, grating, unfeminine voice.

" 'Lo."

"You're there."

"Where should I be?"

"Stay where you are. I'm picking you up."

"You are?"

"I'll pass your house. Stay put. Will pick you up soon."

"You sound like a telegram."

"I'm serious."

"What's the gimmick?"

"No gimmick. I'm coming over to your place."

"Yeah?"

"I *am. Yeah!*"

"Son of a gun."

"How do you feel? You feel OK?"

"Fine, how do you feel?"

"Fine. I'll be right over."

"I'll see it when I believe it."

"Bye bye." I hung up.

Almost at once that shattered feeling fell away. I showered, humming. Got dressed, whistling. Found all my chocolate-covered graham crackers intact and ate a few with sour milk and still felt good. Point being, as Milly would say, that I could see light at the end of the tunnel. For the first time—

light, actual light. And I began to understand. It was, of all people, this girl, this flat, sweet, masculine Milly around whom, for some reason, believe it or not, everything turned. It was she I had to save to save myself. This *had* to be the answer. I didn't concern myself with such things as why. I didn't give a thought about the future. I just wanted there to be one. With a deep and special longing I ached for Philippa, for her warm swarthiness, her recoil-less laugh, her teasing, giving, stunning self, thought of all the easy things we could do today together, nodded, and hurried off to save Milly.

"You're a girl who loves long walks in the woods," I said to Her Majesty, breaking the silence as we were lowered through the building to the ground. What on earth was it that made me keep trying?

She seemed mildly surprised. "Yes, I am."

"You don't like tennis. You have a marvelous temper. You're wisely discriminating when it comes to people."

The red-head turned and stared at me, her haughty, freckled face vacuous in surprise. "How do *you* know?"

"I'm not sure. But from certain people, exceptionally good or very bright ones, I get—I don't know how to put it—messages. Emanations. Waves."

She said nothing.

"You just moved into this building. You're not going to an office. You'll come back here about four. I feel it."

After debating with herself for a moment, "I work at modeling."

"Ah, that would explain it."

The door parted. She studied me as she edged slowly out.

"Good-day," I said and marched ahead of her in a kind of triumph. I was more certain than ever that today, or at so least this variation of the original, would be a very good one indeed.

Until I reached her door, that is and pressed the bell and

stood examining the same identically beautiful sky I had glanced at, off and on now, for six whole days, and then thought, Christ, she isn't buzzing me in! I rammed the button with my thumb and held my breath. Had I let her slip away? Where to? Into her grave yet again? That couldn't be, could it? Well what in hell was going wrong here? It was the morning, only. She was not supposed to kill herself until—

The Buzzer! At last! Up those musty stairs I dashed, two at a time, preparing to give a solid rap on her door which, when I got there, was standing open. Empty. Her storeroom of boxed and rolled-up items was also empty. There was a trail of water coming from under the bathroom door. Quickly I grabbed the knob and pulled. Plastic ensembles of dancing bears and waddling ducks confronted me.

"Be out in a sec," she said, hiccupped, and disappeared to reappear at once. "Sorry I'm not ready. Had (hic) to clean the pad. For you only I do it. Point (hic) point being you don't come over much no more, Boss-man. So it was a real mess. Anyway, pull up a box and sit down. I'll be right out. That is if I don't hiccup myself to (hic) death."

The curtain of bears and ducks closed and I went into the living room to try to adjust to this place where the dead live and banter with guests and the sunlight of the morning-before pours in on the tragic scene of the night-to-come. The bed had been made and was waiting like an open palm. On the shelf was a stack of postcards and an open box of smallish blue envelopes with matching blue paper.

Milly appeared in one of her floor-length skirts. The frizzy hair, the loud, "Hi!" and the touch of dandruff on the shoulder; she was all there, alive, clumsily herself, and smiling— yes, even smiling. And my heart raced at this dizzying spectacle, this second coming of miraculous, mundane Milly.

"Do we go to the office or what?" she asked.

"We play hookey. We spend the whole day together, that's what we do."

"Schmuck, I'll get fired."

"I'm your boss. You will not get fired."

"So *you'll* get fired. That's better? *Then* I'll get fired."

"I'll phone-in sick. I'll say I told you to take the day off. Easy."

Milly threw her beads away and stood looking at me as they swung back and hit her hip. "What's going on?" she asked, cautiously, her voice and spirit sinking.

She had me there. All I knew, all I cared to really think about, was that I must keep her away from pills and misery until tomorrow, keep her away, I hoped, forever, but most important until tomorrow because tomorrow was number one, not me or love or even life, just tomorrow, tomorrow was all. So I kissed her. It was as good an answer as I could summon up at the moment. There was no jolt of voltage as happened that first time, just a refreshing return to a place more pleasant than I had remembered.

"What's going on?" she repeated, pulling away.

"I just wanted to see you, to hold you again. That's all."

"No shit." Anger hardened in her neck. She moved her head with a slight, convulsive twitch as if trying to shake off fleas. "Why this sudden change all of a sudden?"

"It was gradual."

"Gradual? You shot the hell over here fast enough."

"Yes, well that was this morning."

"What was this morning?"

"That which appeared to be sudden but which actually wasn't. It grew, you see, slowly, steadily."

"What did for God's sake?"

"This deep gradual feeling I had that I wanted to, how shall I say, be with you again."

She sat down on a roped carton marked fragile.

"OK. Question: when you first started futzing around—that time in the office when we came here—you said it was like—"

"A compulsion?"

"Yeah. A whole demented sexual type thing until I thought maybe, you know, I should invest in a chastity belt or join a union or something. I mean I heard about Casanova and them, but you were, wow, the Bronx Zoo in heat."

"What's the question?"

"The being in heat and all, is it going to be like that? This sudden slowness or whatever that brought you here today—I mean is it going to be again like it was?"

I couldn't say yes because it obviously wasn't and, besides, if I said yes she might want immediate proof. So I said no, that now it was different, deeper, more peaceful, and so on. My answer seemed very important to her for she stared at me in silence for a time and then said,

"Swear to God and hope to die?"

"Swear to God and hope to die."

She examined me some more. "That means I win, I win after all."

"Win?"

"Win you." She smiled and got up. I let it go. Had to because her mouth was on mine, her arms threatening to snap my neck. Unable to contain herself, she did two pirouettes, beamed a message of absolute joy, and then, on the instant, afraid of ruining her luck, dropped into hiding again behind her most somber expression.

"You seem happy."

"Son of a gun," she said.

"Milly?"

"Sir?"

"Let's go and have breakfast."

"Ho kay." We went to the door. She stopped. She went to the bed, folded down the covers, patted the pillow, said, "For later, Robbela," and took my arm again. Exit.

We walked down Broadway, ate at La Crêpe, kept the conversation light, took The Circle Line around Manhattan, had burgers for lunch, studied the fixed and vivid animals in the Museum of Natural History, had cocktails on the East Side, supped at The Forum of the Twelve Caesars, and went back to my place because the thought of using her bed chilled me.

I felt weak. It lasted all day. She wanted no one but me and I wanted someone who wasn't there. So all day I talked and laughed, attentive and polite, except most of me wasn't there either. Gradually her love came out of hiding. Soon it got out of hand. Wherever we went, it happened. People turned to look. A dozing museum attendant awoke startled. Children in a playground grew hushed. As a rule of thumb, the happier Milly felt the louder she became. A casual joke provoked a jungle shriek. Even her sotto voce could travel a city block. Shhhh, Milly. And she would answer, "Fuck 'em, I'm in love."

It really didn't matter. She was happy; that's what mattered. That and not letting her out of my sight. No sense taking chances. What an irony it would be if she got run over now by a truck. When she was finally ensconced in my living room, I knew I had the game all but won. In a few hours it would be official.

I brought out the Chivas, put Segovia to work in the background, listened to a number of Milly's endless monologues, and thought, for the most part, of Philippa. At this very moment she was beguiling an attentive gentleman at that dinner party given by her friends, leading him most bewitchingly with her soft, almost tactile voice into a lengthy discussion of the supernatural.

This was pure speculation, of course. More substantial was

the fact that my phone didn't ring as it had all the other times this evening at ten-fifteen. Officer Dunne would have no cause to try to reach me. The bathtub was empty because its occupant was sitting on my couch. She was holding a glass of club soda, having allowed me to pollute it just slightly with scotch, while I took the stuff straight and refilled my glass often.

Her conversation struck me as becoming increasingly surreal. It wasn't the effect of the Chivas, I don't think. The Chivas in me, I mean. It was the thought that this girl who at this time was dead now sat stirring her drink with her finger and giving me a disconcerting wink as if she was in on the joke. Surreal because during these first hours of her reprieve she talked about, of all things, a dress that needed mending and how all the pizza of late had added on three pounds, and not mentioning at all the recent crisis between us or that terrible swamp which had, in the end, drowned her.

The only truly normal part of the whole evening was her obsession with getting me into bed. More than drink or food, going to bed together, for Milly, was the true form and substance of celebration. And when Milly was in the mood she was never at a loss to find things to celebrate. Even such events as the successful balancing of her checkbook or the arrival of the vernal equinox was cause enough, and off she would go unbuttoning her blouse as she went. Can you imagine, then, what there was to celebrate this evening? More than she would ever knew. Her life, my freedom, time itself, and good works in general. But to her mind it was quite simple: we would celebrate the resumption of our celebrations. "Well, Robbela, speak now or forever hold your what's-its." There really wasn't any way I could say no. When I pleaded fatigue her face was stricken with such doubt as to my devotion that I was crushed and immediately gave in.

So we trooped into the celebration chamber where she pro-

ceeded forcibly to undress me. Every article that she was able
to remove and toss into a corner was accompanied with a loud
olé. Then she took me by my what's-its and led me to the un-
made bed and made me. Her almost-scotch-but-mostly-soda
was at her side leaving a surely permanent water stain on my
table beside the tape recorder. Since we were celebrating
something of the first rank, something very special (a "real
magila" as she would say), she paused while riding on top of
me ("flagpole sitting" to use her words) reached out and refreshed herself with her drink. A true crowd-pleaser she was,
riding me like the best of women jockeys, upright in her
saddle, the big race about to begin, throwing kisses to her only
audience, a silent audience since I had already given her a
standing ovation.

She was riding her heart out. On and on. Horse and rider.
Down the stretch. She fills the room with asthmatic gasps. I
feel it coming, belatedly, regretably, and hallelujah, pulling
us inside out, that marvelous, maddening volcanic moment at
which point I find myself becalmed and alone in bed. Then
on my feet, with all my strength, I try to smash a chair against
the insidious machine that goes on and on no matter how hard
I strike, no matter how hard I try to decimate this thing that
speaks in my voice while I weep in voiceless rage, pounding
again and again until the thing finally stops, the chair splin-
ters, and then, out of breath and on my knees, I hit the floor
instead, again and again, for my having reached time's end
and not a new beginning, helpless with fury, flailing the legs of
the chair with all my might until someone pounds up from
below telling me, God damn it, to stop.

9

If I had thought it would change my life in some way I would have killed myself then and there. What was the point? A leap off the Brooklyn Bridge would only land me back in bed. I was never so safe in all my life or so desperate. All hopes I had, Milly had killed—because saving her didn't matter a bit. I had no answers now. I was totally stumped. Overheating with self-pity and feeling like the complete failure that I was, I had myself a private, hopeless cry.

The thing to do was to climb in bed, which I did. The tape recorder, as luck would have it, had held up pretty well. The chair was in pieces, one of its legs still in my hand. I threw the club across the room. Fuck the furniture. Fuck good works. Fuck life. I pulled the covers up to my chin. A bad case of shivering had taken hold. Was this a nervous breakdown or just the onset of a cold? My eyes took in the reproduction on the wall. Calm as a saint, it was. Sacred in its cool quiet.

Amazing how in all this horror that damn Vermeer never lets me down. Of course the sunlight was annoying me again as its shadow-line nipped the upper edge of the frame.

Then it happened. A revelation kicked me like a horse. It all but knocked me out of bed. Hunting for my watch (it was on the dresser with my wallet), I checked the time: seven thirty-five. At this same moment every morning during the last seven days the line of light and shadow thrown by the morning sun through my window fell across a different part of the wall, covering, or not covering, a different part of the Vermeer. It all came back. I remembered.

"But this couldn't be," I said. "If everything was exactly the same, it couldn't be."

I jumped up and peered out of the window. Tar roofs, brick walls, and the sun coming up over Flushing Meadow. Except on each of these identical days it must have risen at a different time. I sat down heavy with the significance of this, a significance the meaning of which I hadn't the foggiest. There was, however, an implication here that frightened me and it simply frightened me too much not to be true. It was that something was wrong with the solar machinery, time had run aground, damage had been done, and I was the freak born of this collision and like it or not here in the wreckage I would remain. Not one bit of this did I understand. It made no difference. The irrevocable nature of fate is in no way lessened by one's lack of understanding.

Not bothering to shave, meeting no one in the hall, well ahead of the accident in the street, so desperate that I must have looked a sight, I cried out how I loved her and wanted her. She took me in at once, for something very terrible had obviously happened.

"Why on earth didn't you come sooner?" she asked, becoming Mother Earth and holding me close as I sat beside her on the couch. She eliminated the coffee and white wine. We went up the stairs together. The room was indeed a mess but now she didn't care. Not only had a great love burst into her pampered life but a great drama as well. A man now wanted her so very much he was actually in tears. This was the stuff that epics were made of. Legends, perhaps. We had beer and sandwiches in bed. We spent the whole day in bed. There was no mention of Murray's possible return for lunch. She was suddenly all courage, passion, and love. I was absolutely transformed by her devotion, healed and made happy again. And this time, in my arms, late in the day, she astonished me. She actually *offered* to leave her husband! It was *her* suggestion! Philippa will save you, she said. We will be inseparable. She throbbed with purpose. For her the future suddenly made sense. For me all joy was smashed.

"Shall we?" she asked. The plan was for her to move in with me tomorrow. "Oh, shall we? Say yes."

"Yes." It tasted like sludge. Here was all I ever wanted. "Yes," I said. "Yes."

"What will it be like, Robbie? Us together. Tell me."

"It will be a series of endless beginnings."

"Will it?"

"It will."

"Beautiful. What could be better than falling in love and starting a passion over and over with the same man, the only man?"

"Yes."

"Oh, don't look sad. Why are you sad?"

"It's nothing, really. I love you."

"Promise me something. Promise me we'll fall in love again and again. Oh, that will be so lovely."

"Yes."

"Promise?"

"I promise."

"And smile."

"Yes."

She had the future all planned and all I wanted was to be with her this evening and of course I couldn't have that either. Murray might get suspicious, she said. And difficult. But tomorrow she would move in with me. She would need most of the day to pack. It was too late for that now. So she would go with him this evening to a dinner party. But tomorrow she would be mine.

"Sure," I said. "Fine."

At five I left her house and purposely didn't look at the blood-spilt spread of sky. I walked ten blocks through what seemed to be an exceptionally vibrant home-going crowd. At Milly's I sat on the front steps and waited, not at all in the mood for what was coming. To uncork a bottle was all I wanted. I couldn't, though. There was always that problem of Milly's last hours. I simply had to intervene. It made no difference that she would walk into the office the next morning. Her misery this evening would be real enough and the memory of how she looked during those last weeks when she knew I didn't want her anymore was now impossible to forget. How could I let her climb those stairs and go through it all again?

Ten minutes passed. I braced myself against her inevitable mood of misery and recrimination. Then, in the very middle of this thought, there she was running down the street in manic excitement. I went stupid with surprise. She saw me and stopped. "Son of a gun. Where you been?" "Playing hookey," I answered. "Came to say hello." But this didn't interest her. I was truly baffled. Where was her overcast sky of despair? That bottomless swamp of sorrow? She smiled and tapped the newspaper under her arm. "Isn't it awful?" she asked, in a keen breathless voice. When I looked suitably puzzled, she bubbled with delight for here was that delicious opportunity to impart news of great impact to someone in total ignorance.

"You don't *know?* You didn't *hear?* Where've you *been?*"

"What, what?"

"Are you ready?"

"*What?*"

Her delight was uncontrollable. "The world. They think maybe it's like gone haywire."

For all her preamble, the shock was stunning. So they finally discovered what I had known all along?

"It's a catastrophe unparalleled in world history," she recited like a child in school. The *New York Post* was held up like an eyetest. TIDAL WAVES STRIKE WEST COAST. FRANCE, THE BRITISH ISLES AND MEXICO ALSO HIT. MILLIONS BELIEVED DROWNED. OCEAN SHIFT IS WORLD WIDE.

I looked at Milly.

"It's terrible," she said.

A slow nod was all I could manage. We went up to her room where she had a Sony, given to her by the Mad (though generous) Mathematician. There was no TV set. Perhaps it, too, was packed away. We turned on the radio. All stations had discontinued their normal programs. We were told that most of Los Angeles was under water. Large areas of Southern California were flooded. San Francisco and Lisbon, standing on hills, had escaped with minor damage. France was particularly hard hit, however, and in some areas, intoned the grim voice of the announcer, the ocean had rolled far inland. There had been no advance warning. The cataclysm had taken all nations by surprise.

I changed stations and caught an hysterical lady from Big Sur telling how she had nearly been swept off a cliff overlooking the Pacific by the retreating water pouring back down into the sea after the first assault of the tidal wave had spent itself. Missing were her husband, her three children, and her two-story, wood-framed house. The news from South America described riots and looting. In Ireland an ocean liner had been deposited in downtown Galway. The River Thames had backed up and flooded large areas of London. All outside contact had been lost with such diverse localities as Acapulco, Lima, Bombay, Wake Island, Bermuda, Reykjavik, Amsterdam, and Cape Twon. From all over the earth there were reports of billions of dollars worth of property destroyed and untold millions of people killed or missing. Fears had been expressed that the end of the world was at hand. Some said God was punishing man for his sins. The Pope had delivered prayers for our salvation. From all governments came a plea for calm. One noted scientist was quoted as saying that the rotation of the earth on its axis had been suddenly altered because of the increased weight of the oceans due to mounting water pollution. The stock market, of course, plunged.

In all this terrible devastation I felt a tentative suspension of sorrow for I had been corrupted by incontestable proofs that life's shattered pieces would always be put back together again. But previously each repeat had been identical right down to the last human murmur and casual flick of ash. Now this. What did it mean? Milly read my mood as one of shock at the radio's Gotterdammerung. But what I was thinking about was the sunlight on my bedroom wall. Of other things, yes. Of how, while making love with Philippa at noon, the sea had struck. Of my eagerness for the morning, even to hearing the sound of my hellish voice. Of how I was grateful to this mysterious catastrophe for yanking Milly out of her swamp and fixing her mind on life again, if only for a little while. But mostly, if the truth were known, I was thinking of the sunlight on my bedroom wall.

We spent the rest of the evening listening to the news and not once was I forced to speak of love. At the coming of midnight with both of us on the floor beside the radio eating pizza delivered from around the corner and drinking a can of beer discovered in the back of her fridge, I felt a bit sentimental and said, "Good-by, Milly." The second hand was climbing toward twelve and I said good-by because I had enjoyed being with her this evening and knew that I cared for her very much and wanted to see her happy. Milly was alarmed. "You leaving?" I quickly assured her I wasn't. Now all her pre-empted fear welled up and to assure herself that my presence in her life was permanent, she leaned over to kiss me, stretched to join my lips with hers, and never did.

The shadow-line passed right through the very center this time. Significant? I hadn't the slightest idea. I ran to switch on the radio. It promised traffic jams in the morning and in the evening, rain. The air, it said, would be unacceptable. The voice droned on about the American ambassador kidnapped in Brazil. With great relief I snapped it off. What in God's name had yesterday meant? I shrugged. Milly rang. I didn't answer. I waited until the crash was heard in the street. When all was clear, eating a chocolate-covered graham cracker, I hurried off to see the one I loved.

My need for her was no less than the last time I appeared at her door except this time I must have lacked that special headlong desperation which had made her want to leave her husband and live the rest of her life with me. This time she remembered to offer coffee and to waste good sweet time getting sufficiently convinced. Later she suggested the white wine and climbed the stairs ahead of me to tidy the room. What she was about to offer was a good deal less than her fervent best and I couldn't help but feel deprived. She lay in my arms like a skilled courtesan and cherished the surface of my needs with roving hands. But not once did she plan for tomorrow. I desperately suggested the idea myself. If I couldn't have the future at least I wanted the best today. "Move *in* with you? Je-*zus*, you are a speedie one. For three years, nothing. Then, in three hours, you want it all." She laughed, clearly displeased. I could almost read her thoughts. Was she being asked to start an affair that would get out of hand? Was I a lover who would commit indiscretions? She turned flippant to create distance between us. "But, sir, there is so much about you I don't know."

"Like what?"

"Well, your middle name, sort of thing."

Since she would allow nothing but gaiety now, I gave in to put her at ease.

"*This* is my middle name." I placed it in her hand.

"It's a short name. I suppose it'll grow on me."

"Very likely. It has an Anglo-Saxon root."

"Yes, I can feel it when I pull. Is it hard to pronounce?"

"Not if you mouth it as many of your players do."

"Ha! Well, I'm glad to meet the little fellow." And she gave her new acquaintance a hearty handshake.

"He says, likewise, I'm sure."

"Friendly sort, isn't he?"

"That he is. In fact he wants you to move in with him."

"I see you're two of a kind. Well, tell him your bedroom will be a lovely place to visit but I'm sure I wouldn't want to live there."

"He'll be very sad to hear that."

"I'll make it up to him."

"You realize, he and I, well we love you, we really do."

She leaned back on the pillow and stared at me. "Wow, you two really are one fast pair of pricks."

"You think I'm kidding you. Why? Why would I?"

"To get me to dump Murray," she said quickly. "To have that feather in your cap. Then you get second thoughts about me moving in and I'm left with egg on my face."

"Never."

"Often. Believe me. Anyway it's all too desperate, as if you're trying to convince yourself as well."

"I see. You think I'm playing games."

"Are you?"

"Absolutely not."

She locked us into a long hard hazel stare. She sat up.

"Know what?"

"Tell me."

"I'm hungry. Shall we go to lunch?"

Snapping my fingers. "Sure. Why not."

Trying to infuse some passion into today's casual escapade, I foolishly asked her to pick some romantic place I might take her to and quick as you please she named a restaurant above The Bronx, nearly an hour's ride away. She drove and I sat beside her trying to make the most of an annoying abduction. It was called Friday's. There was a large parking field and a narrow stairway up the side of a hill to an outdoor patio with tables and chairs that overlooked the Hudson. It gave us a splendid view of tiny sails and streaks of sun and tall cliffs, all touched by a gentle wind that moved the miniscule boats and Philippa's hair and even stirred a bit of hope in me again.

It was lovely. And three hours later things were even lovelier because then we were back in bed again. It wasn't quite the same as when she was willing to abandon all but it was good enough and I could live with it. At least the oceans stayed put and the millions who drowned now continued their frail dry lives. Then, while sitting on Milly's front steps, it went all wrong. Half the evening was spent trying to pull her out of the swamp because she just couldn't believe that I had returned to her for good. She was certain I was just passing through. When I finally convinced the girl and got her, thank God, to smile, she clung and chattered and insisted on sex, which I kept putting off until this, too, nearly dumped her back into the swamp. It was awful. My heart wasn't in any of it. Keeping her alive was one thing. Making love to anyone but Philippa was something else again. Nor would she go out to a movie or a restaurant. Just wanted to sit in her room at the edge of her swamp and eat pizza and drive me mad.

After three more days of this I got so desperate I tried to phone Mrs. Hawkmann hoping perhaps to convince the old hag to sit in for me. Your daughter's depressed. I can't take it. Go and help her, damn it. It was all academic. I phoned her cottage in Vermont: no answer. When I asked Milly where in town her mother might be, she said she didn't know and what's more she didn't give a fuck.

Well, at least the days were mine, as was sweet Philippa. Although it got a bit tiresome, all that bitter coffee and ice cold wine, I soon learned to avoid the important pitfalls and to accept what was there to be had: and a fine swarthy thing she was too. I loved her. And looking on the bright side I tried to tell myself that after all I wouldn't have to worry about the future ever again.

It was then, as I was gradually beginning to adjust, frightening as it was, gradually coming to terms with something that I knew I could not ever understand or alter, it was then—and I almost missed it—that it happened. Philippa and I were in a Cuban restaurant on Columbus Avenue. The idea, which I was already getting tired of, was for us to be out should Murray return home for lunch. I knew he wouldn't. Philippa thought he might. So off we went, today at noon, again and again. I selected a different restaurant each time. It was the least I could do—for my sake, that is. On this particular occasion (perhaps it was the Chablis) she was more teasing than usual. Would I shoot Murray if she asked me to? Would I promise to write her every day from prison? Would our love survive this mortal life and continue on into the next? I answered yes to each question and, kissing her hand, felt her ankle scraping mine.

"So you'll never leave me?"

"Nope. Never."

"You'll be true even after reincarnation?"

"Easy."

"But how will I know you?"

"I'll wear a red carnation."

"And I'll rub your ankle like this."

"It's settled then."

"I can hardly wait."

"Let's eat first."

"*Men.*"

A shout in the street made me turn and glance through the plate-glass window beside our table. Walking by, idly scanning the customers—a party of four, me, some people behind me—not really noticing anyone, was the hulking, formidable, forward-striding Mrs. Hawkmann.

"Back in a jiffy," and out I ran. Or tried to, for the nearest door was locked, which meant I had to trot into the back where the bar was and use the exit there which opened onto a side street down which I ran to turn the corner at Columbus before I could even start in the right direction. Philippa, sitting opposite my empty chair, was glancing, with a touch of consternation, not at me dashing by, but up at the waiter, who had just arrived with our food. I kept running and for a terrible moment couldn't find that bizarre and striding personage, who, I knew, must be here somewhere. The street was filled with decoys, each a feasible Mrs. Hawkmann who turned out to be, on second glance, a construction worker entering a Deli, a football player in full uniform, two mailmen walking side by side. On the corner of Columbus and Seventy-second Street, masked by a lumbering truck, revealed, then covered up again by a moving bus—in fact running to catch it—was the large lady I so desperately sought. Sprinting, I defied traffic, car horns, and a shouted comment that began, "You fuckin' imbecile, I'd—" But was swallowed in the snarling rage of a sports car. "Hold it," I cried, and whistling in a fulsome soft blast of mostly moisture I reached and boarded (doors closing behind me) the immediately jostling, quivering, semi-crowded east-bound crosstown bus.

A sign read EXACT CHANGE, which, of course, I didn't have. There was some heated debate between myself and the driver as to whether or not I should get off (he even jammed on the brakes to facilitate my departure) while I made a plea to the enclosed masses for someone to come forward with small change. A not particularly kindly little old lady, but one who was eager to get the bus going again, handed me change for a dollar. I paid and pushed past the barrier searching for that one and only face. It was at the back, looking about as inconspicuous as a certain fully grown French general in a high-school graduation picture. I stood beside her. The passing scene, beyond the window, held the lady's interest. I placed my hand on the small landing field of her shoulder. She glanced up, then clutched my wrist, and turned away as if my sudden presence was one of fate's most playful jokes.

"For heaven sake, it's Mr. Blake."

"Good morning, Mrs. Hawkmann."

Hers were tired, bloodshot eyes. Was it a wild night life or too much TV?"

"You look tired," she said, as though mis-reading my thoughts.

"A bit."

"Why aren't you at work dictating letters to my Milly?"

"Lunchtime."

"Way up here? You're almost in The Bronx. Lunchtime, he says. You should eat around the corner like everybody else. What do you do for dinner? Go to Texas?"

"Mrs. Hawkmann, I want you to get off the bus with me. I have something important to tell you."

"Get off? There's a bomb on board?"

"Come on, now."

"Are we at Bloomingdales? No. So why get off?"

"It's about Milly. I must talk in private. Come on."

She gave in. We got off at Fifth Avenue and I took her into the park and sat her down on a secluded bench. I remained standing. She looked up at me and didn't say a word. That absurd hat and gray face. I felt sorry for her.

"Mrs. Hawkmann, your daughter is in a bad way. Very depressed. Suicidal, almost. I've been watching over her for some time now. For many nights. I want you to stand in for me just this one night. OK? I'm tired. I need a break. I want you to go to her place at six and just stay with her. I'll relieve you at midnight. OK? I'll show up and take over. We have to share this thing. I'm afraid for her safety. Are you listening, Mrs. Hawkmann?"

"Suicide?" She stared into a distant, leafless clutch of trees. Then looking at me, "What an awful thing to say. And whose fault is it if she's depressed? It's your fault, that's whose fault it is. Besides," she scratched at something encrusted on the lap of her coat, "besides, Milly won't speak to me. We had a squabble. So you go. It's important that *you* see her. So go." She stared off into the trees again.

I touched her arm. "Listen to me. You're going to do this thing. You're going to do this for *your* daughter. If you want me to take an interest in *your* daughter, God damn it, then *you* take some interest in her too. I want you to do this, understand?"

She stared at me with her sad, closely placed, bloodshot eyes, took a deep breath, and said, "That's funny. You don't know how funny. Take an interest in your daughter, he says. You read that? Where, in a fortune cookie?"

"Well, what's your answer? Yes or no? You don't care, I don't care. It's as simple as that. Yes or no?"

A young woman came by pushing a baby carriage with such care you'd think an open wine bottle was balanced inside.

"Daughters," said Mrs. Hawkmann as though she were identifying a subversive group.

"Yes or no, Mrs. Hawkmann?"

"You're a man of few words." She lifted herself to her feet with a grunt. "And little sense. Talk of economy." She examined my face with distaste. "And I'm not even sure you're a man. My daughter needs you something fierce. And so what do you do? You schluff her off on me. You could maybe transform her whole life. And what's your first thought? Time off. Poor boobie's tired. Tired. You don't know from tired."

"Yes. Or. No?"

"You speak good. Clear enunciation. Schmuck. OK, Mr. Schmuck. OK."

"You'll do it?"

With a sour nod, "Graciously."

"Thanks. I appreciate this."

"Don't mention it. My pleasure."

We strolled to Madison Avenue. Her plan was this: first she must buy Milly a gift as a peace offering. A chocolate-covered nut affair was best, she said. Then I would tag along with her

ONE FINE DAY

to Bloomingdales, where she would do her shopping, which she saw no reason to forego. Finally we would away to Milly's place (Mrs. Hawkmann had an extra key) to ensconce ourselves with a bottle of booze (which I was elected to buy) and together we would wait. My role was to provide moral support, said Mrs. H. When we heard Milly coming, I would quickly duck upstairs to the landing above until Milly had safely entered her apartment. Then, when all was clear, I would skulk down into the street and make a break for it. Did I agree? I agreed.

After a bit of hunting we spied a fancy candy shop, inside of which we saw numerous shelves of lovely little chocolate-covered bait.

"I'll be in there choosing. See that cab parked down the block? Get 'im to pull up in front here to save time."

"And get a few of those little evil things just for us," I requested.

"Will the whiskey be Jack Daniels?"

"It will, it will."

"OK. Go already." And she marched powerfully into the shop. I strolled away signaling for the cab. It drove up to me and stopped. I told the driver where to wait and he moved on and halted in front of the shop. I caught up with him, nodded, and went inside to make sure Milly's mother was buying enough of those tasty tidbits and not just a skimpy two or three. The shop, of course, was empty.

"A large lady?" I all but yelled at a smiling black man behind the counter. He pointed to a door at the far end that said Westminster Hotel. I dashed through it into a lobby and was confronted by a reception desk, a jewelry display, an Avis sign, and several old leather chairs that appeared encrusted with bitter chocolate. A few dazed lobby people were sitting about as if waiting for the resurrection. And, of course, there was a revolving door that led out into the city. I whooshed through, pushing with both hands. A loud street of many moving decoys greeted me again but this time gone for good was the deft and deceitful Mrs. Hawkmann.

I should have known she'd be trouble from the moment I first saw that look of destiny in drag. Who would have thought a mother could be so heartless? She even re-ignited in me the idea of temporary assassination. Think of the joy of watching those two small bloodshot eyes widen at the sight of the gun and blink at the sound of the blast. I spent a good while thinking of that.

Then, in a rotten temper, I took the taxi that was waiting for me in front of the candy shop and went straight to the restaurant—but Philippa was gone, the table all clean and ready for the next customer. She had just left, they told me. She had waited without eating for half an hour, the food slowly growing cold, then she had paid and walked out. I went back to her house, but she wasn't there either. She was completely lost to me for the day. Twenty-four hours without seeing or touching her. It was as if somewhere close by a refrigerator door had been opened.

It's easy for me to tell when I've reached the highest pitch of panic; all I can think of is going to the movies. My first try was a porno film on Eighth Avenue which was about as erotic as a pile-up on the thirty-yard line. I then barged into a Julie Andrews epic in which everyone burst into joyous song like over-ripe musical fruit. That afternoon fatuous happiness and repeated pornography each proved equally deflating.

Next, Chez Milly—where again, minus the uplift of a worldwide catastrophe, she remained as before, and my promises to reactivate our love affair were met by deep skepticism plus an urge for pizza. Afterward, invigorated by a full stomach, she found she could believe again, could trust in the ultimate reunion of lovers split assunder. T'was a happy ending for one if not all. Her face went beatific as though she felt a song coming on. Of course, it was only sex. Her gloom lifted, mine descended. Rescue at midnight was hours away. As always at such reunions she made love like a giddy rapist. And I, damn it, stood fast under the assault and would not, could not, come. I was trapped in my own porno film. That's how sad, wasted, and unending it all was. We were part of a well-oiled machine whose function was not immediately apparent. "Hey, Robbela, you're doin' great, kid." She was a talking piston. "You're lasting like forever." And in mid-flight she made a circle with thumb and forefinger and with her mouth wide open, closed one eye.

And, yes, each morning I woke up as frustrated as ever. Often in life I wished that the night before hadn't happened. Well, it hadn't and that was no better either. I just went back to the same hungers as before without even the benefits, however brief, of release or disgust. And now I had yet another hunger: today at high noon, and nothing could stop me, I would nail the Hawk to the wall.

ONE FINE DAY

Feeling the need as always to push beyond the narrow limits of today, I made a point of catching Her Majesty in the hall and beguiled her with my occult penetration into her life and psyche, depicting her walks in the woods, her occupation, tastes and temper, predicting even the hour of her return, all this and more, which had come to me, I said, in a sudden omniscience. She stood and listened, astonished. Then I swung for the fence. Even greater knowledge was coming to me, I told her, something more, something important that she should know about concerning her future and her ultimate happiness. She watched as if I had demonstrated some incredible trick, as if I had pulled from my sleeve the very pair of panties she had thought she was wearing. If this presentiment did come to me today, as I felt sure it would, had I her permission to knock on her door this very evening to tell her all about it?

The elevator stopped. The lobby appeared. Neither of us moved. "Well," she replied, emerging from her catatonic trance only to fall silent again. The truth was, she didn't know how to react. She nodded and shrugged. "All right," was her slightly rigid reply. "I guess so."

"Fine." Flashing a smile, I marched away.

Now came the hard part. Nailing the Hawk and getting her to open her heart enough to enter Milly's evening of doom. There had to be a plea or threat that would work, plus a way to arrange it, each morning, by phone. Things might even be bearable then. In bed with Philippa by day, then home at night to knock upon Her Majesty's door. Yes, with luck, I might just keep from going mad yet. Yes, just possibly. At this the two cars crashed and I jumped a foot having forgotten all about them, so deep was I in thoughts of escape.

The smartest thing to do would be to go back to the Cuban restaurant, stand in a nearby doorway, and wait. But that meant spending another day without Philippa, which I would

not, could not, do. She was the raft I swam to each morning as
fast as I could. This time, while lounging in her bed, I per-
suaded her to fetch me her photo album, which I recalled
Murray once making fun of in the office. It was a mixed bag, I
had to admit, with some snapshots fastened, some loose and
falling out, and some not even of people at all but of a smooth-
haired fox terrier named Rag. An astonishingly thin high-
school Philippa leaned against a clapboard wall with a be-
witching self-confidence, as if to suggest that if a girl's face was
lovely enough then she didn't really need a body. A more rec-
ognizable Philippa in a baggy Smith-College sweater sat absorbed with three friends at a Ouija board. A few pages later I
was staring sadly at my own dear love during her honeymoon
in Acapulco as she proudly held up a dead fish while Murray
held up two fingers behind her head. There was a group shot
taken at a hectic office party where she appeared in a low-cut
dress and I, third from the left, in a shapeless green sports
jacket. Straining to see and be seen, mouth partly open, half-
buried in a high-neck dress, her face in the dusk of the back
row, stood Milly. In case I had missed this richly comic expression, Philippa pointed it out to me and then went into her
feeling-sorry-for-Milly routine, suggesting I find a few bache-
lors in whom my secretary might become interested. I knew of
none, which was true. What kind of man does she go for,
then? I had no idea, I said. Philippa thought it a great pity that
we couldn't help out. I changed the subject by lifting my glass
so that her right nipple became immersed, after which I breast
fed on chilled Chablis.

"Here's to new ways of drinking," she teased me afterward
in the Cuban restaurant, holding up her glass of champagne.

"Here's to you and chilled white wine," I said.

"Could you possibly make that room temperature red?"

She leaned forward to spear me with her warm, hazel eyes.
"And there's another favor I want you to do for me."

I also leaned forward. "Shoot Murray, right?"

"Well, *there's* a thought. No, I want you to stop looking out the window and pay more attention to me."

"Sorry," I said. But I was unable to stop.

"There you go again."

"Someone is going to walk by. Someone I'm acquainted with."

"How do you know?"

"Just a feeling," I said, staring into the street.

"Oh, who is it?" She was intrigued.

"Any moment now a large woman with a face like Charles de Gaulle. . . . Right . . . about . . . *Now.*"

We waited. And waited.

"Tsh, tsh," she said. "Win some, lose some."

I jumped up from my table. The construction worker, who had been swinging his pick in the street, halted for lunch and strolled into a nearby delicatessen. Then, across the street, a football player in full regalia, marched in cleats toward Central Park and out of sight. I moved to the window and saw two mailmen chatting as they carried their empty satchels.

"What's the matter?" Philippa asked.

I looked up and down the street and up and down again.

"Darling?"

Knocking over a chair, I dashed to the bar, avoided a waiter who was carrying out food, made a left turn, and plunged into the street running hard. I didn't stop until I reached the corner of Seventy-second. I looked in all directions. The truck passed. The bus came. The sports car growled. But no Mrs. Hawkmann. How could this be? I sprinted through the traffic and just made it to the door. This time I had the exact change ready. When I pushed through the turnstile I found Mrs. Hawkmann's seat occupied by a pimply lad in glasses puzzling over a pocket chess set. The bus was moving. I took a seat. I tried to think. A furious joy seized me, and I jumped up to gouge the bell. Set free, I jumped off and sprinted to the nearest phone. I listened to the ringing. It went on too long. I hit the glass wall with my palm. "Be in, damn you." More ringing. *Be in.* Be at your desk eating a sandwich, please. *Please.*

"Social Responses, Mr. Blake's office."

Dear loyal, hard-working, good sweet girl.

"Milly, it's me, Rob."

"You're late," she said from somewhere deep inside her swamp.

"Milly, how do I get in touch with your mother? Where does she stay when she's in the city?"

"Question. Why do you want to know?"

"I haven't got time to explain. Just tell me, where is she?"

"Dough no."

"What do you mean you don't know?"

"She stays here, she stays there. I couldn't care less. Why do you ask?"

"I'll explain later, Milly. Bye."

A cab took me none too swiftly to Grand Central Station, for the streets were swarming with a lunchtime crowd. The next train to Vermont was not for another twenty minutes, so I squeezed my way toward a food counter and, standing up, ate a sandwich and tried to keep nearby elbows from spilling my brimming orange drink. I thought of my delicious meal growing cold on our table uptown and of Philippa getting desperate. Poor abandoned lady. Yet all I wanted, cared about, was nailing the Hawk to the wall.

Beautiful countryside rolled by the train window as I tried to think of some reason why she hadn't walked past the restaurant window. It should have been as inevitable as Her Majesty going to work in the morning or those two autos loudly colliding. I could think of no reason except that the Hawk was as free as I was. This idea sat inside me like a meal I had eaten too quickly. As free as I was. But why was she hiding? Why?

The air was cool when I stepped from the train. Then the trees near the station were savaged by the wind and for a moment it was winter again. A man seated in a parked taxi lay like a crash victim on the steering wheel. I brought him back to life by slamming the door. After I recited the address he drove without a word through leafless woods and followed a climbing, curving stone wall, past a mailbox with its flag up, a covered bridge, an immense barn, and something small with fur that lay dead in the road. There were glimpses of valley and sheep and the snarling sound of a chain saw.

We stopped at the gate for I had asked him not to take me any farther. He agreed to wait. There was a garbage can with a rock on its lid; a good sign, I thought. It seemed like a very long walk up the narrow dirt driveway to the stone porch. A peek through the living-room window and a bold stare through the glass in the kitchen door gave me a sinking feeling. Everything was locked. I held my jacket against a rear windowpane and struck with a brick that I had up-rooted from the flower bed. It made less noise than I feared. The window rolled up easily, and I climbed into the living room, holding my breath. The pendulum of a grandfather clock marched in loud portentous steps. Mail, pushed through the door, lay on the carpet untouched. The cubbyhole where Milly and I had slept was tidy as a motel room. The door to Mrs. Hawkmann's room was closed. I knocked. Twice. Opened it. Even wider. No one shouted or screamed or jumped at me. The bed hadn't been made and on the table was an empty coffee mug. A dresser drawer hung out with its tossed salad of underthings. On a TV set were two framed pictures. In one, Milly was young enough to be her own daughter. In the other, taken at a portrait studio, she was so pretty that she looked like someone not even related. There was also a book *Hitchhiking Through the Holy Land*. Inside was inscribed, "To Mom from Milly."

There was a plant in a pot on the kitchen table. The soil was dry. Some apple strudel sat in the pantry. Very tasty. But if I stayed there much longer I would be depressed indeed so I left, using the front door. I stopped on the graveled path at the bottom of the steps that led down from the porch and looked at the cottage again. It was a pretty little place with a Spanish-style roof and prim white walls. Where would I go to find her now? And why in hell was she hiding? I took a last look at the windows, hoping perhaps to spy her peering out. Only then did I notice the two smaller ones, at ground level, both boarded up. *The cellar!* I dashed back, climbed in, and made a quick search behind a number of doors each revealing only a closet. One, however, was locked. With a hammer and screw driver, which I found under the sink, I removed the hinges and, with a little judicious pulling and cursing, yanked the damn thing free. A stairway led down into an enclave of night. Rising up to meet me was the dank whiff of a tomb. There was a switch. I snapped it from OFF to ON. Nothing changed. I made another lengthy search and, on the floor of the closet by the front door, found a flashlight.

Why bother? Surely she would not be hiding in that blind, chilly vault. Yet why were those wooden planks blocking windows that were themselves too small for a man to crawl through? So I descended, thrusting ahead of me the long beam of light that jumped through darkness to find the cement floor, a sink, a garden hose, some old rags, two beach chairs, a ladder, a fusebox, and cobwebs. The white eye swung in a long column across the void and found a wall, splashed through a stack of window screens, hit a post, then dove into darkness again to something made of dull silver with knobs, tubes, pipes, and a small door. The furnace! And that was all. Ice skates, empty bottles, junk. A long dangling string appeared near my face. There was a shoe horn hanging from the bottom and a bulb at the top.

I pulled and there was light. Not that it did much good. The basement leaped together like a jigsaw puzzle, but one whose picture made no sense. It was just a basement mad with clutter. Nothing more. My foot touched something. I looked down. I was standing in the middle of a large circular band of black material with words printed on it. ELOHIM was one. TETRAGRAMMATION was another. My shoes had come in contact with a black-hilted knife. Nearby was a glass ball, a chalice, a long and beautiful sword. Four candles stood at different points on the cloth circle. Several other items were simply a mystery to me. But riveting my attention was the large round face of a clock lying flat on the floor. The hour and minute hands were pointing at the number 12 and they and a small straw doll were all bound firmly together with a colorful hand-painted necktie that was similar if not identical to one of my own. The feet of the doll were tied separately by a long set of stringed beads that looked suspiciously like Milly's. Scattered over the face of the clock were the remains of a yellow canary. It had been, I'm almost certain, pulled to pieces by someone's bare hands.

As I stared at all this, not moving a muscle, I shivered with a sudden convulsion as if bathed for a moment in Satan's cold breath. Then I stomped on, broke, and scattered everything. I tore the black cloth to pieces. I shattered the crystal ball against the wall. I waited. Nothing happened.

Next, I went upstairs and made a long-distance phone call. My watch had stopped again, this time at five past one in the afternoon. Portentous steps pulled my head around. It was five-twenty by the Grandfather clock. I prayed for Milly to answer. She did. I said I had something important to tell her and that I would be at her apartment sometime this evening to explain what it was. Would she wait for me? She sounded as if she had taken some pills already. "Who knows?" she mumbled. I became desperate.

"Milly, this is Goddamned important. This night might be for keeps. You must wait at home until I get there. Understand? And don't do anything rash."

"Like what? Elope?"

"Like kill yourself, you idiot."

"Over what? You? Pooh."

"Milly—"

"Why'd you want my mother?"

"So I could strangle the ugly bitch."

"Oh, I see. Care to say why?"

"Tell you when I see you."

"When will that be?"

"At ten tonight, maybe. Or eleven. Depends."

"On what?"

"On when I get there. Now will you wait for me? Will you?"

"Maybe yes, maybe no."

"I am very serious, Milly."

"Oh, that's different. He's serious."

"Will you wait for me? I want a straight answer."

"Sure, kid."

"You will wait, then?"

"No sweat. Upps, here comes Scanlan. Got to run. Bye."

"*Milly!*" She was gone.

Now I started to run. Out the door I went and down to the taxi and then to the station, but even so I had to wait one hour for the next train. I asked several drivers at the hack stand to take me to New York, but no one would. I sat on a bench on the platform and ate a bar of chocolate. Could a man go crazy,

I wondered, just waiting for midnight? Just waiting to see what the new day would bring? Sure he could. I felt it. Just as I could feel, like the sharp Vermont wind, that Milly was suddenly in danger.

I didn't believe in witchcraft. Certainly I would never have believed it capable of doing such things as were done of late, even to bringing back the dead so we could anguish once more over losing them again. I wondered if the dead ever dream of returning, however much we believe that the dead don't dream. Hang on, lad. Don't let the mind wander, it might not come back. And don't blow a fuse trying to answer questions. There was only one at the moment that was at all worthwhile: the question of Milly.

At Grand Central Station I sprinted to a phone booth and dialed. It was ten-thirty. I wanted to assure her I was coming, to tell her to hang on because in twenty minutes I'd be there. Just be a good girl. Just wait. The phone rang twice.

"Yeah?" came a distracted voice.

"Milly, you OK.?"

"This is Police Officer Dunne. Who is calling please?"

It was as though I had kissed a wrong, though willing, mouth.

"My God."

"Who?"

"Has she . . . is she dead?"

"Who is this?"

"Damn it, *tell* me. Is she *dead*?"

Pause. "She is."

"Oh, Jesus."

"Now, who is calling, please?"

After hanging up, I stood in the booth staring at the number 911. I saw myself far away decimating a circle of mysterious objects, destroying in the process a life I had become dedicated to saving. Nausea hurried me into the men's room, where I stood rotting and waiting. Soon I was only waiting; the other had subsided. Wanting only sleep, I decided to hazard the trip home. A thought of Philippa slithered through me and was gone. I caught the train to Forest Hills. Life around me went on with its usual maddening indifference. I was no better. Was I a hero who had saved the world or only a terrible blunderer? I could not keep from seeing her lying beneath that sheet. She was done with gestures, she was fixed in time like stone. Would I ever rid myself, I wondered, of her stillness, her silence?

The elevator took Milly and me to the fifth floor and she floated at my side down the soundless hallway. As I reached for my key a door opened and Her Majesty stepped to the incinerator. She saw me and stopped, holding her bag of garbage as if it were an offering. The door to her apartment bounced a few times on its lock.

"I waited," she said. "Now I'm going to bed."

"Just coming," I replied as I took the garbage from her, got rid of it, and, to escape Milly, hurried into Her Majesty's pad, holding the door for her to follow. True, I didn't want anyone but Philippa. Except now, even more than I needed her, I needed not to be alone.

The television was on. A Pan Am 707 had been lost at sea with all on board believed to be killed. I turned it off. Plants lurked in corners. On the walls were photographs of a red-haired beauty, glamorous under a cloche hat, healthy and bare-headed in the wind, vulnerable with a half smile, regal in respose. The living perpetrator of all these various selves stood in the vestibule stunned by my bold entrance. She wore a blue terry-cloth robe. The almost-orange hair hung loose and lovely. The slippers were furry white animals. With all make-up removed, hers was the pleasant face of a total stranger instead of that very familiar glamor mask.

"I don't know your name," I told her.

"I thought you knew everything. I thought you knew all about me."

"A name is nothing. One can ask for a name."

"Oh, I see," she said, skeptically.

"I have a bottle of Chivas Regal. Shall I get it?"

"Well, I don't know."

"Could use a couple of shots."

"I have some Johnnie Walker, I think. If that'll do?"

"Very nicely, thank you."

I settled into her leather couch, and it seemed so impressed that a man, any man, was here at all that it whistled softly. She brought the drinks and chose, perhaps for safety, or because she seemed so right for it, a chair that looked for all the world like a throne. I lifted my glass and aimed at her over the rim. She did the same. We drank. There was a silence. She was waiting, eager to be astonished, willing to suspend judgment (a considerable task for her, indeed), longing for some magic to enter into her unremarkable world.

"Lovely." I indicated her several stunning disguises on the walls.

"You said you came to tell me something. You said you had a message."

"I have nothing." Tasting her scotch again, I balanced the drink on the arm of the couch. "Not any more. There was a moment—you might *call* it a moment—that seemed destined to last forever. A bit of sabotage is what it was. It's over now. Death has come back. Good and evil have returned. When they were gone, I found love. But at a price. Someone I know killed herself. Someone I should have saved. The truth is something I must explain but which can never be understood. Yes, I have secrets. You and I went through a series of reincarnations together. In the elevator, no less. Oh, it's hopeless. I have nothing to say."

"Then why did you come here?"

"Why did I come here? I think I was actually hoping to sleep with you."

She turned away and back again as if it took an effort to look such hopeless ambition straight in the face.

"For a long time now a terrible trick has been played on me and I have yet to find out why. I have come to believe in miracles. You opening your door just now was a miracle. You came out with the garbage and I thought, This is a miracle. At least it's one I can understand. At least it's one that has done some good. See the tricks the mind plays? The jokes we don't even let ourselves in on."

"You're a strange one."

"No, only one to whom strange things have happened."

"Well, something very special must have happened."

"It *has* been a long day, I'll say that."

"I notice your hand is trembling."

"Christ, yes, look at it. A nervous breakdown is all I need."

"You poor man. You are in bad shape."

She seated herself beside me to replenish my drink. Somehow a radio had been turned on. A graveled voice sang of how the days dwindle down to a precious few. The blue robe had parted to unveil, on her thigh, a scratch the color of her orange hair.

"To your beauty," I said, lifting my glass.

"To your recovery."

"The chances are rather slim of my recovering from your beauty."

"Oh, I think you will."

Now even the slow, soft graveled voice seemed caught in the snare of her presence. *And these few precious years and these few precious years and these few precious years . . .* Her Majesty's eyes poured their warm green ink into the air.

"Someone scratched you, I think."

"Did they?" She pouted as her finger traced the damage.

And these few precious years and these few precious years . . .

"Your Royal Majesty." It was another toast.

She straightened, regal and pleased.

"Tell me, is your skin as smooth as it looks?"

Her palm slides down her thigh a bit and up slightly and down again. Her eyes catch mine. Her lethal ink inflates me with promise. The room has contracted a fever.

"You must never try to seduce me," she says in that familiar haughty voice.

On hearing this I am deep in grief again.

"Because you see," lifting her glass to her lips, "you don't have to try."

She sips her drink, good cheer faintly chiming in her glass. I reach and touch her orange wound in the white sea of her heat. Her fingers pluck at the hairs on the back of my hand. At that moment, somewhere in the city, another hand lifts the singer's broken voice out of the room. Slowly my palm moves along the milk and freckles of her flesh. Her hand shelters mine as my fever casts its lecherous glow on all the walls.

"We don't have to hurry, do we?"

"We have all the time in the world," I tell her. "All the time in the world."

11

"Be out in a sec," she said, hiccupped, and disappeared to reappear at once. "Sorry I'm not ready (hic). Had to—"

"Never mind." And I yanked from behind the bears and ducks her starkly dripping self, threw a bath towel around her shoulders, and pulled her into the storage living room, her sad yellow shower cap still on her head.

"What the (hic) hell are you doing?"

"Milly, sit down." I indicated a carton marked fragile.

"I'm dripping."

"Go right ahead."

"Thank (hic) thanks a whole lot."

"Milly, I went up to your mother's cottage yesterday."

"Alone? Boy, you really are avoiding me."

"I went because you wouldn't tell me where she's staying."

"You never (hic) asked."

"You forget but actually I did."

"What are you talkin'? You never did."

"All right, all right. Then where *is* she staying?"

"I never said I'd tell you. I just said you never as (hic) asked. Shit." She slapped herself twice on the back, her elbow pointing straight up.

"Why won't you tell me, God damn it?"

"'Cause I don't know myself, God damn it."

"You're lying."

"Who says?"

"Milly, do you know what I found in the basement of your mother's cottage?"

"Mice? Look, I'm dripping all over the fuckin' floor."

"I found out that your mother is a witch. That she deals in Black Magic. That's what I found out."

She was drying her shoulder. She stopped. "You've lost all your marbles, you know that?"

"No good, Milly. I was there. Broke into the place. I actually saw it."

With a shrug, "So the old lady's nuts. Always has been. Swear to God and hope to die. Really, nutsville. Astrology, hypnotism, you name it. Years ago she tried sending me messages by ESP. Told me to wait in my room at midnight. I told her, stop trying to save on a phone call."

"Tell me where she is."

"Look, I said I don't know."

"Milly, if you don't tell me, I'm walking out of here. For good."

She put her feet on the box and her chin on her knees. "Walking out?"

"That's right, Milly."

"Well, I mean you haven't been around here a whole lot lately, anyway."

"Well, I'm here now and unless you tell me what's been going on, I'm never coming back, ever."

"It's over anyway, isn't it?"

"It is *not* over. But it will be if you keep lying to me. Now *talk*."

"Talk, he says."

"OK forget it. You know what I'm going to do? I'm going to send you the hell back where you came from. Back to the math department. And don't let me see you in my office ever again. Good *bye!*"

It's easy to bluff when you can change the script the next day or throw out the whole scene and start over. I was out the door and starting down the stairs when she called.

"Boss-man. OK, come back."

In her room again, I pulled up a box and sat down.

"Go ahead," I said.

"Go ahead, he says. He thinks it's easy."

"Milly, start talking."

She did, finally, in her flat voice—half calm, half comatose. It had all to do with love and it had all been done to her before. A spell had been cast, she said. It resulted in a sweet and sour little man, a poor lost soul, going suddenly, one rainy morning, into heat. Milly and her mother had met the guy by accident in B. Altman's and Mrs. Hawkmann took a liking to him. Said he was nice. Milly shrugged. She guessed so. There the matter was dropped. But a few days later Milly gave a yelp in the office stockroom, whirled, and told the little man to keep his fucking hands to himself. It was too late. The Mad Mathematician was crazed with Milly-lust. He persisted. Milly prevailed. The thought that there might be a dark side to this sexual farce never entered her mind. "Just figured he had galloping brain cancer or something." When it happened again and the crazed one was her boss she wondered if brain cancer could be catching. "Then *I* caught it," Milly said. "Wow, pain, yuck."

"It was your mother, then, who—"

"I should have guessed but who could think straight. Point being I was too busy gettin' screwed to think straight. Then one day we went up to the cottage together, remember? And you went for a stroll in the woods and I stayed in with a cold. Well, I'm hunting around for the aspirins, right? Poking into this drawer, that box, here, there, everywhere. Suddenly I find this wax doll with a pin stuck through its tit. S'got eyes, nose, you know, all drawn in with ink. And not only that. It's like very explicit down in the groinal area. Swear to God and hope to die. OK. Are you ready? Written all across the damn thing is my name, *my name!* I absolutely plotzed. I never felt such fear. Then I remembered having dreams of being stuck with pins, remember? Maybe I didn't tell you. Terrible dreams. Now I know why. Well, I was sick. I dashed into the kitchen and showed the doll to my mother and I could see from how her face nearly falls off that she's as guilty as sin. She denies everything, of course. In all the screaming and yelling that follows I decided to tear the fuckin' doll to pieces. I take hold of its head and I'm trying to pull it right off when my mother screams, "Stop! Don't!" But no one has to tell me to stop 'cause suddenly its like somebody wacked me in the neck with an ax. I'm on the floor in agony, and my mother rushes to the side of who? Me? No. To the side of the doll. She fusses with the thing, mumbling some mumbo jumbo, and wamo, the pain is gone."

"Christ."

"To say the least. Well, now she comes clean. Has to, you see, or else I'll tear my head off."

"What did the old bitch say?"

"A whole lot. Loves me, says she. Wants me to be married

and not lonely like she is. So she puts a spell on both of us. First you, then, when I resist you, me. A spell on both of us. How do you like them apples?"

Milly stops, examines a toe, then me, then the toe.

"How did you get her to turn it off?" I finally asked.

"By screaming a lot. I told her it was humiliating. I told her I didn't want you this way. It was like, I don't know, corruption in high places. Besides, it felt like I was living in a steamroom. She said if she turned it off you'd leave me. I didn't agree. I was sure it would continue. It was so lovely." She examined another toe. "I was wrong."

"I'm very fond of you, Milly."

"That's nice. Anyway, the rip off is that it only half worked. I stayed in love. I'm still there."

"Your mother is one Goddamned interfering Jewish mother."

"You sound like an anti-Semite."

"How do you know she isn't lying to you? That she hasn't still got you under her spell?"

"I don't. But if she was going to pull a fast one she wouldn't keep me with a pin in my tit and let you free. Would she?"

"No, I guess not."

"Hey, look at the time. We'll be late for work."

She rose but I pushed her down.

"Where is your mother, Milly?"

"Why do you want to know?"

"Because your mother *is* pulling a fast one. In Vermont right now she has in her basement, in one of those magic circles or whatever you call them, she has a clock and a straw doll; the hands of the clock and the straw doll are tied together with one of *my* expensive silk ties—the red one you always liked, remember?—and there's a string of *your* beads—"

"The brown and black ones?" she called out. "The ones you always hated?"

"Yes, are they missing?"

She stared at me as if noticing lice.

"Milly? Hello?"

"I'll kill her." She nodded in calm, dedicated certainty. "I will kick her ass."

"Where *is* she, Milly?"

"A clock, you say? What does it mean?"

"That's what I want to find out."

"The Westminster Hotel. That's where she is."

"The one with the candy shop?"

"That one. Hey, what's the rush?"

"Phone her," I yelled. "Keep her talking."

"Can't," she yelled after me. "We're not speaking to each other."

While running down the street, I was hit with a sharp whistle and saw Milly's head sticking out of the window with a finger of each hand in her mouth. I waved, kept running, and eventually saw a cab. I was still breathing with effort when the driver reached the park. This time the Hawk would not get away. I swore she wouldn't. The end of the mystery was near. I swore it was.

A man with wind-blown hair, standing on Fifth Avenue beside a shabby briefcase held together by rope, was handing out leaflets from inside a sandwich board that read WORLD COMING TO AN END. If you only knew, I thought, oh, if you only knew.

We stopped at a red light. The feel of Her Majesty's thigh was still in my blood if not in my hand. I remembered my shout of joy when I awoke. Milly would be alive! Alive and torturing me instead of dead and torturing me. I didn't even think of Philippa. There was room for only one obsession at a time and Mrs. Hawkmann came first. I was accosted in the elevator by Her Majesty's deep freeze and haughty silence. I didn't have the strength to use my omniscient deceits and pseudo-miraculous snares, although I had to restrain myself from telling her that last night I had gotten as far as her left thigh and with better timing I'd get further yet so she need not look quite so haughty.

"Westminster," said the driver. We were there.

"Is this cab free?" asked someone on the sidewalk.

I push past and make for the building in a nervous sprint. The lobby is as dusty and dead as I remembered.

"Whuroom Msaukmannin?" I fling at the desk clerk.

"Vot?"

"What room. Is Mrs. Hawkmann. In."

"Ah, ya. Zees eez ze big lady, no?"

"Yes, ah huh, yes."

"Meeszees Awkmanns. Vun moment." And he went down the open book with his bandaged finger. "Ah, ya. Meeszees Awkmanns I yam sawry has left ze 'hotel for goot zees morning at eight o'cluck. She go fast, phew."

"Forwarding address?"

"Vun moment." The frayed finger moved along the page. "Ah, ya. Forwarding address eez not 'ere, no."

Soon I was standing in the street, squinting in the sun, knowing I had lost, feeling it sink in like old age. Hard as I might try, there was no way on earth I could ever get to this hotel from my apartment in time to stop her. Every morning she would check out at eight and safely elude me. The reason 'why she go fast, phew,' was because she wasn't sure just how much time she had to spare. She needn't have worried. Here was one race she would always win should this morning dawn a million times.

Hands dug into pockets, I drifted up the street in shattered bits and pieces. There was that light-headed feverishness again, that racing boil of frustration perpetually unresolved.

Was I losing my grip? Oh, probably. Why the hell not? Lovely trays of chocolate in the candy shop caught my eye and soon I had in my hand a little white bag of goodies which I ate as I walked. Little square brown pacifiers to keep my mind on the problem instead of tumbling away in jagged pieces with the wind. Let me see, I could phone the hotel before eight but the Hawk wouldn't answer, of course. I could call the police but what would the charge be? I could phone Milly—here the farce begins—and beg her to hurry over to restrain by force a mother with whom she was not on speaking terms. Futile, let's face it.

I popped another milk chocolate with its soft caramel center into my mouth, chewed and prayed, stopped, chewed more quickly, swallowed, and began my prayer, properly, attentively, from the beginning. All I could think of was the usual "Please, Lord, help me 'cause I'm lost, at my wits end, and very much afraid. Please show me the way or make me bright enough to figure it out alone so that everything can go back to how it was before it all went wrong. Please, Lord, how about it? Fair is fair?"

I felt just as I did when I prayed as a child: exhibitionistic and ridiculous. I suspected, though I couldn't prove it, that no one was listening, or if someone was, He was giggling. After all, consider the nature of my request. "Save the world, sir, since I am in it. The devil has pulled a fast one. A tour de force, if you don't mind my saying so. Something's gone wrong." As if He didn't know. What a joke. How does one pray and keep a straight face? Now even I was laughing. But I was laughing uphill.

I popped another pacifier into my mouth, hailed a cab, and gave Philippa's address. "Hurry," I said, for the bubbling was getting worse, as if the flu was coming on. "Right-o, Captain," said the driver as we swung into the park, where for a moment, through the window, flashed the prophesy of doom and the outstretched hand, quivering slightly, with its leaflet.

There was all that talk about shooting Murray and wearing a red carnation during my reincarnation and she rubbed my ankle with hers as the football player and the two mailmen appeared and disappeared in the street. I half wondered if by some miracle the Hawk would appear as well. Then the food came and we ate and I told her again how much I loved her.

"But exactly how much?" She was smiling. "I mean on a scale of one to ten."

"On a scale of one to ten I would say, oh, ten."

"Wrong!" was her retort. We both smiled.

"Perhaps we should ask Vince what the correct answer is."

Philippa shook her head. "Trouble is you can't trust anything he says. He's terribly disreputable, you know."

"Oh, how do you know that?"

"I read it in the paper. A few years ago. Vince and some others were arrested for robbing a bank. Really. Vince was in the get-away car, but his buddies were nabbed inside, where a couple of plainclothes men were standing on line to cash their checks. Fantastico, no? Well, they nabbed Vince as well, but none of his buddies ratted on him, as they say, so he went free for lack of evidence. All they could get him on was double parking."

"Was he working the elevator then?"

"He was, and Murray wanted to get rid of him but the union said he hadn't been proved guilty of anything."

"Except double parking."

"Except double parking. Actually there are those in the office who are glad he's still with us. He sells them grass."

"I never knew that."

"Neither did Murray until just recently. It seems Vince will do anything for money. I even suspect Murray has changed his opinion of Vince. I think he feels that someone truly disreputable is good to have around. You never know what you may want him to do for you."

"That's *it*." I slapped the table.

"That's what?"

"Is he in the phone book?"

"Vince? I suppose so, why?"

"Oh, it's just that I have a little job for him to do."

She looked worried. "You're not thinking . . ." Her eyes widened. "You're not thinking of having him do some harm to Murray? Rob, I was just kidding. Rob, what's so funny?"

That evening before climbing my way to her third-floor swamp, I phoned my way through a phalanx of Vincent Lewises until I arrived at the V. E. Lewis on Twenty-second Street who said, "Hello, Chief. Pick a number from one to ten."

"Vince," I said, "pick a number from one to a hundred dollars."

The wind of his wit died down at once. He was a good listener. Mine was an involved story about needing someone to shadow a certain middle-aged lady tomorrow morning. I gave no names, just a description. I said I preferred not to explain why but that I wanted him to trail the woman in question from the Westminster Hotel, where she would be checking out on or before eight o'clock, and to keep following her wherever she went. Then he was to phone me at home and I would hurry over. One hundred dollars was his if it all went according to plan.

"No sweat, Chief. I'll call in sick so I can give all my time to it. You should hear from me about noon. Easy."

You'd think I had asked him to buy me a quart of milk.

Good old Vince. Of course this was only a trial run. I'd have to phone him when this morning came back again to set it all up once more. But it was a relief to know he was willing. I just hoped to God that Vince would be there and awake and ready to go at seven-thirty and that it was even possible for him to get from Twenty-second Street to the hotel on such short notice. I'd find out soon enough.

The rest of the evening was its usual disaster. I was too nervous and tired to be of much help to Milly. My thoughts kept wandering off like disobedient dogs and I would find one of them nuzzling up to Philippa, another prowling about the Westminster Hotel or giving a low growl at the sunlight on my bedroom wall.

Although earlier in the day Milly had admitted what her mother had done, this did not bring us closer as I had hoped. It only made the truth that much more difficult to avoid. I was not now nor had I ever been in love with her (passion induced by magic was inadmissible) and since I understood that this was so, she was now obliged to face up to it as well. She did so rather poorly. My suggestion that the two of us begin again didn't revive her as it had before. She knew I was only trying to cheer her up and this reduced all hope to the squalid truth of cold pizza crusts and hollow beer cans and now she, too, seemed nervous and exhausted.

She hinted that I should leave. I stayed. She saw my presence as an intrusion and insisted that I go. I still refused. She grew morose and wouldn't talk. I squeezed her thigh. She asked me to cut the shit. I did. There were long silences as I sat on the floor with my back against her bed, sipping beer. Occasionally, she would break out with a sudden, "Haven't you left yet?" Or a simple, philosophic, "Fuck." She made it quite clear that I would not be allowed to stay the night. I said I would stay only until twelve.

"Twelve? What's so big deal about twelve?"

"No reason. Just want to."

"You make a bet with someone or what?"

"I'm just not leaving until then. Period."

"What's this, a sit-in?"

"I like being with you."

"That's very funny. I'm tired. I want to sleep. And you won't leave."

"That is correct, ma'am."

"At twelve you had better leave or I scream."

"Agreed."

"Well, I'll see it when I believe it."

"Something like that."

She waved me away with disgust. "Enough said the better."

"Exactly."

The rest was silence except, of course, for the dripping faucet in her tub.

This time I was in such a rush I didn't even stop to turn off the tape recorder. As I dialed Vince's number in the hallway I heard my voice in my bedroom giving out with the familiar, monomaniacal, "Hop to it. No more late start for you buddy. Come on, come on, wake up. Today you're going to get places. This is it. On your fuckin' feet. Get into your clothes and get movin' kid. Today is going to be a big day or I'll know the reason why. Today is going to be—"

"Hello, Vince," I said. "This is Robinson Blake."

"Hello, Chief. Pick a number from one to ten."

Chocolate-covered graham crackers helped somewhat, as did black coffee laced with anisette. The *Messiah* turned on loud is the music best suited to keep one from going bananas while waiting. Actually there was no need for Handel just yet.

I was doing all right. At least so I thought. A few more graham crackers and the act of getting dressed calmed me considerably.

Then Vince phoned and I was on it, dropped it, found it, put it to my ear, and yelled, *"Hello!"*

"Hello, yourself. What are you shouting for?"

"Milly."

"Son of a gun. He remembers my name. OK. Question: Did you just phone me a minute ago or not?"

"Milly, I can't talk now."

"'Cause by the time I finished breaking my leg getting to the phone it went dead. Since you never call at night anymore, I figured maybe he's calling me by day."

"Milly, I said I can't talk now."

"I heard you."

"I'd love to chat—"

"Who's stoppin' you?"

"—but I'm waiting for an important phone call and—"

"Really?"

"Really."

"Boss-man, faretheewell."

I was debating whether to continue getting dressed or to have another cracker first and had decided to combine both activities at once when I did neither and rushed to the window to watch a bald-headed man climb out of a maroon Dodge and watch that other gentleman, too, in the plaid trousers, but most particularly to observe the expensive fur jacket, the impeccable upsweep of her red hair, and that imperial walk of hers as if she knew that secret cameras were recording her every move. I felt I had lost a needed friend and the emptiness of this coming evening seemed terrible indeed.

The phone went off like a gunshot in a footrace.

"Hello!"

"Did she call yet?" This time it was death speaking.

"What do you mean?"

"You seeing her tonight?"

"Damn it, I haven't got time for this."

"But do you have time to wait for her call?"

"I am waiting for a call from Vincent Lewis, our elevator man."

"Oh, sure. Of course."

"Milly, when you go to work this morning—that is if I don't fire you on the spot—you will find that he is not at his post making jokes as usual but out somewhere trailing your worthless, witch of a mother."

There was a vast silence. "My mother? Why my mother?"

"Because she sticks pins in dolls and screws up people's lives and I want to find out what else she's been doing so I can stop that shit too."

"Who told you about the dolls? Did she tell you?"

"She told me nothing. She's been ducking me for days, if you must know."

"Then who told you?"

"Look, I'll explain everything later but you must get off the damn phone and *now*."

Silence.

"Milly?"

"Can I ask one question?"

"Hurry up. What is it?"

"Are we . . . are we through?"

"No we are not through, God damn it, and will you stop asking me that damn question?"

"Stop? I never asked it before."

"I know, I know, I know, now will you get off the God-damned phone?"

"You don't have to shout. I mean shouting is for vulgar people."

"See you, Milly."

"Good," she said, "bye."

She hung up and the knot in my gut was cinched even tighter. Will she do something rash before the day even begins? No, Milly's a good girl. Not the type to kill herself on company time. Let us dearly hope not. I kicked the wall. Again harder. Vince, phone, would ya? Would ya phone?

Dressed at last, my tie knotted into my throat, I sat waiting on a scaffold of silence until I could take it no longer, got up, stacked the *Messiah* on the hi-fi, and turned up the sound. Calcified with expectation, I am Abe Lincoln seated in his glory with waves of music, like history, breaking over him. Or I am a condemned perfectionist diligently practicing for the day of his electrocution. I listened to how Ev. Vry. Va. Halley. Shall-be-exhau. Haulted. But all I wish to hear is Vince! Phone, Vince, would ya please phone?

He finally did, right at the beginning of the Hallelujah Chorus. I had to clamp my free hand over my free ear to catch anything at all. "What?" I kept yelling, "What?" "Enemy" was what I heard. She was *at* "enemy" or *an* "enemy." I was about to tell him to hang on so I could scramble into the living room and kill Handel with a twist of a dial when I caught on. *Kennedy!* She was at Kennedy. "Hurry Chief. Not much time," he said. That, too, I caught and, after agreeing on where to meet, I was out the door as the voices bellowed, "Ever and ever, Hallelujah, Hallelujah," and by the time my door swung shut, cutting Handel down to a muffle, I was already into the waiting elevator with my thumb on G and my free palm slapping the wall.

I ran to the intersection, where I usually have good luck snaring cabs. Now there was nothing. I waved at every taxi (they were all occupied), and one driver, the S.O.B., actually waved back. I curse. I hover. I stand there doing a lot of dynamic waiting. The Midway theatre is playing *Escape from Al-*

catraz. A large jet roars in steady grandeur westward. Is the Hawk in it? Sweat runs its tongue down my spine. I search the traffic for a glimpse of yellow. Longing to hear Philippa's voice (even a few words would comfort me), I spot a row of empty phone booths and am forced to tell myself to stop behaving like a child. By now, of course, she is seated in her black stockings on Murray's couch and suddenly into the street I run, waving as if a war has ended. The rear door won't open. The driver has to reach back and lift the button.

We move not nearly fast enough along the monotonous expressway. A sign for Liberty Avenue is soon followed by another suggesting the Aquarium.

"Gorgeous out," says the driver.

My mouth is like a sandbox; my chest, rusted metal. Sweat continues to reappear on my face until I simply give up and put my handkerchief away.

"You don't get lotsa days like dis here."

"No, you don't."

I clutch my wrist. Thirty thumps in fifteen seconds. Multiplied by four that makes, Christ, a pulse of 120! Take deep breaths. Think of pleasant things. Sweet Philippa is evoked and hovers lovingly until I am crushed under the reality of her absence. The back seat seems enormously empty and noon is filled with invisible darkness. Pain pins a morbid warning to my chest. Thoughts move slowly against an undertow of worry. I long for Milly's life-giving energy but it is all packed away like everything that is hers. For years now her whole life has been boxed up, ready for removal. There is only one last box to fill.

The taxi has stopped. I throw him some money and run into the building. I collide with someone, apologize, and keep going. Time is evaporating. Planes are leaving. Perhaps she has gone already. I yelp. A hand has grasped my shoulder.

"Hey, Chief, slow down."

In his sky-blue Byron shirt and zebra pants, he looked far more disreputable than he ever did in uniform. Instead of his elevator cap he had shining black sinful hair.

"Where is she?" I asked. "Is she gone?"

Vincent's face squeezed out a conspiratorial smile as he led me to a ticket booth. He pointed at the wall board.

"Leaves in ten minutes, Chief."

A line of print leaped at me like an assassin. Pan Am flight 428 bound for London.

"Just in time, eh?" said Vince.

I stare at Death's lottery number on the wall. Was all this insane scrambling simply to get myself on board *this* plane? That which was best and most cowardly in me advised that the really smart thing to do was to let her have this one. Toss in my hand and go home. Wait for a new deal the next time around. Perhaps she would lead Vince somewhere else, to a hotel in the Catskills or a flight bound for Miami, places where I could follow and confront her and not have on my mind the horror of a bomb and a terrifying plunge into the sea. Or if she persisted in going to Kennedy and getting on this plane then I would try getting there first to stop her at the flight desk.

Vincent's eyes were watching me. Even his wart seemed to be watching me. Over his shoulder I saw the phone booth I had used once eons ago. I ran to repeat my bomb-threat phone call, with Vince trotting after me like a puppy. Someone was inside talking and laughing. A short Chinese gentleman with a high giggle. There was no other phone booth in sight. With Vince still following me, I ran back to ask the ticket clerk how much time I had left. She peered at her watch. There was no time left. I would have to sign on now or not at all. I slapped down my passport and credit card. She gave a sigh. She got to work.

"Vince," I said, moving him out of earshot. "When that phone booth over there is empty," I lowered my voice, "when it's empty you phone Pan Am and tell them there's a bomb, *a bomb!* hear me? on board this flight. Get it? If the plane takes off before you call then—"

"Luggage?" asked the lady behind the desk.

"None," I shouted and dropped my voice again. "If the plane takes off, you phone them anyway. They'll turn around and come back. Promise you'll do this, Vince. Look." I produced my check book and wrote him out twice the amount promised. "And there's still another hundred in it for you if you do this thing, all right? Vince?"

His suspicious eyes peered into me and I wondered what madness he found there. But I could not wait any longer. That was the whole point of it. My patience had come to an end.

"Vince?"

"Your ticket, sir," said the lady.

"Vince." I pushed my check into his hand.

"Don't worry, Chief. Leave it to me."

"Sir, you will have to hurry."

The Chinese gentleman was leaving the phone booth at last. I pointed. Vince noticed. We both waved good-by. I ran and didn't look back. A woman in uniform frowned at my ticket, said, "Oh, dear," and led me rather frantically across the carpeted lounge, through a crooked tunnel and into a massive, four-engine jet. A pretty blonde stewardess had all but closed the door.

"Good for you," she said and laughed.

I explained that I was hoping to surprise my dear aunt who, though afraid of flying, was going to Europe for the first time. Would she kindly arrange for me to sit next to this lady? It would be such a comfort for the old dear to have me with her. I exuded a benign and retarded saintliness. The stewardess touched my arm and promised to try. She went up the aisle, leaned over, and spoke to a youth with YALE writ large upon his chest. He got up willingly, perhaps gratefully, and was led to a different seat. The door to the plane, as upon a vault, slammed shut.

I couldn't help thinking that all these people, just recently dead, seemed disconcertingly alive in the same way a movie star continues to perform with charm and wit though buried for decades. The stewardess turned and smiled. I winked my thanks and quickly slipped in beside the Hawk.

12

We hurtled forward in a rash thrust of power until all was gently lifted only to be tipped and yanked steeply into the sky. When we were high over the ocean, level with the earth, fixed on our course, I noticed in the sunlight a single footprint on the wing. My neighbor kept her face to the window. We were allowed to unfasten our safety belts. *Vince hadn't phoned yet and why hadn't he phoned and had something stopped him?* I quickly plugged up this hemorrhage of worry. I must remain in control. The stewardess demonstrated how to inflate a lifejacket. Unable to wait for Mrs. Hawkmann to notice me, I tapped her on the shoulder.

"Oy!" she said, clutching her heart.

"The game is up, lady."

"You shouldn't scare people like that."

"I said the game is up."

"Who's playing games?"

"I know all about your meddling with Milly and with me. Now talk."

"I don't wish to talk."

"Look, everything has gone *wrong*. What the hell have you *done*, for crysake?"

"I am not conversing with you. That's all, that's it."

"Oh yes you are, lady, and you know why?" She stared straight at me. "First of all, day after day, I've prevented your dear daughter from killing herself. That was no fun game, let me tell you. Well, now I quit. Whatever happens, count me out. Second, I will hound you and hound you until you do tell me what's going on. And I have all the time in the world, don't forget. Third, if you don't start talking right now I will punch you in the fucking mouth. Are there any questions?"

"You argue good. Logic, it has. Polite, it's not. Should have been a lawyer. Or a criminal."

"Well?"

"You'd punch *me*? Front of all these nice people?"

"Four or five times hard before they stopped me. Six times maybe. Much blood, loose teeth, the works. Yes, I would."

"Man of action."

"Come on, damn you, *talk*."

The long, sagging, big-nosed face seemed almost amused in that sour dyspeptic way of hers. Now the eyes were alert with fear.

"You'd abandon Milly?"

"As of this instant."

"That's cruel."

"Lady, I want answers or I just don't play any more. I want things explained nice and orderly and I want them explained right now."

"Order. That's you all over. Poor Milly. I'll tell you something, Mister. Order kills as much as chaos."

"Philosophy later. Now facts. And hurry. We may not have much time."

I wondered what speed my pulse had reached. Then I plugged up that thought as well.

"Not much time?" she asked.

"Forget it. Come on."

"You look worried, Mr. Blake."

"Will. You. Come on?"

"Ah, Mr. Enunciation again."

"Or do you want that rap in the teeth?"

The stewardness appeared and smiled beatifically. "He really cares for you," she told Mrs. Hawkmann. "It's so wonderful to see."

I hurriedly ordered double bourbons, and the stewardess went to get them.

"What's with her?"

"A bad judge of character," I replied.

"Must be on pills." She folded her hands in her lap. Then looked at me. "How'd you know I was on this flight?"

"Mrs. Hawkmann!"

"All right, all right." She gave a sigh. "Well, here goes."

Yet for a few moments she said nothing. The sea burned with distant patches of bright silver. The engine hummed loudly and out of tune. Not far off was that enchanting Dickensian child whom I had seen at the airport the first time I phoned and reported the bomb. He stood in the aisle, dressed in white, as his mother sat and combed his curls. The exquisite creature smiled at me as if he knew full well he was the world's wonder—one of those delicious tots, rare as unicorns, who talk like a sage while dressed like a fop. How sad that he too must perish. I cursed Vincent for being the incompetent bastard that he was. Had something gone wrong? Or had he simply run out on me? I plugged this up and shivered. The little angel was smiling at me again in boundless, beatific trust.

"Do you know anything about witchcraft, Mr. Blake?"

"Very little. But I'm learning."

"I won't give you a long schpiel. We're not supposed to blab about it anyway. But *white* magic is for the doing of good works. Do you understand me? A white witch can do many fine things. I myself once cured someone of cancer. I have often helped people in need. Believe me, I have. Then I discovered that my own daughter was in need. And I helped her too. Don't look like that, you putz. I did help her. Except she found out. Is it my fault she found out? She's got too much pride, that one. God forbid I should fix her love life for her and make her happy. Oh, no. She wants to do it *her* way. Her way, *ha*. Wants to find a man all on her own, she says. OK, OK. I do as she asks. I stop helping. So what happens? Everything turns to turd, that's what. Could have *killed* her. That's how *mad* I was. *Furious*. Then one day something very scary happens. It really gets me frightened. Now and then I receive messages. I see things. You know, *things*. Bits and pieces of what's coming. Of the future. Sometimes I understand. Sometimes not. This one is going to break a leg. That one is going to lose his money. Simple things, clear things. One night I see something terrible, something I don't understand at all. I see her completely submerged in her tub, her hair spread out and floating like black seaweed. She has killed herself. Such a scream, I give. Well, I fainted dead away. Really. I wake up, remember, and again I faint. Oy, what a night. The worst I ever had."

The stewardess brought our whiskeys as if to give Mrs. Hawkmann strength after such a night. And still the plane hadn't turned back.

"Then what happened?" I asked.

"I became obsessed," she said in a raw whisper. "All I could think of was to summon help."

"Help?"

"To use the power. To command. Don't ask questions. If I tell too much I could be cursed. Doubly so. More than I am already, that is. To save her I had to do something I had never done before. I was terrified, believe me. Because what I had to do, you see, was to go, was to delve, into, into the dark side." She sipped her drink, the ice silent in the plastic cup. "I made, I finally made a . . ." She gestured with her hand, ". . . an agreement."

"A pact."

"Refrain from interrupting, please."

"Sorry, go ahead."

"Actually, I didn't think I could. Go ahead, that is. I didn't believe it possible. Talk of chutzpah. But then I was told that it *was* possible."

"Told?"

"Told," she snapped.

"I think I am finally beginning to understand."

"I had just minutes to go before midnight struck. I made the pact just in time. Otherwise it might have been too late, not possible at all. I promised my service. In return. In return for having my baby. Saved. I asked him how long I could have it repeated."

"Him? The devil?"

"Tsh! Shhhh!" She looked around furtively. "I asked because my request was until—"

"Until I saved her."

"Yes. I was in my cottage in Vermont and I was in the very middle of saying, asking, if it would really go on until—"

"And?"

"And I woke up in that damn hotel in Manhattan where I had gone to bed the night before."

"The Westminster."

She nodded. It seemed she was having a little trouble breathing.

"I got on the phone right away," she continued. "Right away I got on the phone. And called her. It rang and it rang. I died. I just absolutely died. Then, Gutzi dunk, she answered. She answered. I couldn't—"

"Speak?"

She nodded and turned her head away. I patted the long log of her arm.

"And you hung up without speaking, didn't you? Milly phones every morning, afterward, to see if it was me. I thought she was just making it up."

Mrs. Hawkmann shook her head.

"So that means you phone every morning too, at the same time, just to make sure, don't you?"

Her head rocked forward and back. As I waited for her to regain her composure, I noticed the white thread of an invisible jet pulling westward. Mrs. Hawkmann's bottomless love made me want to sound the depths of my own. There was a steady painful emptying in me as I moved farther and farther away from Philippa. By now she'd be reclining in his chair and he would be pressing close to those parted lips that he would prefer to kiss, but instead he would drill into the hard whiteness of one of her teeth thinking how marvelous she was and how witty and glamorous and altogether disturbing and he would speak to her and say, "Take water and rinse." I sipped some whiskey, tried to smile, and failed. I wished I could hold her hand now for comfort. The flight hadn't turned back. I was going to die. At least we were going to crash. Would there be much pain? Vince had an hour yet. But could I be sure? Well, we'd all end up back in our own beds again anyway, wouldn't we? Could I be sure? My drink trembled and I propped it on the armrest. I hated him. I hated the bastard more than I ever had anyone in my entire life.

"You know what went wrong?"

"What?" Thinking she meant with Vince.

She shrugged just as Milly would, fast and reckless, almost with petulance. "Thought you'd tell me." Again the shrug. "Who knows?"

"Mrs. Hawkmann, I have saved her a dozen times or more. And *still* it goes on."

"I don't know why," she whispered. "I just don't know."

"Summon him again, damn it."

"Shhhh."

"Again until everything is back—"

"I tried. I did try."

"You tried?"

"Many times, believe me."

"Well, what happened? I don't understand."

"What happened? he asks. Saved she is, screwed we are, that is what happened."

"How?"

"I only wish I knew." She put her head back and closed her eyes. The aircraft droned onward. I tasted more whiskey.

"The fly in the ointment . . ."

"Yes?" I asked. "Well?"

". . . I thought . . . still think, is what's-her-face, Mrs. Black Legs."

"Philippa?"

She glared at me, her Gaullist nose all but tilting with mine. "You're so busy schtupping her that when it comes to saving my Milly you are putting into it no heart. Oh, you poor bored putz. How tiring it must be and you just with guilt to keep you going."

"Ah, I see. If I love her like Prince Charming then the manic-depressive Princess with the suicidal tendencies is rescued. If my heart is pure, she lives. Is that it?"

"You degenerate. Taking someone else's wife and schtupping her silly. Mazeltov. My Milly needs help and you, you misery, what are *you* doing? Aah, you make me sick. Look, is it too much to ask to save a girl you *don't* love?"

"Shhhhh."

"A punch in the teeth, that's your speed. You're all heart. What a prize. God forbid."

She stared out the window. There was only the groan of the aircraft now and the others turned slowly back to their own business. A lunchwagon came down the aisle with several hostesses pushing. Neither of us wanted food, and they pushed on, leaving a whiff of roast beef. I watched the others eye their trays and begin to eat. All those poor souls soon to go spinning down amid continued screams of terror. There was no point in mentioning the bomb to Mrs. Hawkmann. Why start her agony sooner than the others'? Only I knew what was coming and I bore the weight of it less well with every passing moment. It seemed futile attempting personally to make them turn back. Why on earth would someone board a plane he knew to be a death trap, keep his own counsel, and then suddenly warn everyone in mid-flight? Who would buy that? They'd think him deranged. So there was nothing to be done. Perhaps I even believed this. Perhaps it was even true. Anyway, I didn't feel up to making a fuss, just as one doesn't struggle when the noose is fastened. For what is death after all if one wakes up again almost at once? Perhaps I believed that one as well.

Yet how I ached for them. That angelic child. The two young ladies serving food. A honeymoon couple sharing a spoon and occasional kisses. A portly chap lovingly tasting his Beaujolais. An old man reading the salt packet with a magnifying glass. Two teenagers grimly sawing their rolls in half. All of them in a shattering moment with stricken faces would learn that here was doom. We would all be thrown into the breathless cold, clutching at space in that intolerable tumble above the vast sea, in that final mighty burst of life.

I decided to make a fuss, after all. Try at least. Reach the pilot now. Make him go back. The waiting. It was impossible. It was a torture I just could not take any longer. I lurched forward so as to spring out of my seat when I saw the Dickensian child standing at my side, holding my arm rest, beaming his joy. The clean pure eyes held me for a moment like sky-blue jewels. I started to move. At that point, he spoke. "May I whisper into your ear, please, Mr. Robinson Blake?" Again that ostentatious grin, the voice disturbingly self-assured. I was summoned closer with a small finger. Two lips brushed my ear. "Follow me, please, sir. It's to do with a Mrs. Scanlan." The child strolled away. He began to skip, tapping each arm rest as he passed. I jumped up. It was as though an outrage had taken place, an incredible, tasteless practical joke. No one even glanced at me. The child had stopped. He looked back, gave a commanding toss of his curls, indicating that he expected me to follow, and went inside one of the toilets and closed the door.

I ran and, with the help of a slight momentary tipping of the aircraft, plunged into the tiny cubicle. The child, as if on a pedestal, was standing on the closed toilet bowl, his little eyebrows raised in surprise at my clumsy entrance. I slammed the door and we were alone. At that moment the overhead light went out.

"Damn."

In the cramped dark the child's saccharine voice offered advice. "There is, I believe, just above your head . . ."

My hand moved in a circle hitting and losing something weightless and thin. Catching hold, I gave a tug. The bright cubicle, to my astonishment, had become a closet full of clothes. Holding my breath, I gingerly pushed open the door.

Here was an exact replica of the entire room. Even the Vermeer was there. Everything was there. I dashed to the window and found Flushing Meadows, the purple lake, ribbons of moving cars, everything. I turned to view the bed, the tape recorder, my own shadow on the wall. My heart hammered in relief and alarm. Here, surely, was the total madness I had been anticipating. Yet odd how nothing was distorted. In fact my mind seemed, as always, normally, boringly lucid. I went into the other rooms and found nothing uncommon there either. Handel's *Messiah* was at rest on the turntable, the machine having turned itself off. There was no sign of the golden child.

A drink was called for. It was, you might say, mandatory. I fetched a glass, threw in two pieces of ice, and started to pour out some Chivas Regal, when the bottle spilled whiskey all the way across the dining-room table and into the sugar bowl. I had lurched as though slapped. It was the doorbell.

Putting down the glass and bottle, feeling scotch seeping through my shirt front, I reached the knob, took a deep breath, and pulled.

"Your Majesty!"

A thin, reshaped eyebrow rose, as the child's had, in mild surprise.

"Do you have a moment?"

Without waiting for my reply she came right in. She didn't stop until she reached the living room. Her clothes were still those of this morning and she got rid of her fur cape by dropping it on a nearby table. Now she looked more a queen than ever with her up-swept hair, her bare arms, and her now, fully revealed, black, off-the-shoulder dress.

"May I sit down?"

I waved her to the couch, but she chose instead my leather reading chair. The lovely, frosty woman seemed faintly sad, as if worrying about something entirely unconnected with her presence here. Remembering my existence, she gave me a smile radiating, to my surprise, actual warmth.

"It would have been more fitting to step into the elevator," she said, "and squeeze your bum. An eye for an eye, as it were. But there wasn't time."

I must have been the very picture of astonished stupidity.

"You remember . . . ?" I brought out then stopped, wide-eyed. "You remember what happened?"

She leaned back against the black leather in her black dress and her pale freckled face and limbs seemed disembodied.

She smiled. "Perhaps you had best get that drink. I'll wait."

"Would you care—"

"No, not for me, thanks all the same."

In a daze I fetched the bottle and glass. Her Majesty was sitting just as I had left her, not a muscle had moved, and the glazed look, that vacant, unlit stillness reminded me of a catatonic. I managed a sip from my drink. I sat down and waited.

"All set?"

"I think so."

She crossed her legs and interlaced her fingers just under her chin. "Well . . ." Her green eyes found me again after examining the wall above my head. "I am here to apologize."

"Apologize?" I actually laughed. "What have *you* done for God's sake?"

"Not for anything that happened in the elevator or afterward. For *that* you should apologize to *me*."

"Yes, so for what?"

"Well, for all this unpleasantness you've gone through."

I was unable to find the beginning of any appropriate declarative sentence. I peered at her. She nodded.

"I don't—"

"Take some more whiskey," she advised. "It'll relax you."

I did. It didn't. The hammering in my chest was alarming.

She leaned forward. "Your heart's racing. There, there. It's all right. It's all over now."

"Over?"

"Yes, over. I am here to explain."

"Look, who sent you? I want to know."

"Consider my being here in the nature of a public service." She leaned back and studied my reaction. Just as I was about to speak, she beat me to it. "To begin with, I'm afraid you've been rather harsh on poor Mrs. Hawkmann. She is legitimate, though somewhat atypical. She spends a good deal of her time, as do most of them, going through a series of primitive rituals—you know, a coven of twelve people dancing 'skyclad' as they say and all the rest of it. But she does good works. Small but good. Then, unfortunately, she ran into some exceptionally bad luck. She cast some spells, bungled, and tragedy resulted. Desperate, she did the only thing she could, she summoned the help of an old friend of mine."

I broke in, "Look, I hate to be suspicious but are you . . . are you the Devil or . . . or what?"

The smallest of smiles played upon and disappeared from her lips. "Delphine would be delighted to learn that someone had suspected her of such cosmic renown."

"Who?"

"Delphine Bedford. The lady across the hall. The lady you're now looking at."

"Listen, if you're not the Devil," I said, "which I'll have to accept on face value, then you're not this Delphine person either, are you?"

"Delphine has had a hard day under the lights, as she would say. She came home a few minutes ago to take a nap. So I borrowed her for a while to bring about our introduction. Just as I borrowed that child in the plane, the one you were so taken with."

"Borrowed?"

"Did you really expect a bearded old man? A total stranger? What would I have said at the door? Or should I have descended through the ceiling accompanied by trumpets? You would have had a coronary, believe me."

She looked away and seemed to lose interest.

"You're making fun of me."

"Well, I sometimes find it difficult not to lapse into irony during these discussions."

"You're God, then."

This sounded so foolish that I regretted it at once.

"For the purpose and duration of our discussion, that tiresome name, childish and melodramatic as it is, does, I admit, more or less, cover it."

I stood up, but only to refill my glass. The idea occurred to me that all this was simply a schizophrenic collapse. My visitor seemed totally relaxed and eager, almost hungry, for conversation.

"You sure you wouldn't like a drink?" I asked. This too seemed monumentally fatuous.

"No, at least Delphine doesn't. Not this early, anyway."

"Ah, I see." I sat down. "Are you male or female?"

"It varies. But you'll get confused if we go into that."

"Well, all right. I suppose we should get back to your, as you put it, apology."

"Yes, let's get that over with." Her Majesty shifted about in the black leather chair and a momentary look of discomfort appeared and made real the dull symmetry of her face. "I see Delphine has a slight case of back trouble." She crossed her legs and leaned on the chair's left arm to get more comfortable.

"You all right?"

"Yes, yes. It's this poor girl who's got the problem."

"Cure it, why don't you?"

"It's not in the Concordance." Her eyes widened in exclamation. "That would be obstruction." She waved a finger as
she shook her head.

"Obstruction?"

"Interference."

"Hell, snatching me back from a plane that's half way—"

Her finger worked like a metronome. "If I am allowed to
proceed then perhaps you'll understand."

"OK, OK."

"The universe is not like a watch, as some of your more
mechanical minds have postulated. Flattering, true, but
wrong nonetheless. Nor is it," with a grandiose wave of her
hand, "a *thought!* Ha! No, it is exactly what it seems to be. A
mess. While we're on the subject, let me say that neither is it
an accident, a molecule, a vast tomb, an heirloom, or any of
those other theories—which brings us back to the first point.
This mess came about, quite frankly, as the necessary setting
for a wager—one that grew out of a philosophical dispute as to
whether animals with sophisticated intelligence, if allowed to
go their way unhindered and unhelped, could actually survive
the problems they would make for themselves. Do you see
why the experiment is so interesting?"

"More or less."

"Good. The universe then, to put it bluntly, is—"

"Big bang? Steady state?" I was trying for high marks.

"—in constant need of repair," she concluded almost pa-
tiently.

"Repair?"

"For example, the earth's spin of late has been slowing
down. This was even detected not long ago by some French
scientists. A fraction of a second was being lost each year.
However, the deceleration would not have continued in terms
of fractions of seconds. Beyond a certain point, the earth

would have lost speed quickly and then completely. The result, a catastrophe. I had to step in just as I once did centuries ago. Yes, it's not the first time this has happened."

My hand had all but turned to ice. I remembered my drink, loosened my grip on it, drained some scotch and put the cold glass on the mantelpiece. At that point I was asked a question, and rather sternly, I thought.

"The Bible, do you know it?"

"Well, to tell you the truth, sir, that is, madam . . . what I'm saying is, I don't really. Skimmed a bit. Here and there. A little Genesis, a little Matthew, you know."

"Damn silly book. More trouble than it's worth. The heavens and the earth were created in seven days, were they? Ha! Just this little adjustment *today* took almost a month. Anyway, the Bible does mention a time of great calamity and flood."

"Noah's Ark," I snapped.

"A children's story. Charming. Yet the flood *was* real enough. It happened again, as you'll remember, just a few days ago."

"You mean those tidal waves all over the world?"

"I was a purist once. I tried to adjust the spin in mid-flight. Trial and error. Except one such error sent the oceans up onto the land. These days I take no chances."

"So you made time stop."

"No, I can't do that. I just reran it. Since there has to be movement, stopping would make adjustment impossible anyway."

"Of course, yes. That's what I meant to say. Except how is it—"

"How is it I have trouble with the spin of a small planet and yet can repeat a universe of incidents?"

"Well, yes."

God stood up and pressed her hands into the small of her back, arching out her breasts and frowning.

"Can I get you or, rather, Miss Bedford something? An aspirin?"

She smiled. "No, thank you. It'll be all right." She stopped to fix me with her deep, light green eyes. "If you wanted to repair a damaged 35 millimeter motion picture film, the hard part would be to retouch thirty or forty frames, the easy part would be to rerun those frames to see what progress you were making."

"Is that how it's done?"

"No, but the parallel is not inexact."

"I thought—"

"No, it was Man thinking he was omniscient who decided that I was omnipotent. Anyway, it was hard work, tedious and boring."

"I'm sorry."

"Don't be absurd."

"Well, why do you fix the earth's spin and not Miss Bedford's back?"

"One is maintenance, the other—"

"Obstruction."

"You're learning."

"And it's all part of some sort of Concordance."

"Very good. And *that* is where Mrs. Hawkmann comes in, I am sorry to say. That is, as a matter of fact, where all hell breaks loose."

13

She plunged and touched her toes several times. Arms akimbo, she bent to the left in repeated tugs and then to the right. Holding arms straight out she twisted at the waist in quick rotating swings until one hand accidentally knocked my newly filled glass of scotch from the mantelpiece to the floor. Or toward the floor, because she quickly threw up her hand, palm open, as if stopping traffic, and the glass halted just inches from the carpet. The spilt scotch looked frozen as in a high-speed photograph. The suspended piece of ice shone in the sunlight from the window. Then, as if all this were attached to her hand by a string, her arm moved abruptly, as when snapping a whip, and the whiskey spilled into the glass as it rose and landed in her waiting hand, which she moved just a bit to the left to catch the ice.

Shaking her head sadly, "Magic. I should never have agreed."

She held the glass as far from her as she could, and it took me a moment to realize it was being handed back to me. My guest wandered over and stood by the window as I examined, smelt, and eventually sipped my bewitched but otherwise un-altered drink.

"I agreed to witchcraft and patriotism so that I, in turn, could have—you won't believe this—humor and poetry. Little good they did me."

The voice was surprisingly melancholy. She turned from staring into the street and showed me her pained emerald eyes.

"Perhaps religion," I said, "eventually will—"

"That, least of all. We each had one final endowment to place like buried treasure in the future. I decided on music. My friend thought a long while, like a grandmaster at a chess-board. Then, smiling, he said that for his last choice he would have Man conceive of the idea of God." Her Majesty shook her head.

"You mean—"

"Brilliant, wasn't it?"

"Didn't you *want* Man to know about you?"

"Never! Thousands of years of decimation and torture, not only in my absence but in my name: that synonym for car-nage, and, to add insult to blasphemy, expecting a reward, *the* reward, of life after death."

"Is there any? At all?"

"You must be joking! Isn't *this* bad enough? At any rate, he was right. I was wrong. We're experimenting now on a new model. A humanoid with less creativity and more empathy. He'll be duller but, we hope, better. You know, I honestly didn't believe that men and women would develop such an absolute genius for rationalization."

She sat down, slumped in gloom. I, needless to say, was crushed beyond speech. A blur of rock music pulsated in the distance.

"You see, to give religion a fighting chance, there would have to be just one, any one, but only one. Except I had no endowments left. Let two religions occupy the same place at the same time and what do you have? Hell. Unless, of course, you defuse them both."

"I see." But I didn't want to see or do anything for a while.

Head back, her eyes on the ceiling:

"Witchcraft is to my own powers what model trains are to interplanetary travel. But even an electric toy can short circuit an apartment building and black out the East Coast."

"Hum," I grunted. The prospect of flinging myself through the window seemed pleasantly soothing.

"And that short circuit turned out to be Mrs. Hawkmann."

The image of myself spread like jam in the street vanished. I looked up and found her, fingers interlaced, legs crossed, as when she first came in and took her seat.

"The old lady tampered with her daughter's love, and it ended badly. Then she called upon my friend to put into operation this mad and totally impossible plan to have the fateful day actually repeated, *repeated*, until such time as you came and saved her. As she herself might say, the plan was facocked. Except for one thing. The daughter accidentally picked as the day to kill herself the same twenty-four hours that I, for other reasons, decided to stage a rerun. You see, it was set to happen anyway only she couldn't possibly have known that. My friend, of course, knew it. And therein lies a tale, as they say. From my point of view, a short circuit took place. Mrs. Hawkmann summoned up her powers, but in actual fact all she was granted was memory. As were you. All the rest I did and *he* got the credit. You should have heard his laughter. And I couldn't do a single thing about it. I still don't know why you didn't end up in a padded cell, particularly after you did 'save' her and *still* nothing happened. How could it? I had yet to get the spin right."

"You talk about a padded cell. Well, why didn't you come and tell me all this sooner?"

"It's against the Concordance to give any member of the human race substantial knowledge of the future even if, for a while, there is to be no future."

"And now?"

"Now I'm finished."

"Will Milly be safe? Will she?"

"It's all in your hands, I'm sorry to say. It's too tangled for a simple resolution. You have Mrs. Hawkmann to thank for that. I just came to explain, apologize, and leave again. The previous todays before this day began have, of course, all been stricken from the record."

"And Philippa?"

"Good luck."

"That's all you came to say?"

"Isn't it enough? Usually I say nothing, and that has annoyed I can't tell you how many." She stood up. "I do hope I've thought of everything." She picked up her mink cape, slung it over her shoulder, and strolled away. I followed. At the door she turned; an ugly gloom had pulled down the corners of her mouth. Her silence made me aware that something important had not been said: a question asked, perhaps, an assurance given. I had an obscene feeling that a part of her had reached into me to erase what I was trying to remember.

"You told me too much," I said. "I feel done in."

One hand was on her hip, the other held the mink as it hung down her back. Sorrow still shaded her face. Her green eyes took me in with a compassion I found terribly off-putting.

"I feel I wanted to ask you something but that it's slipped my mind."

"You'll remember as soon as I leave."

"What if I come running after you?"

"If you're very quick, who knows?"

Again that look, melancholy and amused. She actually patted my cheek.

"Well," she said, "have a good life."

"Sure thing," I laughed until I saw she hadn't meant it as a joke. Soberly, "I'll try."

"Of course." The way she said this gave me a chill.

"Well, then . . ." Should I have offered my hand? Conveyed thanks? Registered a protest? Too late. The door had closed although I didn't remember her leaving. I was alone again and confused as if groping my way out of sleep. The missing ingredients of myself drifted together until that piece of what I wanted most to remember floated back. It was the frayed end of a rough thread of worry; I pulled and out popped the face of Mrs. Hawkmann. Of course! Her Majesty must do something to stop the bomb. Hadn't I the right to make at least one request? All those innocent people flung into the sea. "Wait!" I pulled open the door and ran out into the hallway only to bang my knee against the bowl and slap both palms against the wall to keep from falling. I did a one-legged dance of pain, holding the sink for support and hearing the astonished, commiserating intake of breath from the ventilator. The sight of the toilet propelled me back into my own home again, where in neat rows were hundreds of heads and many portholes filled with blue.

"We're about to hit some turbulence," smiled the stewardess. "Would you return to your seat, please, fasten your safety belt, and observe the no smoking sign."

A man in a garish sports jacket had entered the toilet. The door said *occupied*.

"Oh, my God." I looked around wildly, knowing that there was no escape. "Oh, my God."

"There is really nothing to be worried about, sir. Just a little atmospheric turbulence."

"We're going to crash, explode, yes, we are."

"Captain Gaybell is very capable. Turbulence is not dangerous. Just a little bumpy. Now, please, sir . . ."

Pushing past a man who had stood up to put away some
hand luggage, I found my seat and knelt on it with one knee.
Mrs. Hawkmann was staring out the window as if she hadn't
moved since I left. My resolve not to mention our impending
destruction took hold again. She turned and saw me.

"You look like death warmed over."

I could sense the metal, the air, our limbs, our lives at any
moment, exploding, my wide eyes were already part of that
imminent, loud, jolting detonation.

"*What*, already? What *is* it?"

"Bomb," I chittered. "Bomb. Gorna blowis up. Any minute. Bomb. On board. Here. With us. Really."

"You poor putz. I phoned them about that from my hotel
before I left. It's true. I figured heartless you are but dumb
you're not. To take a ride on a plane that's been crashing every
day for a month, is dumb, am I right? OK you're dumb. I'm
sorry. I thought you were smart. You're dumb. That's all,
that's it."

The ceiling was a cool spread of riveted bliss. As I lay back
in my seat I managed to whisper, "Why didn't you tell me?"

"As far as I'm concerned, on speaking terms, we're not."

I began to shiver and twitch. Feeling sorry for me, the
stewardess personally fastened my safety belt. My terror at all
this approaching turbulence was something she found almost
endearing. Poor thing, she kept saying, would I like an
aspirin? A blanket? *He'll be all right*, she mouthed silently to
Mrs. Hawkmann, who ordered a refill of our drinks.

Then it was as if my reprieve had brought back to me all of
life again at once in such a mighty rush that I was bounced
and jostled in the very overload of exultation. All the other
passengers seemed stoically joyful as well, quivering and shaking without stop in happy, sporty turbulence.

It even shook some sense into me. I squeezed her log of an arm. "Oh, Christ. We've got to get hold of Milly!" Mrs. Hawkmann calmly observed my new hysteria. I told her we were free. Tomorrow would come at last. What happened now, this evening, was final and would never be erased. Her eyebrows joined and curved in an arc of disbelief. I explained about the earth's spin. At the mention of tidal waves she looked shaken.

"Can't be," she insisted.

"It is."

"No."

"Wait and see."

"It's really over?"

"Yes, it is."

"It can't be. An agreement was made."

"Your Black Magic had nothing to do with what happened to the world."

"It did so."

"It did not."

She pulled her arm free of my hand. "Who told you all this?"

"God," I said, wincing at the sound.

"Well, who *was* it?"

"I mean I was *told* by God." I pointed vaguely at the roof of the plane. "He came *down*. He *spoke* to me. I had no choice in the matter."

"*Tsh!*" She clearly had not believed me.

"Oh, I get it. You can talk with the Devil but God is out, is that it?"

Her eyebrows made another furry bridge over the prow of her nose.

"It wasn't me, then—"

"No."

"—who did it?"

"No."

"Gutzi dunk."

"So when we land I must phone long distance. I just hope we're in time. Must get her to hang on, not do anything. I'll think of something. Have you any suggestions? She's *your* daughter."

The stewardess brought us our drinks. The crowded tunnel of the plane was being readied for a film.

"No," shouted the gruff voice beside me.

"What's the matter?"

"Don't phone her."

"You're kidding?"

"It'll upset her. Don't phone."

"Up*set* her?"

"I know what I'm saying. So don't."

A terrible doubt hit home. "Look, I certainly will unless you come up with a damn better reason than that."

She stared at me in the semi-darkness looking more than ever like Charles de Gaulle.

"You chickened out. Wanted *me* to sit with her while *you* went schtupping. Well, I would have. But I couldn't. She hates me. Yes, it's true. So I disappeared, hoping you'd go to her again like you were supposed to. But just in case. Just to be sure . . ."

"Yes?"

"At the airport, just to be on the safe side . . ."

"Yes!"

"I sent her a telegram."

"You did?"

"In your name."

"In *my* name?"

"'Fraid so."

"Oh, no."

"It said—"

"Don't tell me."

"I must marry you."

"Oh, no."

"I adore you. Cherish you. Can't live without you."

"You didn't."

"With all my love."

"Oh, no."

"Robbela."

I soon realized that she fully intended to follow me wherever I went. Her fear, I suppose, was that I would phone New York and tell Milly the truth. At the airlines terminal, I dashed from the bus to a waiting taxi and had him drive at length around the West End to make sure no one was following. Then I gave the name of the only hotel I could remember, an expensive one near Regent Street. I entered in triumph. She was sitting in the lobby.

I signed the book and took the elevator to my room. How could she prevent me from phoning Milly now, I wondered? The door was locked. I was alone. Well, she would have stopped me somehow, of that I was certain.

I had a sandwich sent up. I read for a while. I went to bed. Sleep, however, stayed well out of reach and after a while I climbed back out of bed, put on my clothes, and went for a walk in the chilly night. Shaftsbury Avenue at four-thirty in

the morning was more dead and deserted than I would ever
have thought the heart of a major city could be. I kept walking.

My watch said it would be midnight in New York in twenty
minutes. I stood on the island in Picadilly Circus, the wind
biting through my suit. I waited. At two minutes to twelve I
gripped the railing with all my strength. A bobby strolled by,
asked if I was all right. I was and he went away. The fate of the
future rode on the minute hand of my watch. I trusted no one
these days, not even God. The railing would keep me here. It
must. Now there were only seconds to go. Four. Three. Two.

My eyes were shut. I opened them. I was in London. I
waited. I was still in London. I squealed. A near faint swept
over me. Hot damn. I would actually have to *fly* home. I was
grinning and dancing in moronic glee.

"You're acting a bit dotty, mate." It was the bobby again.

"I am going home to bed, sir."

"I would if I were you. And straight away."

"Good night, officer," said I, delirious as a sweepstakes win-
ner.

"Mind your step."

At the door of my room, with the key in my hand, I was
grabbed from behind and lifted clear off the ground. Then
came that laugh like a mad bird.

"Put me down," I shouted in a whisper.

She did and, swinging me about, took hold and danced
down the hall with my suit while I, inside, followed wherever
it went. "It happened, hey hey," she bellowed, "it happened,
it really really happened."

The phone rang and someone, ostentatiously English, said,
"Good morning, sahr. It is seven o'clock, sahr. Thank you,
sahr." I went down to the lobby and paid with my charge card.

In an attack of generosity, I paid for Mrs. Hawkmann as well. Then I took a taxi all the way to the airport while parts of my brain kept dying and coming alive again. The driver shook me awake: "Heathrow, governor."

The seat assigned to me was a good one by the window up front. As I should have guessed, there was a delay due to "technical difficulties," and we were all marched back to the lounge. When the passengers were allowed to board once more, Mrs. Hawkmann was among them.

A man next to me was reading a newspaper. A peek at the date assured me it was Tuesday, April 16. Happy birthday, Rob, I smiled to myself and fell asleep. I awoke to find a hostess fastening my belt. Soon Philippa in a blue bikini had taken her place. She claimed she remembered that marvelous day and all the things we did together. I longed to touch her. I hesitated. Somewhere a clock struck twelve and all at once I was holding a metal fence in the middle of Picadilly Circus.

It was raining in New York, which raised my spirits at once. The trouble was I had landed with Milly in my lap. I ran to the first phone I could find. The door was open. Inside sat Mrs. Hawkmann.

"*Shhh, shhh,*" she hissed. "Calling her right now."

The sight of that great hulk stuffed into that narrow space, so helpless, so afraid, stole all my anger.

"*Shhhh! Waaunn,*" she counted, nodding in rhythm with the sound of the ringing in Milly's room. "*Tw-ooo . . . Threeee.* Come on, come on, will you. Oh, pick up the fucking *four-or.*" Her arm shot out and made a fist. Caught inside was a bit of my shirt and tie. Her eyes were shut. She pulled me close. A faint and distant Milly gave forth with a happy hello. Mrs. Hawkmann hung up, her forehead falling against the coinbox. In a soft but spirited clatter the machine returned her dime.

"Alive," I whispered, more relieved than I had thought possible.

With her head still pressed against the coinbox, she quivered.

"Don't cry," I said.

She shook even more. I patted her shoulder. She took my hand.

"Don't cry. She's OK."

"But for how long?" The inflamed eyes stared at me, awash with joy and grief.

"Go to her," I suggested, smiling encouragement.

"Me? *You. You* go to her, you *putz*." She threw my arm at me.

"All right. But you must stop meddling."

"I don't mean to, believe me."

"Then why did you delay the plane?"

"I overslept."

"You promised Milly you wouldn't tamper anymore."

"I am only trying to save her life."

"If you hadn't meddled in the first—"

"I know, I know, stop hocking me."

"If you must tamper then for crysake get her to stop *loving* me."

She replied very slowly, "Believe me, I have *tried*."

"No progress at all?"

She shook her head as her tears left lines of mascara. It was as if she had lost all of France in a card game.

"Use this," I told her, offering my handkerchief.

"Oh, dear."

"Look, over there is a ladies' room. Go. I'll wait."

"Tsh." And she dabbed at the farce of her features with delicate maidenly concern. "Oh, dear. Thank you, Mr. Blake. Oh, dear."

I escorted her to a door marked WOMEN, SENORAS,

MESDAMES, DAMEN. She went in but not before I had retrieved my handkerchief, remembering how she had once made use of my tie. One couldn't be too careful, I decided. It was this very principle, when the door had swung shut, that sent me running out into the rain to find a cab and shout her address as I jumped in, still holding my handkerchief.

It proved to be the worst ride of my life because I would be late no matter how quickly I arrived. I so very much wanted things to be as they once were. She had complained that I had made her wait for three years. Surely one more day would make no difference. Wasn't that so? It had to be so. I reran hard-core memories of us in bed and heard again that climactic cry as if she'd been shot. There was even time to remember how we sat on the grass in the park when she called me Robbie in her husky voice. Or how she touched my arm for no reason in the Cuban restaurant giving me all of her mute endorsement, reaching into me with her lovely hungry eyes.

At the same time I was sick at heart about Milly. How could I ever step out of her life so that once gone she'd have cause to stay alive? How, indeed.

Well, one trauma at a time. I slammed the cab door, ran up the steps of the browstone, rang her bell, and waited. Not a sound. Variations on disaster occurred to me. She might have gone out. The Scanlans had moved. Or had she simply acquired another lover?

"Yes?" It was that none-too-pleased voice, and my spirits soared.

"Robinson Blake. I've got to speak to you."

The door opens on its chain. She peeks out just as she always does each time I wake her.

"It's me. Rob."

"Ahhhhh. So *here* you are." She is like a mother relieved and annoyed at the tardy appearance of a wandering child.

I was let in and it took an effort not to kiss her. She wore a green sweater and black bell-bottom slacks. The change of outfit gave me a shock. Her hair was combed as well and she wore shoes. A mug of coffee was already in her hand.

"Where have *you* been?" she asked, amused and disapproving. She let me into the living room without waiting for an answer, and we sat with the trampoline-sized coffee table between us. Could she get me something? "No, thank you," I said. She took a sip from her mug and winced in pain. I asked what was wrong. A new filling, she said. She waited. I could see she was terribly interested in what I had to say.

My opening statement was, by now, memorized. For three years I had desperately wanted her. It was fear alone that kept me quiet. Apologizing for this inexcusable reluctance to show my love, I then mentioned the dream in which the two of us had shared a hammock; that little invention of mine that never failed to get her. It was the full pitch. Her eyes narrowed.

"You love . . . *me?*" She seemed incredulous.

"With all my heart."

"And what do you suggest we do about it?"

"Become lovers."

She snapped her fingers with a graceful movement of her hand. "Just like that?"

"We've waited a long time."

"*Have* we?"

"Yes, we have, actually."

"Then there's no point in waiting any longer, is there?"

"Not if two people want each other."

"Fan-*tast*ic."

"Do you agree?"

"Fan-*tast*ic."

"I adore you, Philippa. I really do."

"We could do it on the coffee table. It's close. Save us time."

Her tone was all wrong and I didn't know why, or how, to change it. The future was slipping away.

"We don't have to make love at all. But if we did I think upstairs would be a better place. Or my apartment. Listen, we could just take a walk in the park, OK?"

"But we'll end up screwing, won't we? I mean it's not fresh air we're after."

"Look, I'm deeply in love with you. That's what I came here to say. All I want is for you to understand."

"Fan-*tast*ic."

"Why do you keep *say*ing that?"

"Why?"

"Yes, why?"

She laughed. "You are some sweet bastard. You really are."

"Why do you say that?"

"You want to know why?"

"*Yes.*"

"Because you're engaged to Milly, that's why." She leaned forward. "I saw the telegram. Milly showed it to me herself." She sat back and all that was inside her sweater, far away, nodded once.

The room was sinking.

"I didn't send it," I said calmly. "Her mother sent it."

"Her mother? Her *mother?*"

Philippa's laugh chilled the air. My thoughts couldn't move quickly in such a cold place. Nor did standing up help me think. She stayed where she was, leaning back against her pillows. Once we had made love on that couch after strolling in the park on that perfect, almost immortal day.

In the midst of my paralysis I blurted out, "I'll explain."

"Don't bother. Milly told me all I want to hear." She nodded. "So you were having an affair with her. How very discreet. You sly dog. And no one knew. Of course, no one was supposed to know, were they? Milly wasn't sure if even she was supposed to know. Seems you carry discretion to extremes. So the poor thing had to get up courage to ask if you were through with her. Oh, no, you weren't through. Or so you said on the phone just yesterday. You even sent her that telegram. Then I guess you got cold feet. Tsh, tsh. Guess you thought if you slipped into bed with me you'd be too busy to get married. That it?"

"No, wait. Wait, wait."

"Don't worry," she purred with a mock show of wide-eyed, condescending patience. "I'm not going anywhere." She grinned and waited. I was being encouraged to condemn myself even further since she was already determined to disbelieve anything I might say.

A different ploy was needed. To win her back and have her in my arms once more, why not take her in my arms and that way win her back? If talk can lead to passion why not circumvent the talk and, after the passion, when all is easy, talk then? (You can see how clearly I was thinking.) I went and sat in panic, beside her, on the couch. Now, go and take hold of her. I jumped to my feet. The front door had gone off like a cannon and Murray, tall with fury, plunged into the room.

He marched directly to a chair by the front window and snatched up some papers he had obviously been working on late last night only to leave without them in the morning. With a full swing of his arm he threw them into his attaché case and slammed it shut.

"I see you finally got your ass out of bed," he snarled, turning to discover me there instead. The refrigerator began to groan in the kitchen.

"Hi, Murray," said I, hoisting both eyebrows while trying and failing to smile.

"Look who dropped in," Philippa declaimed, her arm stretched out toward me, palm up.

"You worthless fuck," he whispered. "Where the hell have

you been? I had to do your work. Myself. At night. And you, you fuck, you don't phone, you're not home, you are no-where."

"I was sick."

"Shit, you were sick. How come you can send telegrams proposing marriage but you can't say where the hell you are or when the hell you'll be back?"

"Because he's trying to wiggle out," Philippa said. She sipped some coffee and winced.

Murray's baby-face digested this distasteful information slowly and with effort.

"You're *not* gorna marry her?"

For Milly's sake, the pretense of our engagement had to be maintained. There was no other way, at least for a while, so I couldn't speak, although I almost screamed.

"Fantastico, no?" Philippa had placed her chin in her palm.

Murray's rage increased. "Then what's all this about, fella? What are you doing here, anyway?" His finger stabbed my tie. "I don't hear you talkin'. Make the jaw move, fella. What in holy hell is goin' on?"

I had just faced God, death, and Mrs. Hawkmann. I had been bounced about by the devil's own magic and metaphys-ically force-fed with some poisonous truths, and yet I still found that a furious Murray Scanlan was as disturbing as ever. Too much, I suppose, like my father, whose anger had struck like earthquakes. Or perhaps it's just that Murray was a crude S.O.B. and that the secret of success for crude S.O.B.s is that they are, if nothing else, frightening.

"Come on, come on." And once again his finger tried to gouge my heart out.

"All right, I'll come on," I told him while telling myself to shut up. "You want to know what's going on? All right, I'll tell you. Here it is, Big Murray," I continued, while that weaker, saner part of me sent out dozens of desperate alarms. "All right."

"I'm really dying to know."

"Shhhh."

Murray waves her away. "Well?"

"You won't believe this." I glance at her. "Neither will you, in the beginning." Turning to Murray, "But your wife and I had an affair. We love each other. Or we did. I still do. We were in bed together."

She is staring at me in bemused amazement. "He's gone ga ga."

"I'll prove it. You have a scar here on your rump. In heat you flow like mad and soak everything. You like to be touched here and here and you use your own hands just like men do. And when you have an orgasm it's like someone shot you with a gun."

For a moment no one moves. Philippa digs a sharp look into her husband. "Did—?"

"I didn't tell him anything." Then to me, "How do you know these things?"

"I just told you how."

Murray whirls to look at his wife, who snorts,

"He never touched me."

"Yes, I did. You just forgot. And we talked. You told me you settled for Murray after a great love in your life died long ago. Some married man long ago who died. Murray couldn't have told me that, now could he?"

Philippa's eyes looked glazed.

"Could he?"

As if to herself, "No, he couldn't."

Now, caught in a stampede of enthusiasm, I found myself chanting, "Philippa with bread, Philippa with meat. Philippa with anything, we've got to make her eat."

"I might have mentioned *that* to you *any* time."

"But do you remember when?"

"No, I don't."

"Once you said you'd give up everything, including your husband, and move into my place."

"*That* doesn't sound like me."

Murray puts down his attaché case and stands straight again. "I want to know when all this happened."

"It never happened." Philippa glanced at me for confirmation.

"It did happen. It did."

"How in holy hell—"

"Shhhh." She waves her husband into silence.

"It did."

"How *do* you know all this?" she asks, perfectly composed.

"You must believe me, we were trapped in time. Really, we were. Inside one long day. We lived that day and variations of that day again and again. Black magic had something to do with it. We fell in love. It happened. You know it did. We did fall in love. We still can. Half that love still lives. Your half is waiting to be born again. I tell you ours can be a great passion. I know because I just lived through it."

"You are ab-solute-ly mad," says Murray grimacing.

Philippa lifts her hand. "Wait. Go on, Robbie. Mention some other things no one could have told you."

Can it be I have her hooked? Plunging into the past like a scavenger, it suddenly comes to me: "Hammocks!" Almost with a shout, "*Hammocks!*"

Scanlan frowns. "Hammocks?"

I point right at her. "Your dream. The night we went swimming. The two of us in a hammock together. Kerplunk, remember? You fell asleep by the pool, and he carried you to bed to make love. But then I came knocking on your door, and this gets Murray so furious that he—"

In an instant I am thrown and held, thrown and held, seeing only the radio and the kitchen door, the radio and the kitchen door, while my neck is being crushed in agonizing pain.

"Liar, liar, liar."

I struggle, Philippa screams, and Murray, clutching me with all his might, crashes heavily upon the apparently unbreakable coffee table. Through the glass top I study the brown rug beneath us as one of my fingers finds its way up Murray's nose while the other hand tries to break the death lock on my throat. Screaming, "Stop it both of you," Philippa pulls Murray's hair so that my finger slips out of his nose, into his mouth, then out again before he can bite. I search for his eye, find his ear, and hang on. An ashtray thumps to the floor. Philippa's feet appear under the table. While she is yelling, "Stop it, stop it," and he, "Liar, liar," I discover that even more frightening than pain, or suffocation, is my total inability to utter a single sound. I am being strangled in my own absolute silence. I will die mute and absurd, watching my murderer with large, curious, desperate eyes. My foot finds his chest. I push. We burp apart and fall to the rug on opposite sides of the table. Landing on her coffee mug is like getting a kick in the ribs. Murray and I stare at each other under the table. His nose is bleeding. I still can't speak. Philippa gives one last, "Stop it."

Murray, on all fours, grabs for me and misses. We both rear up with the table between us. Philippa screams, "No!" Murray circles the table to get at me as I circle it to get away.

"Nose," I croak. "Blood." I even point at his head.

He stops, touches his face, checks his hand, is aghast, produces a handkerchief. It keeps him busy.

"Philippa!" I sound like a Hollywood gangster or an ex-boxer.

Her lovely frightened eyes swing to take me in.

"I love you Philippa." My voice gruff and filled with gravel.

"Yes, I know, I know."

"Well, what do you say? I want you. Come. I adore you. And need you. What do you say?"

That slight bemused smile of hers. She lifts her chin to speak to me, very gently, "You're insane, you know. You should rest."

"You're fired!" says Murray from behind his handkerchief.

"Oh, God." She turns to beg him not to.

"No, Phil. He's through. Finished."

She looks at me again. "See? What you've done?" Turning her head. "Murray, wait."

"I'm firing him."

"I need you. Listen to me. Will you listen?"

She shakes her head, eyes shut as if in pain. "Please go, Robbie. *Please*."

"I'm afraid we must ask you to leave," Murray announces in muffled pique.

"Oh, Philippa."

"Please, Rob. Go. *Please* go."

"I'm afraid we must ask you to leave."

His crumpled handkerchief had blossomed into a rose. Philippa had turned her back to me.

"I'm afraid we must ask you to leave."

15

It was a while before I remembered the rain. Then I noticed it falling softly into the small street-puddles of sky. Pain helped to distract from the misery. When I looked right or left, it got me in the neck. When I took a deep breath, it found me in the ribs. She had sent me away without my life and without realizing what she had done. But this wouldn't last. She would be with me again. She would hold my hand again. We would sit together and be enthralled, exhausting laughter, squandering love.

Two men and I entered the building together. Vince gave me a queasy nod and then for our mutual edification revealed that if Hope Lang married Bob Hope, her name would be Hope Hope. No one cared to reply.

When I entered my office, she was standing by the file cabinet.

"Milly!" It took at least five seconds to get up the courage to say even that.

She spun around. "You scared the *shit* out of me."

"Sorry."

Taking a deep breath, she exhaled and was herself again. But happy. I had forgotten that look. Both fists clutching her beads, she bit her lip and said, "Got your telegram."

"Ah."

"Were you too shy to ask in person? Poor Robbela. Poor me. Cried my heart out, I did. Promise me you'll always come right out with problems or shyness or anything. Promise?"

"Promise."

"Ho kay."

"Milly," I began, walking about and touching dust on the file cabinet, "there is, in fact, something I should tell you. A thing that happened. A terrible thing."

"I know," she confided with a conspiratorial understanding that astonished me. She shook her bereaved head with stoic courage. "You got fired."

"You know that already?"

"The whole office knows. Scanlan phoned in the news just twenty minutes ago. And no one was told why. Just fired, he said. Just because you stayed out without phoning in? I mean you were all nervous proposing marriage and like that. Look, I'll go to Scanlan and explain."

"Milly, no. It's a basic disagreement over something and really it's better that I leave."

"You *wanna* get fired?"

"I want to get a new job so I won't have to take crap from him any more."

She nodded. "Ho kay. I'm coming, too. We'll quit together."

"Milly, there's no point in us both being unemployed."

"Me work for that prick with ears? After he kicked you out? Ho boy would I never." And Milly, in fierce loyalty, lifted in the general direction of Murray's office, a single slender middle finger. Then to me, "Are there any questions?"

"Yes, one. Your loyalty, is it to me or to him?"

"You."

"Well, then, *I* tell you *not* to quit. OK?"

"Shit, I never get a chance to do anything dramatic. All right, Boss-man. Since I'm going to become your wife, I'll stay. My mother, at least, will be happy. Which reminds me. Did you find her yesterday or no?"

"I found her," I said, not knowing what I would say next, knowing only that I was unable to decide what on earth I would do with this girl. "I talked to her."

"So?"

I sat on my desk. I picked up a pencil. "Well, she admitted all those things you evidently never wanted me to know."

Milly tugged at her lower lip in grotesque contrition.

"And she says she's not going to interfere anymore," I concluded for want of knowing how to start.

"Ha! What she say when you sent that telegram? How did she like them apples? I was right, wasn't I? In my heart, here, I knew it. I was miserable for a while. But I was right, wasn't I? You thought it over. You came back to me, you really did. Son of a gun. I'm so happy. Listen, why aren't we kissing?"

Well, what could I say? And so she stepped up and had at me. I grunted. It was the throat again. I told her I had somehow acquired a stiff neck. She apologized and let go. It was then that it dawned on her.

"You seem low," she said. "Why are you low?"

"Jet lag," I replied, knowing I couldn't just toss the truth into her life like a bomb and then rush in to save what was left.

"Jet lag?" she asked.

I got off the desk feeling in my hand the pencil's sharp

point. "I had to follow your mother to London before I could get her to come clean."

"You went and came back in a day?"

"That's right."

"Poor guy. Listen, leave it to me."

This was her plan. I would do nothing. She, everything. I had been fired, had I not? So screw 'im. She would go through the files, empty drawers, dump stuff out, pack stuff up (she was good at packing, she said, it was unpacking that was her tragic flaw), while I just sat there, getting rid of jet lag and quietly drinking my morning coffee, which she would now order for me, OK? Sit down.

I did. She returned from her room with that purple, gift-wrapped package she kept bringing with her when she first appeared in the office again and again yesterday morning. She handed it to me, grinning.

"A joyful thirty-fifth."

"Thanks."

"Many happy returns of the day."

"Thanks."

Inside was a book. *Hitchhiking in the Holy Land* by Irving Blackstein.

"Remember? I mentioned it to you on that drive to Vermont. It's real exciting."

"I remember. And really, Milly, thanks."

She went back into her office and shut the door, leaving me to watch a man, small in the distance, leaning backward into space, held by straps, ruffled by wind, peering into a silent world of seated people whose job it was never to cease shuffling white sheets of paper. I was also free to watch the electric clock blinking another number into place, and the wall calendar with its picture of Vermont. I stood up. The chair gave a cry of pain. I had finally concluded what I surely always knew, that my only hope was to wait for the elusive Mrs. Hawkmann to free us, if she could, and if she couldn't, if Milly was never to be released, ever, from this obsession then, just to keep her alive, I would have to marry her. That thought and the weight of the rest of this terrible day came down on me like a crash-landing. I wanted nothing more than to be in my bed asleep. To tell her of this change in my plans, I went to her office door and opened it.

She was at her desk sandbagged behind a stack of files. She would glance at a sheet of paper, judge it of no value, and drop it into a wastepaper basket, giving a simultaneous whistle imitation of an incoming artillery shell followed by a deep-throated explosion. She dropped another piece of paper and another loud screech was followed by another moist and simulated detonation.

"Milly," I said timidly enough for her not to hear me. "Ah, Milly."

This startled her. The phone rang and startled her again. Her hand reached out. "Four nine nine seven." She looked my way. "Hello, Mrs. Scanlan." She lifted her shoulders and held them in mid-shrug, her eyes quickly questioning me. I was almost too stunned to react. I hurried toward my desk, closing the door. There was another squeal as I fell into the swivel chair. I was hectic and immobile, hot and chilled, numb and afraid.

"Hello!" I flung this out hoping it would skip lightly over the surface of the void but it sank at once. Philippa also said hello but as if doubtful of its meaning.

We both waited. Milly hung up. We were alone again.

"Murray just left."

"He left you?"

"He left the house."

"Ah."

"He's on his way in."

"Is he."

"I couldn't talk while he was in the room."

Now it was I who was unable to talk, my heart hammering frantically.

"Rob," she said, in her most secret, husky voice. "Will you meet me for lunch?"

"Where? I'll be there."

"Rob, I'm going to mention a restaurant. Please tell me if the name has any meaning for you."

She was speaking slowly, ominously.

"What is it? What?"

"A place called . . . Friday's."

I was flabbergasted. She was supposed to have forgotten. A violent joy seized me.

"Of course I remember."

"Fantastic," she said in flat astonishment. "Rob, oh Rob."

"Yes, Philippa."

"Can you meet me there at, say, one P.M.?"

"All the way up there?"

"Yes, all the way up there."

"Sure. Can I come and get you first?"

"No, I'll meet you on the patio. The rain has stopped. It'll be lovely. One P.M."

"One P.M."

"Beautiful." And she hung up.

I kept hold of the phone for a while as if it were her hand. Brush strokes of pain flicked across the inside of my chest. The order of things, such as it was, had been up-ended again. Why on earth hadn't she forgotten? I ran and opened Milly's door.

"Going out. Be back in a while."

The news that she would not be sharing her lunch hour with her fiancé somewhat deflated her.

"Going out?" she repeated with a forlorn curiosity.

"Something important has come up," I explained and since she knew it was Mrs. Scanlan who had just called, I implied that the appointment had something to do with my being fired. I even hinted that there was a faint possibility of my being reinstated and on my own terms. For all I knew, it was true. For all I knew, everything was true.

She nodded. "Good luck, Boss-man."

I waved. With her mouth open, an eye clamped shut, she joined thumb and forefinger to give me a farcical little fare-theewell, a cheerful signal of solidarity.

Vince was not at all pleased to see me step into the elevator.

"I phone them like you said, Chief. I really did."

"And?"

"They said they'd look into it."

"Is that a fact?"

"I wouldn't lie to you, Chief."

"Surely not."

"They promised me they'd look into it."

"Perhaps they got tied up with other things."

"Yeah, perhaps."

I was too filled with the promise of Philippa to care about past treacheries. Perhaps some other time. I stepped from the elevator and turned to look at him. It was a wild shot.

"By the way, do you have a car nearby I could borrow?"

He was suddenly all smiles. Evidently anything was better than my asking him to return the two hundred dollars. He left the elevator unattended and took me down the street to a rusting Pontiac and, with protestations of good faith and long friendship, he pressed the key into my hand.

The vehicle started with a death rattle, died, and rose from the dead to shake and tremble with mechanical palsy. The first thing I had to do, of course, was to buy the bastard gas.

As I headed north on the West Side highway a column of sunlight broke through the overcast sky up ahead to spill patches of dazzling silver onto the river. Vince's radio (it actually worked) gave sound to this flaming halo of promise, and the sound it gave was *The Symphony Fantastic* of Berlioz, which filled me and the Pontiac and the whole Hudson Valley with its mounting, throbbing *March to the Scaffold*.

Most of the tables were not yet ready for lunch. Two young men deeply engrossed in sharing the same menu leaned together on a white tablecloth and took turns pointing out interesting selections. With them sat a disgruntled-looking woman, who sadly studied a menu of her own.

Only one other table was covered with white linen. It stood at the far end by the low stucco wall beyond which, in the far distance, were steep cliffs and clusters of trees. She was seated alone, chin resting on her hand, staring down into the great spread of river. She wore a cream-colored, sleeveless dress, and her shoulder-length hair was a careful, cared-for turmoil of lush weight and vibrant black. She saw me. She stood up and waved as if I might miss her. I had never seen her so happy. We actually shook hands.

There was so much she wanted to say or wanted me to say to her, and there was so much I had to ask before I could say anything, that the result was a delicious silence.

It was broken by a waiter asking if we wished to order drinks. I sent for a bottle of Chateauneuf-du-Pape and glanced across the table to see if it struck a chord of memory. She said nothing. I peeked at her low cut display of spongecake. She squeezed my wrist. I felt her cheek. She kissed my palm. The current went right through to my toes.

"Do you have something to tell me?" she asked, with caution.

"Yes. That we loved each other in a different time, during a forgotten day."

"And what happened to us there?"

"We were interrupted."

"We became separated."

"Yes," I said, "that's right."

She seemed very pleased. "Are you suggesting that we should take up where we left off?"

"That is exactly what I've been suggesting."

She looked so terribly happy that I thought she might actually float away with well-being. That is, if I didn't first.

"I love you."

"Are you sure?" she asked.

"Absolutely."

"Yes, I remember our love," she said, touching my wrist once more. "How could I ever forget it?"

I felt an almost painful tremor of relief. "You do? You really do?"

"Oh, Rob, I can't believe this." She shook her head as if dizzy with pleasure. "I just cannot."

"They do happen sometimes—miracles. Believe me, I know."

"Fan-*tastic*." She squeezed my hand with both of hers. I had to restrain myself from letting loose a giggle of triumph. And from kissing her.

Luckily the wine came and there was much to do. I had to okay the label and watch him uncork it and offer a bit of what was inside of it to be tasted. I tasted it. He peeked at her spongecake. I watched him fill up both glasses. We both watched him leave.

"To miracles," I said, lifting my glass.

"To our reunion," she replied, lifting hers.

We touched glasses and sipped Burgundy together. She winced slightly and pressed her cheek with two fingers. "It's this—"

"Tooth," I said, hoping one last time to impress her with my pseudo-mystic powers.

She looked surprised.

"You went to a dentist yesterday."

"Oh, yes, I told you this morning, didn't I?" Which she had, only I had forgotten.

"Well, you seem to know all about me. In bed and out. How does it feel suddenly knowing so much about me?"

"Makes me want to know more."

A lazy, throaty laugh; then she made as if to dip her finger into the wine and sprinkle me. She seemed disappointed I didn't do the same to her. I just beamed happily into those intriguing hazel eyes.

"Perhaps it'll sound silly," she said, "but I want to ask you a question, a very special question. The answer will prove once and for all—"

"That I love you."

"No." Her face was solemn as she circled the rim of her glass with a finger tip. "Prove that this really *is* a reunion."

"Hell, that's easy, We're here, aren't we?"

"Are we?"

Some hectic sparrows flew across the patio above the two young men, who were slowly testing each other's apparently delicious appetizer while the woman, seated with them, stabbed soulfully with a bent straw at the bottom of her cocktail glass.

"After lunch," I suggested, trying to get things onto a less metaphysical level, "let's have a reunion in bed. What say?"

Philippa looked up at me with a hopeful expression. "The old Robbie would never have had the courage to ask that, would he?"

"Well, he's a new man now."

"Is he, really?"

"Yes, he really is."

"And how did it come about?"

"Love, for a start. I hear tell it does strange things."

"You mean you loved me so much you just had to come back?"

"Well, yes, of course."

"But how is it that it happened? I mean, how did it all come about this way?"

"It's a long story. Ask me an easy one."

She exhaled in a mocking, slump-shouldered, despair. "All right, I will."

She sipped some wine, charming me with the sight of her trembling hand.

"Are you ready?" she asked with a nervous smile.

"For what?"

"That special question. You see I want you to convince me it really happened."

"I don't understand."

"To make sure, that's all. When you said those things about sleeping with me, how I—what did you say—cried out as if shot?"

"Yes."

"There's only one way you could have known that."

"Exactly."

"Robbie, the last time we saw each other, that time long ago, you gave me something. What did you give me? I'm sorry for asking but I just have to make sure."

"Make sure of *what?*" I asked with annoyance.

"That you're . . . who I think you are."

A terrible doubt began to wind its way toward my great new joy.

"Tell me, Rob. What was it you gave me? Just name it, that's all."

"When? Gave you when?"

"That last day."

"I gave you a lot of things," I insisted, in a calmly spreading panic, having no idea what she wanted, knowing only that it was somehow terribly important.

"Not a lot of things. Not really. Just your love, mostly. But there was one gift. It was special. To me."

"It was?"

"Come on." She was growing impatient. "Don't tease me."

"A recipe for Quiche Lorraine?"

"I said don't tease."

"Something *I* gave *you?*"

"Yes."

"But you gave to *me.*"

"I know."

"Coffee, wine, your car, your bed."

"I said, I know."

"I took you out to restaurants."

"I'm not *talk*ing about that."

"What, then? A good time in the sack?"

"Tsh, don't get vulgar."

"I'm not getting vulgar, I'm getting desperate. What in hell am I supposed to say?"

She seemed as stricken by all of this as I was. "Rob, please. Don't let me down."

I was trying to control myself. "Where the hell *was* I when I gave this special thing to you?"

She winced. "Here, at this table."

I was stunned, for it was certain now that there was nothing to remember.

"Tell me," she demanded, "tell me."

"Why is it so damn important?"

She leaned closer, "How else can I be sure that you're *him.*"

A breeze tousled her hair and drew several strands across one eye. A paper doily blew away, but her words hung there, and I felt the chill one gets when a sweet and benign companion is suddenly found to be deranged.

"Him?" I repeated quite softly.

Her eyes were wide as she fixed me with a hurt, vengeful look. Lifting her right foot (it took an abrupt, unladylike contortion) she dumped it with a jolt on the table, shoe and all, shamelessly, like a drunken derelict, and the red wine rocked in unified rhythm inside the stemmed glasses.

"*Philippa!*" I rasped in a spasm of shame.

She pointed accusingly and in mute rage at a delicate, unfamiliar, silver slave bracelet, whose inscription TILL DEATH DO US PART flashed in the cool sun.

16

Peering into her lap, she used my handkerchief to dab at her eyes. What happened had gone unnoticed. The two young men, waiting for the next course, were smoking Gauloises, complacent as kings, while the woman, using a folded dollar bill, was brushing breadcrumbs from the tablecloth. Our waiter asked if we wished to order. Not as yet, I said, and he refilled our wine glasses and went away.

The face was much improved when she returned the handkerchief. She sipped her drink. She sat back and tossed her hair with a quick left-to-right up-shake of her head. Her cheek bones appeared to have swollen slightly with despair. The voice sounded as if she had little strength left.

"There was a man, once, long ago. My first and only passion. He was fat and married. It was all wrong and, yet, so right. I was a foolish little ninny. He even said so. To play games with someone else's man would be, I thought, great fun. I've been trying to recover ever since from that little bit of fun. I learned what passion was. I never did learn where to find it except with him. So love became a drug. I accepted the pain because I needed the pleasure. Because I needed him. One night he put a slave bracelet on my leg. How appropriate. The only present the bastard ever gave me. Then at seven o'clock one evening he left me and started his drive home to his family, just as he always did on Saturday night. Half an hour later, while I was still lying in bed writing him a letter. Telling him of my love. He got. He got caught in a. In a pileup. Turnpike. Fog. . . . He was the only one among all those cars. Thirteen cars. The only one. Dead." She brushed something away from her face, blinked, and again accepted my handkerchief. After a few moments she added,

"Willa Cather once wrote, 'where there is great love there are always miracles.' Ha!"

"Oh, Jesus. And you thought this fat and married friend of yours had somehow gotten inside of *me?* Oh, Jesus."

"He was a man," she rasped. "Not a little boy afraid to touch the candy. He was a true man."

"Oh, cut the crap."

"And how *did* you find out all about me? In bed and everything. Who told you?"

"Dear Lady," I said, heart bleeding, as I looked now at my own lost love. "Dear Lady, *no* one told me. We have been in bed in love in your home upstairs time and time again together, that's how I know."

"Tsh, such a stupid little lie. I think you must be mad."

I shook my head. It was pointless. As if to make it all the more unreal I saw, in the high blue spread of day, like a subtle mistake no one had noticed, the faint, milky, half-disk of the moon, beautiful and nearly transparent in its corner of the sky like something dead and decomposing.

When I looked back at her she was staring past my shoulder.

Her eyes shifted a bit and were now looking hard into my own.

"Yes, he was a man." She leaned slightly forward. "He was not afraid to touch, like you."

This, too, I could not believe. Her voice had become actually playful.

"Are you afraid to touch?"

"No," I said.

"Do you still love me?"

"Who wants to know?"

"Give me a kiss, now, Robbie." It was the Philippa I thought I had lost.

"Right now," she added. "I would hate not to have kissed you at least once."

We joined our lips like two people on either side of prison bars. She pulled away and left me hanging over the table. I leaned back.

"Now," she said, getting up, "I will go back and try to explain again to Murray that nothing you said was true. And you? You go and explain to your sweet little Miss Fiancée over there what *our* little kiss just now was all about. Voilà! We're even, as they say. Good! *Bye!*"

Behind me are tables. Behind them, at the far end of the patio, instead of a wall, is a small hill of shrubbery with a backdrop of river. Upon that hill, amid that shrubbery, Milly stands. She is open-mouthed at the now confirmed sight of me, of my naked face, peering at her. She looks to the left and right and runs out of sight.

I dash between tables, knock over a chair, catch a glimpse of our waiter's startled face and make it to the hilltop. Below is an ever-steepening slope through trees to where the ground stops abruptly, high above the river.

Then I notice a garish, full-length skirt billowing down the steps toward the parking lot. I descend the grass slope instead of the steps to hit bottom almost when she does. "Milly!" But she runs as if beating out a base hit. We sprint farcically among the parked cars. It takes a while but finally I catch up to her in the driveway and, grappling clumsily, we both trip over the curb and sprawl onto the grass. We lie at rest, bodies heaving.

"Millyyou . . . muslisten."

"Shiton . . . youboy."

She gets up. I grab her ankle, and down she goes again as if hit. We are kept busy breathing. A full-time job. The sun's warm. The grass, moist. She kicks the hand holding her ankle and is up, running. Cursing, I follow. We grapple in the middle of the drive.

"Stop it," I hiss. "Stop it."

We lurch and dance about. We bump up against something hard. With no small effort I shove her inside the phone booth and push her down into the seat. She pops up trying to get out but I keep pushing her down again until she just sits and gasps.

In all her effort and agony, gutted with exhaustion and anger, she still has a little girl's heartbroken face.

"Saw you . . . kissher . . . yesyou . . . kissher."

"Millycalm . . . yourself."

She pops up and is pushed back again.

"Calmdown."

"Kissher . . . ohyes."

"Millyit . . . was just a . . . kiss good-by."

"Liar . . . he said . . . you pro . . . posed to . . . to her . . . he told . . . meScan . . . lantold . . . told me."

"Bastard."

"You're the . . . bastard."

"No."

"You don't . . . love me."

I shook my head in protest having run out of everything except the truth.

"You don't love . . . me."

"Milly."

"You really don't. You just . . . don't love me."

"Milly, Milly, Milly."

At that moment we both jumped as the phone rang. She began to cry. I touched her shoulder but she shook me off and the phone rang again, loudly, in the narrow booth and kept ringing. We did nothing. We would wait it out, my foot holding the door open, Milly dabbing at her eyes with her skirt. But the phone kept hammering at us until Milly yelled,

"I can't stand it."

I reach for the receiver and Milly, seeing her chance, pushes past me and gets away. I dash after her, trip, and slide, face down, on the grass. This gives her all the time she needs to stop, rummage through her skirt pocket, produce her keys, and open her car door. I am about to give one last pleading scream before she gets away for good when she calmly limps her way back in my direction. She stops and picks up a shoe, which had fallen off in the scuffle. She is examining the strap with mystified attention. She turns to glance at me. Somewhat puzzled, she makes that swift, almost subliminal shrug, and goes back to the struggle with her shoe. When I get to her side she speaks at once.

"Rob."

"Yes?"

"Would you answer that damn thing. It's driving me bananas."

Only then did I realize the phone was still ringing. I lifted her car keys out of her hand, said, "For safe keeping," and walked back to the booth.

"Stop thief," she said, softly, but her shoe had all her attention.

When I put the receiver to my ear, a forceful growl riveted my attention.

"Mr. Blake, relax already."

"You?"

"Me."

"I don't believe it."

"*That's* a big help. Now listen good. I made contact finally. As regards Milly, I didn't do it right. I did it wrong. Would you believe I left something completely out?"

"I don't get it."

"Pay attention and you will get it. For you, it worked. But that was all. Well, how was I to know? Then she says hands off, so it's hands off. But it happens. Things go wrong. Believe me."

"What are you talking about?"

"Milly, you putz. She's not in love with you anymore. Is that clear enough?"

Through the glass booth I saw her try the shoe on and take it off again.

"You don't know what I've been through," Mrs. Hawkmann informed me in a belligerent voice.

"Is that a fact."

"A real mashigana cockup."

"Look, are you sure it's over?"

"Relax, it's over. No question."

"How did you know I was here?"

"I just knew. One knows, that's all. It happens."

"Mrs. Hawkmann," I began.

"Good-by, Mr. Blake. You are at last a free man."

"Wait, wait!"

"And while you're at it, would you maybe do me a little favor?"

"Me?"

"You. Now listen. Please, Pol-*ease*, would you leave my little Milly alone."

"*Me!* Leave *her* alone! Why you Goddamned meddling old—"

She hung up. So did I, rather forcefully. There was a slight, pleasant tumble of silver and I was one dime richer.

Leaving the humid phone booth, I walked up to where Milly was standing, with her bad posture and her problem shoe. I gave her back her keys. She didn't even look at me. While fiddling with the strap, she asked:

"Who were you talking to?"

"Wrong number."

"You always get so pissed off when it's the wrong number?"

"Sure, why not."

"Your trousers are torn."

"Ah, yes."

"Who were you talking to?"

"I told you."

"No, really. Who was it?"

"Your mother."

Milly stared at me.

"Yes, your mother. Claims she just now removed that spell on you. She tried it once before but something went wrong. A slip-up of some sort. She didn't explain. So it seems you're not in love with me after all. You never really were."

"So that's it." She shook her head sadly. "A moment ago I felt, suddenly, like an actress. You know, curtain, play's over, plot's ended, all the shit resolved, costumes, everything, bam, back in the box."

"So your mother *was* telling me the truth."

"Drat, I can't fix this damn shoe."

"Let's have a look."

"See? Broken right there."

As I worked on it, she looked at me.

"Hey, why did you send that telegram? That was really cruel, boy."

"I didn't. Your mother sent it."

"My mother? *My* mother?"

"She thought you might do something drastic while she was away so she decided to make you happy until she returned."

"You know, that makes no sense at all."

"I know, don't talk to me about it, talk to your mother."

"We're not talking."

"I wish I could say the same."

Milly nodded, but I'm not sure at what.

"By the way, how did you know I was up here?"

"I listened in. You thought I hung up but I just diddled the button. So, you've been screwing Mrs. Scanlan?"

"Yes," I said bitterly, "but not so she noticed."

"Frigid, huh? Son of a gun. Well, that'll teach you to judge a book by its tight-fitting cover. Better stick with Jewish girls."

Pleased with herself, she smiled. I gave her back her shoe. The only way I could fix it was to use one of my own laces to bind her strap together.

"But now *your* shoe is no good."

"Doesn't matter. How is it, OK?"

She walked in a small circle like a customer in a shoe store.

"Yeah, thanks."

"Don't mention it."

There was an awkward silence. "Well, that's my car over there," she said, lifting and lowering her chin.

"I remember it."

She walked and I limped in that direction.

"You wanna lift?"

I stopped and patted a crumpled fender.

"Whose wreck?"

"Belongs to Vince."

"It's like that portrait of Dorian Gray except it happened to his car instead."

"You read that book?" I asked, hopefully. "So did I."

"Naw, just saw the movie."

"Ah."

"Listen, I'm bushed." This, after a pause during which she sent her beads on another little flight into space. "Could I maybe have the rest of the day off?"

"Certainly. Yes, sure."

With somber significance. "I've decided to unpack."

"You have?"

"A warehouse is not a home."

I nodded. She nodded. There was another awkward silence. My head ached; my trousers were torn; Philippa was gone; and the wound that was her absence burned terribly. Something else burned as well. What was it? So much had happened. I had talked with God and run afoul of the Devil and nothing in this world was quite as I had thought. We were all of us in trouble; the future was black; hope was waning; and yet here, right before me, brown-eyed and ill-dressed, was a creature who could not possibly do anything but improve. An example as well as an antidote. Soon she would get into her car and drive off and I missed her already. There it was. That's what burned. I would always wonder and worry about her. I just would.

"Milly."

"Jesus, you scared the shit out of me."

"Sorry. Listen, when I get another job would you consider being my secretary again?"

"No thanks."

"I suppose you're right."

"Enough is already too much."

I nodded, not sure at what. "I'm very fond of you, Milly. You're very special."

She looked at me, her face touchingly plain and eager to be otherwise.

"Yeah?"

"True. And some day you're going to be very happy, I feel it."

"Yeah?"

"Yeah."

She shrugged. "Well, I'll see it when I believe it."

"Fair enough," I said.

She went to her car, got in, glanced my way, looked down, and started the engine. She glanced at me again. I was still there. She gave me her one-eyed, open-mouthed, thumb-and-forefingered-circle of assurance that everything was more or less "ho kay." And then drove off.

Alone, exhausted, thoroughly miserable, I climbed into Vince's car and just sat there, head throbbing. Now, I had no one. I saw my entire future grimly overcast with loneliness, broken only with an occasional downpour of grief. Having run aground upon Philippa's loss, here I would stay, stranded and broken, while everyone else moved on without me.

I turn the key. The engine gags but doesn't start. I try again and am able to achieve only a raw and futile grinding away of hope. I feel like weeping. I try again. No luck. I am shipwrecked beyond doubt. Another invisible jet is making its chalkmark on the sky.

Someone pulls up beside me. "Need a push?"

I turned to stone. I turned to look.

"Just want to say how very sorry I am for what I did."

Philippa was at the wheel, the engine of her car purring gently as if she were about to leave.

"I was miserable," she continued, "and I just struck out at you. Will you ever forgive me?"

All I could do was stare at her face.

"I lost her for you, didn't I?" she continued. "I was watching. My car was back there. It was horrible watching. And I was the cause. I was a vicious bitch, I know. But it's not often in life you find someone you love and then lose them twice. Can you understand that?"

Slowly, as if danger lurked everywhere, I climbed out of one car and into the other.

"I do not love her. She does not love me. I do not want her. She does not want me. OK?"

"I'm sorry," she insisted.

"Don't be. It's over. It really never was. And, believe me, I am deeply grateful that it's over."

"I see. . . . your trousers are torn."

"I know."

She touched the rent with her finger. "All that business about having an affair with me—"

"Was nonsense. I lied."

"You just . . . made it up?"

"Out of desperation. I saw I was losing you."

"Losing me? You never had me."

"True, true."

"How . . . how did you know all those things about me?"

"You won't believe this."

"I'm pretty gullible."

"Well, it all came to me, last night, in a . . . a dream."

She stared without blinking.

"We were back at that motel, remember? After I fell asleep in the beach chair, you came out to wake me. Then we went to my room. We made love and you told all about yourself. You claimed you could tell the future. You said Murray was looking for you in his own dream and that soon he would strangle me. But you were the one who was really in danger, you said. That if I was to save you, I must act now, that I must declare my love now."

Her gaze still fastened on me, she blinked twice.

"At which point," I added, "Murray broke in and strangled you to death."

She blinked again. "Fan-tastic."

I climbed out of the car and closed the door. I walked around to her side and opened the door.

"Move over."

She did, still looking a bit dazed.

"I'm going to drive you out to my place," I told her after climbing in.

"*Are* you?"

"Yes, Ma'am." And off we went.

"You know something?" she said.

"What?"

"I've always wanted to see your place."

"Well, today's the day."

She thought for a minute as she peered through the windshield at the wide, glistening river.

"A dream. Fan-tastic."

"Yes."

She looked at me. "*Now* do you believe?"

"In what?"

"In the supernatural, of course."

"Yes, I think I'll just have to give in on that one."

"Well," she said, "it took long enough to convince you"

LEON ARDEN was born in New York City and attended Columbia University for two years before he withdrew to become a free-lance photographer. His previous novels include *The Savage Place*, *Seesaw Sunday*, and *The Twilight's Last Gleaming*. An early play of his has seen three summer-stock productions, and his new comedy, *High Fidelity*, has been optioned for production in London's West End. Mr. Arden is married to an English journalist and has a four-year-old daughter. He and his family divide their time between London and Connecticut.